# OUTSIDE *the* LINES

## Book three of
## Girls of Summer

## by Kate Christie

Second Growth Books
Seattle, WA

Printed in the United States of America on acid-free paper
First published 2018

Cover Design: Kate Christie

ISBN: 0-9853677-6-8
ISBN-13: 978-0-9853677-6-3

# DEDICATION

To the women who have spoken up
and to those who haven't:
*We got this.*

# ACKNOWLEDGMENTS

To the fans of Emma and Jamie's story who reached out to let me know they wanted to read more: Thank you! This novel and the next in the GoS series exist because of you.

# CHAPTER ONE

"Hand me a baby wipe, will you?"

Jamie glanced around the living room. A baby wipe? Where the hell was she supposed to find a baby wipe?

From her vantage point on the corner of the couch, Emma uttered a quiet laugh that cut off as Jamie's gaze skittered back to her. "Maybe bring me the diaper bag?" Emma suggested, her tone suspiciously neutral.

Of course—the diaper bag and its endless contents. Why hadn't Jamie thought of that? She reached for the battered black bag peeking out from under the coffee table, its sides decorated with fading Dr. Seuss characters, and took a calming breath. It wasn't like Emma had asked her to change the baby. *Thank god.*

As Emma made short work of the newborn infant's diaper, Jamie couldn't stop the disgusted sound that escaped the back of her throat. Seriously, how did someone that small produce that much excrement? Emma rolled her eyes at her response, and Jamie felt a flare of irritation. She had *told* Emma they were too new to do the baby thing. She didn't have the foggiest idea what to do with an infant. But Emma had only smiled and said, "That's okay. I do."

And it was true, she did appear to know how to take care of a squirming, squalling newborn. In her eight years on the national team, Emma had obviously embraced her role as adopted auntie to the half dozen children whose player moms had lugged them to tournaments across the globe. Yet somehow this knowledge did little to assuage the panic that rose in Jamie's chest every time she thought about holding the baby herself. It wasn't her thing, a fact that Emma didn't seem to find relevant.

"Can you take her?" she asked, tucking the soiled diaper into a plastic bag. "I need to wash my hands."

Jamie tried to school her features into less deer in the headlights and more confident adult doing normal adult things. "Um..."

"Come sit next to me." Emma nodded to the couch cushion.

Warily, Jamie approached. At least the baby—no, she corrected herself, *Julia*—had ceased her pitiful mewling now that she was clean and dry.

"Here." Emma held out the tiny infant. "Don't worry, you'll do great. I'll help you. Okay?"

Reluctantly Jamie extended her arms, arranging them as Emma directed. And then Emma was smiling softly into her eyes and placing the baby in the cradle of her arms.

"See? You're a natural. Make sure you support her head. I'll be right back."

Alarmed, Jamie looked up. But Emma was already retreating down the hallway leaving her alone with the—with Julia.

For a moment Jamie closed her eyes. You couldn't break a baby, right? Like, that wasn't a thing, was it? Unless you dropped it. Or inadvertently smothered it... Her eyes popped open and she quickly checked the baby, relieved to see herself being watched by eyes that slid in and out of focus. Outwardly the infant's airway appeared clear, and there was every reason to believe that was the case inwardly as well. Jamie forced her shoulders to relax. She could do this. The baby couldn't even move on her own. If Jamie could go one-on-one against Phoebe Banks, the best goalkeeper in the world, she could hold a baby without breaking it.

Huh. She hadn't known a newborn would be this small. She stared into Julia's flint grey eyes, so unlike her mother's hazel ones, and let herself feel the heft of the tiny creature in her arms, warm and soft and incredibly light weight. Were newborn bones hollow, like a bird's skeleton? She would have to Google that.

Slowly, as the seconds passed and Baby Julia watched her with a permanently confused, wondering gaze, Jamie settled into the couch. This wasn't bad. In fact, it was pretty cool to bear witness to the beginning of a life. Hard to imagine it now, but one day this baby would become a girl who would walk and then run and then, more than likely given her parentage, chase a soccer ball across the first of many fields. She smiled as she imagined watching the future girl enter a stadium in her crisp American uniform; cheering her on as she tracked down an opposing player the way her mom had done for years; celebrating as she lifted a gold medal high in the air, her teammates around her.

No pressure, though. Maybe the kid wouldn't even like sports. Some people didn't, a fact Jamie had long acknowledged to be true (her own sister and mother, for example) but had never quite been able to accept in her heart.

Julia gurgled, almost like she was trying to assure her that she would—*duh*—like sports, and Jamie murmured, "Of course you will, little one. Of course you will."

The baby's mouth formed a slight "O" at the sound of her voice, and her eyes landed again on Jamie, who felt the weight of her stare like a physical touch. This tiny creature was relying on her for protection and safety. Not like the baby had a choice, but still, she could have been screaming bloody murder. Instead she was snuggled into Jamie's arms like she belonged there. Like they both belonged in this moment, together. Jamie felt her own breath slowing, her heart rate evening out. She wouldn't let anything happen to Julia, not on her watch. And all at once she felt it, this new sensation that had been steadily creeping over her ever since she'd decided to move home: She was ready for the next stage of her life, whatever it might bring.

Julia gurgled and squirmed, mouth twisting. Jamie rocked her experimentally, watching her face. The movement seemed to help, and she smiled, inordinately proud that she had managed to relieve the baby's discomfort. She had thought about babies in the abstract plenty. She'd known since college that she wanted to settle down one day and start a family of her own. But babies in theory were considerably less daunting than one in the actual flesh. Although now that she was holding this particular one, *daunting* felt like the wrong word. Entrancing was perhaps better, or fascinating, or even incredible. Because the miracle of life? Turned out it was aptly named.

She was so focused on the infant in her arms that she didn't notice Emma until she swooped in beside her and rested her chin on Jamie's shoulder.

"Hello again, Baby Julia," she cooed. "Are you my sweetest girl?"

Jamie's open mouth rivaled the baby's. "I thought that was my nickname!"

"No, you're my sweetest *woman*."

"I see how it is—already giving away my nicknames."

"Guess you'll have to learn to share."

She watched Emma tickle the baby's cheek. "You're beautiful," she said.

"So are you." Dimple evident, Emma leaned in to kiss her.

Jamie yelped and drew away. "Dude! Not in front of the baby!"

Emma huffed out a laugh. "Why not?"

"I don't know. Because!"

"You're weird," Emma said, and pecked her cheek before pulling back. "Do you want me to take her?"

Actually, she didn't. "Um, no?"

"I told you, you're a natural."

Emma rested her arm against Jamie's shoulders and they settled comfortably together, alternately chatting and fussing with the baby. Soon Julia's eyes began to close, and Jamie felt her own eyelids grow heavy, almost as if the baby were hypnotizing her.

"It's okay," Emma murmured, slipping her other arm under Jamie's to help support the baby. "You can go to sleep. I know you're still jet-lagged."

Jamie started to protest, but Emma was warm and the couch was comfortable, and Baby Julia was full-on dozing now. She gave up the fight and let her eyes fall shut, settling in more fully against Emma. "Maybe just a short nap."

She felt Emma's lips press against her temple, her breath fan across her forehead. "Sleep well, my sweet girls."

Maybe they *could* do the baby thing, after all.

"Damn, you two don't waste time, do you?" an amused voice commented at much too high a decibel for someone that close.

Jamie blinked awake to find Ellie standing over them, her grin teasing, as Grant Baker lifted a bag of groceries onto the kitchen counter. In the near distance, she heard footsteps galloping down the stairs to the lower level of the house. They were back.

"Again, Elle," Emma said, yawning and stretching beside her, "we've known each other longer than you've known Jodie."

"Yeah, yeah. How's my goddaughter? I missed you,

5

Julia," she added, sitting down on Jamie's other side and bending her head to inhale the baby's downy hair. "God, I love how babies smell."

Jamie frowned. "Everyone always says that, but she smells sort of sour to me."

"Thanks a lot," Tina Baker said as she climbed the stairs from the lower level, her two sons trailing in her wake. "That *is* my child you're talking about." She stopped, lifting her hand to her chest dramatically. "Wait. *You're* holding her, Max?"

"I am capable of holding a baby." Although she wasn't sure how much longer that would be true. Her arm was asleep.

"I don't think it's the capability she's questioning," Emma said, "as much as the willingness."

Everyone paused as the boys accosted their mother for a snack, but Grant intervened. "I've got it," he said, giving his wife a quick kiss.

"Thanks, love." Tina sighed as she settled on the couch next to Emma and hefted her feet onto the coffee table.

Ellie leaned forward, eyes on the exhausted mom. "Speaking of love… Aren't these two almost disgustingly cute?" She waved at Emma and Jamie.

"They are," Tina agreed. "Awfully domestic, too. What do you gal pals call it, U-hauling?"

Emma rose. "And on that note… Jamie, do you want to get going now that Mama Bear is back? By which I mean you, of course, Ellie."

The national team captain held out her arms eagerly. "Come to Mama Bear."

Jamie almost didn't want to relinquish her charge, which she knew was silly. She would see the baby again in a matter of hours. Steeling herself, she smiled sadly down at Julia and handed her over.

"Sorry again to crash your date," Tina said. "But can I just say I thought you were together at January camp?"

"They claim they weren't," Ellie said, gaze fixed on her goddaughter. "They were being clueless, weren't they, widdle wun?"

"Where are you going tonight?" Tina asked, ignoring Ellie's lapse into baby talk. With two older kids, she had undoubtedly seen it before.

Jamie shrugged, slipping her phone and wallet into her jeans as she followed Emma toward the front door. "We haven't decided. By the way, did you get any sleep down there?"

"I did. It was lovely." Tina smiled. "Thanks for loaning me your room—and for babysitting."

"Anytime." Emma slipped her hand into Jamie's. "See you guys later."

"Have fun," Tina said.

"Don't stay out too late, kids," Ellie added, but her attention was clearly on the little girl dozing in her arms.

They grabbed their jackets from the front closet and then they were outside, following the paved path to the driveway where Jamie's hatchback was parked. Ellie's Explorer and the Bakers' minivan were in the other half of the driveway, shiny and new and big compared to her more modest set of wheels. Emma's car, meanwhile, was parked on the street. Jamie was kind of happy she drove something as low-key as a Subaru.

"Sorry about that," she said, waving toward the house. "I didn't realize Tina would be here today."

"Are you kidding? That was a perfect way to spend the afternoon. Well, almost perfect..."

As they neared the driveway, Jamie felt hands propel her forward into the side of her car, and then Emma was turning her and moving in for a long kiss. Jamie's body, already on notice at Emma's proximity, immediately went on full alert, and it was all she could do not to groan into the kiss. It had been too long. She and Emma had made out plenty in California, among other things, but with the nature of her injury at January camp, she hadn't been up for anything strenuous. Well, that wasn't entirely true. She would have been only too happy to have her way with Emma, but Emma had insisted on waiting for their first time until they were both healthy.

If Jamie had known it would take *this* long to be in the same city, she would have pressed the issue. Somehow weeks had turned into almost two months apart as they kept missing each other. First there had been Emma's road trip with the national team, during which Jamie had remained in Berkeley for physical therapy. By the time her leg was fully rehabbed and her dad had helped her move up to Portland, Emma had a meeting in New York at the children's medical charity her family helped fund—for real this time. After that, she'd left directly from the East Coast to join the national team in Portugal for the Algarve Cup. They'd joked that their planes had passed somewhere over the Atlantic, but it was literally possible: The same day Emma returned from Europe, Jamie headed to London to prepare for Champions League. She'd only gotten back to the States a few days earlier and launched immediately into the remainder of NWSL pre-season. Today was Emma's first day off from the Reign in a week, and here she was at last, and here they were kissing—at last.

When they finally broke apart, Emma smiled up at her. "I've been wanting to do that ever since I got here."

"Me too," Jamie admitted, almost shyly. Which was ridiculous, because she and Emma had been official for a while now. But ridiculous or not, the time apart had led her to wonder how Emma would feel when they were finally in the same room again. Judging from her kiss, she still felt the same.

"Are you hungry?" Emma asked, body still pressing

into Jamie's.

She swallowed, tempted to make a crass quip. They weren't quite there yet, were they?

"And before you go all Angie Wang on me," Emma added, leaning in to breathe against her neck, "you should know that I intend to ravage you later. But for now," she sucked lightly on Jamie's earlobe, "I need actual food." She pulled back, dimple flashing mischievously.

Jamie closed her eyes and tilted her head back, shaking her head at the ash-colored sky. "I swear, Blake, you're going to be the death of me."

"Drama queen. Now come on. What's the plan?"

In anticipation of Emma's visit, Jamie had mined Ellie and Jodie, her fiancée, for Portland restaurant recommendations. As they slid into the car she asked, "What type of ambiance are you in the mood for? Like, candles and low light, or bright lights and diner food? Or something else?"

"Um…"

Jamie was backing down the driveway, but she could hear the hesitation in Emma's voice. "What's wrong?"

"No, it's—I'm not sure I'm in the mood for the whole restaurant thing."

They were out on the road now, a quiet street in Southwest Portland situated midway between Providence Park Stadium downtown and the Thorns practice facility in Beaverton. Jamie braked, slowing their descent into the city, and glanced at Emma. "What are you in the mood for, then?"

"Honestly? I would love to get take-out and find a park or someplace else with a view. I just want to be with you."

Jamie pondered the request. The spring day had been fairly warm, and it hadn't rained recently. She kept a blanket and a couple of camp chairs in the back of her car they could use if it got chilly, and anyway, she had never been a huge fan of supposedly romantic restaurant dates. They seemed forced somehow, like the participants were playing a part in a show that was more for other people. Emma being Emma meant that there was always the risk she would be recognized, too, especially in soccer-crazy Portland. Better not to risk having their limited time together interrupted by star-struck soccer fans.

"Let's do it," she said, smiling over at Emma. She was *here*, her brain marveled. In Jamie's car! Preparing to take a meal with her! And, you know, do other stuff later. Holy crap. *Holy crap, crap, CRAP*. But Jamie swallowed down her mixed nerves and anticipation over the end of the date and focused on the more immediate question: "What kind of take-out?"

A little while later they were camped out on a hillside lawn in a park not far from Ellie's house, the city spread out below, legs tucked under a shared fleece blanket as they washed down copious amounts of Whole Foods sushi with water and miniature bottles of wine. The sun was still a ways from setting, but low clouds blocked the view of area peaks. Supposedly this was the highest point in Portland. From her daily runs around the neighborhood Jamie knew that on a clear day both Mt. Hood and Mt. St. Helens—as well as a few other Cascade volcanoes—were visible.

Sushi was an excellent finger food, Jamie decided, although Emma wielded chopsticks like a pro as she said, "Tell me more about London. Did you have fun with Britt?"

"Sure, if you don't count the whole losing thing."

Arsenal's 2013-14 Champions League campaign had ended in the quarterfinals. This was good news for her NWSL commitments because if Arsenal had won this round, they would have played two more matches in April and, potentially, the finals in May. Still, Jamie couldn't pretend she wasn't disappointed by the result. Arsenal had been her home for the last three years, and the final loss at home to Birmingham City meant her time in London was over for now. She'd actually teared up when it came time to board the plane for the US. The thought of seeing Emma soon, though, had consoled her as she'd traversed the Atlantic for the fifth time since December.

"Tell me about it. I hate losing." Emma expelled a frustrated breath that Jamie easily interpreted. The US team, currently ranked number one in the world, had failed to win a single group stage match at the Algarve Cup on their way to finishing in an embarrassing seventh place.

"Right? It's *literally* the worst," Jamie dead-panned. She had heard Emma rant about their generation's willful misuse of the word "literally" on more than one occasion, but it was still amusing to watch her head list to one side as she tried not to twitch in exasperation.

"Well, maybe not—" Emma stopped, eyes narrowing, and stuck her tongue out. "Jerk."

"Nerd. What's the deal with the team, anyway? Ellie hasn't said much."

Since her return from London, Jamie had overheard muttered comments about line-ups, coaching decisions, and heads that would likely never find their way out of asses, but she hadn't wanted to pry. Getting cut from the program was still a bit too fresh in her mind.

"I think people are starting to calm down now," Emma said, "mostly because we were all sucked into pre-season as soon as we got back. But morale isn't good. We lost to *Denmark*, for Christ's sake, and the World Cup is less than a year and a half away. You know?"

"Yeah," Jamie said, and reached for another piece of salmon nigiri. "I know."

The silence that settled between them felt awkward, and Jamie wished her last comment had sounded less sulky teenager and more supportive friend. Or date. Girlfriend? Whatever. It wasn't Emma's fault that she was on the national team and Jamie wasn't. There wasn't anyone to blame—except maybe Craig Anderson and his coaching staff. *Bastards.*

"Is it bad I don't feel completely awful about how you guys did at the Algarve?" Jamie asked, hazarding a glance at Emma.

"Oh my god." She paused, chopsticks in mid-air. "I can't even believe you, Maxwell!"

"Sorry?" Jamie skewed her face into a cross between guilt and amusement.

Emma shook her head and laughed. "No, you're not."

"You're right. I'm not."

"If it makes you feel any better, I *may* have heard more than a few people say that leaving you off the roster was a bad call. One in a long list, admittedly, but still."

"Really?" Jamie wanted to ask who'd had her back in Portugal, but she restrained herself. It was nice to hear, but ultimately it didn't matter what the players thought. The only opinions that counted were those of the coaches. And the federation, to a degree that wasn't entirely clear.

"Yep." Emma plucked a dragon roll off the plastic tray in her lap. "You have quite the loyal following, turns out."

"Including you?"

"Naturally. President of your fan club right here."

"Ditto," Jamie said, and reached for her miniature bottle of wine. Emma's words washed over her, warm and real, reminding her once again that this was really happening. *They* were really happening. Living and working in different cities might leave more gaps than not during the pro season, but that was okay. Their feelings for each other had survived a decade-long separation; in comparison, a few weeks or even months were nothing.

Well, not *nothing.* Being apart even for a short time royally sucked. But Jamie had faith they would figure it out.

Beside her, Emma popped another sushi roll in her

mouth and chewed. "Anyway, how was it seeing your ex?"

"It was—civilized," Jamie said, remembering the cool smile and brief hug Clare had bestowed upon her the day they met for coffee. "She's dating someone, I'm dating someone…"

Emma looked at her askance. "You are? Who?"

"Shut it, dork."

"You'll have to make me." She checked their immediate vicinity, and then, apparently satisfied they were alone, leaned in to kiss her.

Jamie stuck her tongue out, intending to be silly, but almost immediately she realized that french kissing Emma was not silly in the least. No, it was hot and sexy and soon she was scooting closer—

Emma broke the kiss. "Sorry. We're in public."

"No, I know. Don't worry about it." Jamie squashed a sigh and reached for her wine again. It wasn't like she was a huge fan of public make-out sessions herself. But with their current logistics, she had a feeling they were going to have to seize the moment whenever—and wherever—they could. Speaking of which… "Maybe we should talk about sleeping arrangements. I told Tina she and Grant and the baby could have my room tonight."

Emma blinked at her. "Oh."

"The boys are sleeping on the pull-out in the family room, so that leaves the upstairs couch for us." As Emma continued to stare at her, Jamie ducked her head. "I know, I'm sorry. Ellie swears she told me about Tina's visit right after I got back from London, but that day is pretty much a blur, so…"

"You know what? This is fine," Emma announced. "One more reason we shouldn't stay at Ellie's house tonight."

"It's kind of late to call up Brugge."

Jordan Van Brueggen, a relative newcomer on the

national team, was the other allocated player at Portland. An outside midfielder, she had grown up in Colorado, played college ball in Arizona, and was one of a handful of social and political conservatives in the pool.

Emma scoffed. "No way are we calling VB."

"Then where are we staying?"

"You'll see."

"Emma..." They'd had this argument before in January when Emma suggested she spring for a few nights at a fancy hotel in downtown San Francisco, or even for an average room near Berkeley's campus.

"No, Jamie. I'm not sleeping on a couch with you tonight. For one thing, my back can't take it, and for another, I don't want to have to worry about Tina's boys walking in and asking why Auntie Emma is hugging 'that girl.' Naked."

"That totally wouldn't happen."

"How do you know?"

"For one, Ian is convinced I'm a dude. I heard him arguing with his dad: 'No, that's a boy! He even has a boy's name!'"

Emma pursed her lips, clearly trying not to laugh. "Small fry aren't so good with the gender cues."

"Gee, you think?" Jamie asked, and the conversation moved on to kids and bodies and the hormones that made adults love their children so intensely. Emma did most of the talking on this subject while Jamie sat back, sipping her wine and chiming in at appropriate moments. God, Emma was beautiful. And intelligent. And legitimately loaded. What was she doing with someone who couldn't even afford an apartment of her own?

Jamie had allowed her pride to prevail in January, but now she was tempted to rein it in. More than tempted—this was their one night together for the foreseeable future. Emma was flying to Denver tomorrow for the first of two national team friendlies that would keep her traveling for the next week. After that they would both be in-season through the end of August. Given that Portland's first three league games were on the road and Seattle's second three were away, they might not see each other again until their teams met in mid-May. And even that first match was scheduled for Portland, where Jamie would still be sharing a roof with Ellie.

"Okay," she said after they'd finished the sushi and most of the wine, "you win. Let's stay someplace else tonight."

"Babe," Emma said, her tone a cross between kind and condescending, "that was decided a while ago. Seriously, you need to learn to keep up, beanpole."

"Beanpole? You know you want all of this." Jamie waved at her body, currently hidden by a bulky sweatshirt/fleece combo.

"You're right." Emma moved closer to murmur in her ear, "I do want all of you."

Jamie felt a shiver work its way along the sensitive skin of her neck and down her back. A hotel would be fine. Definitely.

She sprang up, faking a yawn. "Sheesh, will you look at the time?"

"I was thinking the same thing."

"Ready?" Jamie asked, holding out a hand.

Emma took her fingers and pulled herself up. "The question is, are you?"

That was the question, wasn't it?

\*   \*   \*

Emma sat in the front seat of Jamie's car, thumbing through hotel options on her phone while Jamie packed up. She clicked on one that might be promising and skimmed the amenities—suite available with a view of the Willamette River, king bed, and in-room Jacuzzi. That would do nicely.

She booked the room, completing the process as Jamie slid into the driver's seat.

"All set." Emma slipped her wallet back into her handbag. "Do you know how to get to the South Waterfront?"

"Yeah, no. I've been in Portland for a total of ten days."

"GPS it is. Wait. Are you okay to drive?"

"I'm fine."

"I can drive if you want." Not only did Emma weigh more than Jamie, she partook of alcohol a tad more often. Possibly more than a tad.

Hand on the ignition, Jamie hesitated. Then she undid her seat belt. "I'm a better navigator than you, anyway."

Emma pretended to elbow her as they crossed in front of the car. "Nice."

Jamie caught her arm and tugged her off-balance, holding her close long enough to connect their lips. The kiss was brief, but Emma felt it deep inside. God, she had it bad. She pushed Jamie away, ignoring her smug smile.

"You're lucky I"—she started, and then stopped as Jamie blinked at her—"like you." She continued around to the driver's door, face-palming inwardly. That was not how she wanted to tell her. Anyway, did confessing one's undying love qualify as first date material?

Probably as much as getting naked in a hot tub did. And yet, that was where they found themselves an hour later: facing each other from either end of a steaming tub on the top floor of a South Portland hotel, the sky outside the indigo that always reminded Emma of watching the sunset from her parents' old living room.

They had managed to get in and out of Ellie's house fairly quickly. With children present, the adults hadn't been able to tease them too much about their sudden recollection of an unspecified prior engagement in the city, one that would keep them out so late that they would stay downtown so as not to wake everyone else up. Obviously they were doing the house's current inhabitants a favor.

While Tina snorted, Ellie had exchanged a knowing glance with Jodie, her fiancée, who had come home from work while Jamie and Emma were out. But they didn't say anything as Jamie jogged downstairs to pack a bag for the night.

Ellie waited until she was out of earshot to elbow Emma. "Don't mess this up, Blake."

"I have had s-e-x before, you know," Emma snarked back.

And then her smirk faded as Jack, Tina's oldest at six and a half, piped up: "What's sex?"

The room was silent for a moment, and then all the adults busted out laughing. Jack's chest puffed up in pride and he began to dance around the room repeating, "Sex-sex-sex-sex," while Emma—subtly, she hoped—flipped off her friends.

The drive into the city had been oddly awkward, and Emma had searched for conversational topics, discarding one after another. Soccer, the most obvious, was tricky because their pro teams were rivals and the national team was in disarray. She hadn't let on to Jamie how bad it was, but after bombing out of the Algarve, most of the older players were furious with Craig over formation choices and starting line-ups. The grumbling of recent months had grown into a veritable cacophony over many of his decisions, including cutting Jamie and starting inexperienced newbies over older, more seasoned players. With discord running rampant, Craig was rapidly losing the team's respect.

For once Emma would rather be with her club than the national team. The Reign organization was stable, even if the same couldn't necessarily be said for the league. But with financial backing from the federation—something the two previous American women's pro leagues had lacked—the NWSL had a better chance at sticking around for the long term. The Thorns franchise was stable, too, in addition to being the closest team to Seattle. They were lucky Jamie had landed in Portland with Ellie, even if 180 miles sometimes felt like it might as well be a thousand.

Tonight, though, they would sleep in the same room. And right now, they were naked in the same tub.

"Hi," Emma said, sliding one hand slowly up Jamie's taut, firm calf.

"Hi," Jamie echoed, watching her with glowing eyes.

Emma gave her leg a gentle tug. "You're too far away."

"I am?"

"You are." She watched as Jamie's lovely body with her lovely muscles and her lovely tattoos drifted closer, closer, until all she could see was the blue of her eyes.

"I love you, you know," Jamie said, her voice a little hoarse.

The words weren't really a surprise; at some level, Emma had known. But the warmth that seeped into her bloodstream, heating every inch of her and making her throat tighten, that was a surprise. She slipped her arms around Jamie's neck, fingertips brushing the top of her back where the phoenix tattoo started. "I love you, too."

She tilted her head back slightly. "Even if I play for the Thorns?"

"Even so." Despite the teasing words, Emma was deeply, ecstatically happy. Nothing else mattered except the two of them alone in this room—for a little while. "Kiss me?"

"So bossy, Blake," she said, her eyes on Emma's lips.

"You love it."

Jamie didn't answer, only leaned in, strong arms

bracing her as the tub jets whorled and whooshed, and then their lips connected, softly at first and then harder as Emma tugged again. Jamie's body fell into hers, and she gave a surprised gasp that Emma immediately longed to hear again. Quickly the gasp turned to something else as their skin slipped and slid together under the roiling surface of the water, legs entangling, chests pressing, thighs rubbing. The heat inside Emma raced and then settled, pooling low in her abdomen as light flickered against her closed eyelids.

It only took a few minutes of rocking together, mouths and bodies moving in synch, before Emma felt herself tipping and falling, her limbs tensing in the final moment before the orgasm washed over her, forcing a muted cry from her lips. She kept her eyes closed through the delicious waves, only opening them after Jamie pulled back.

"Wait, did you..?"

Emma bit her lip. "Yes?"

"Wow." She ducked her head and kissed her again, lips moving more slowly now. "That's amazing."

"I think that's supposed to be my line."

Jamie pressed her hips into Emma. "Not yet it isn't. I'm not done with you."

Emma inhaled sharply as the heat flared back up. Another surprise—Jamie taking control. She wouldn't have predicted it, but she definitely liked it. Hell, she more than liked it. "You're not?"

"Not even close. We have the rest of the night, don't we?"

"We do," Emma agreed, and tugged her back down.


"Did you set the alarm?" Jamie asked, slipping back into bed and immediately snuggling into her side.

"Mm-hmm." Emma turned her head to lazily kiss Jamie's still-damp forehead. She smelled like toothpaste and lavender bath salts and sex, and it was almost enough to make Emma want to have her way with her, *again*. But it was after midnight and the alarm was set, and despite what they might want they each had busy days ahead—national team training camp in Denver for her, Thorns practice and a pre-season scrimmage for Jamie. They were professional athletes, and as much as they might want to stay up all night, their consciences wouldn't let them.

Still, they had utilized the past few hours to the best of their (considerable, Emma thought) abilities, each learning what the other liked first in the tub and then in the king-sized bed. Emma had finally realized one of her fantasies—kissing her way across the phoenix tattoo that stretched across Jamie's back—and Jamie had reciprocated by paying equal attention to the script on her ribcage and the spiral compass tattoo on her hip. Eventually they'd donned robes and fed each other pita chips and hummus from the "care package" Ellie had pressed into Jamie's hands as they left the house. They'd laughed and kissed as they filled their glycogen windows and Emma had been amazed at how easy everything felt, how normal.

Being with Jamie was what she'd expected in some ways, but at the same time, nothing like she could have predicted. Jamie was tender and sweet in bed, but she was also teasing and demanding, driving Emma to the brink multiple times before backing away and building her back up again. Little remained of the girl who had never been kissed, and Emma wasn't sure if she was insanely jealous of or incredibly grateful to the women who had taught Jamie how to be so comfortable with her own body—not to mention, someone else's. She had felt Jamie's eyes on her as her fingers curled and twisted inside her, drawing gasps and sounds she was pretty sure she'd never before emitted. No first time had ever been quite as meaningful, but then again, she'd never been in love with a partner before sleeping with them. This thing between them was already more serious than most of her past relationships combined.

How serious had become clear during dinner at the park near Ellie's house when the conversation had shifted to Baby Julia. With the sky overhead slowly darkening into a soft purply gray, Emma had explained about oxytocin, the "love hormone" triggered by physical and emotional connection with others. Newborn babies, she'd told Jamie, tend to bring it out in anyone who gets near enough.

"That is one awesome evolutionary development," Jamie had commented, "though I suppose it's necessary since babies are incapable of self-care."

"Toddlers, too. It takes years before a kid can dress herself or wipe her own ass."

"Nice," Jamie had said, wrinkling her nose.

And then, for whatever reason, Emma had found herself blurting, "You've said you want kids, but are you sure?" As Jamie looked at her quickly, she'd added, "I know, this isn't normal first date fodder. But the baby thing is a deal breaker for me."

Jamie had nodded, gaze unwavering. "I'm sure. That's doesn't mean the idea doesn't terrify me. But so did trying out for the national team, and I wouldn't change that, even if it didn't work out."

"You never know. The door might be closed now, but stranger things have happened."

Jamie had hesitated. "You don't always have to fix everything, you know."

"Oh. Yeah, I know." And she did. But knowing she didn't have to and preventing herself from trying were two very different things.

They'd eaten in silence after that, and Emma had been relieved by Jamie's answer even as she'd wondered if some overly defensive part of her brain was attempting to put the kibosh on their relationship. She hadn't really needed to ask about kids, had she? If she'd had any question, Jamie's sentiment toward children had been on display since Emma had arrived at Ellie's earlier to discover Tina, Grant, and their three offspring visiting. While Jamie had been wary of the newborn baby, she had rough-housed and rumbled happily with Jack and Ian, the two older boys.

Emma hadn't been the only one to notice Jamie's way with the brothers, either. Shortly before Grant and Ellie took the boys to the store, Tina had commented, "They've only met her twice and they already love her."

"They do," Emma had agreed.

She wasn't surprised by Jamie's capacities when it came to engaging children, not after watching her work her magic on Steph's young son at residency camp. It was more that Jamie didn't strike her as the maternal type. But was that completely true? Even as a teenager, Jamie had been amazing with Emma's little brother the week after their father died, hanging out with him and generally helping distract him from his grief.

Anyway, being kind to children wasn't only within the scope of "maternal" types. She chided herself on her own bias. For women like Jamie who fell towards the middle of the gender spectrum, it was a disservice to assume they wouldn't want to be around kids just as it was a disservice to assume that men wouldn't, either.

Now Jamie burrowed closer, her face on Emma's shoulder. "I love you," she said, her voice drowsy.

"I love you, too," Emma whispered back, kissing her forehead again.

"Sweet dreams."

"Sweet dreams to you, too."

Jamie sighed, the sound happier and more relaxed than Emma had ever heard from her. *She* was responsible for that, and no one else. The corresponding rush of emotion that surged through her body was equal parts love and oxytocin mixed in with a tiny amount of terror. Because if she loved

Jamie this much now, what would being with her for months or even years be like?

The thought would have been more frightening if she hadn't felt at peace in the dimly lit hotel room, Jamie's warm body flush with hers under the soft cotton sheets, the sounds of the city of Portland lapping against the building's exterior as they fell asleep together, legs and arms entwined.

## CHAPTER TWO

Jamie stood under the hot spray, practically moaning as the warm water eased the chill from her extremities. It was her own fault she'd gotten this cold. Playing soccer in rainy, fifty-degree weather wasn't the problem. Driving home in wet clothes without showering first at the Thorns practice facility, on the other hand, hadn't been her best decision ever. But she'd wanted to get home ASAP. Emma and Ellie and the rest of the national team were playing China in Colorado, and she couldn't wait to watch.

Unfortunately—or perhaps fortunately?—Jodie had texted to say that her work function was going longer than anticipated. Which, hello, it was Sunday. But Jamie wasn't one to talk since she'd technically had to work that afternoon as well. At least she would get time off tomorrow after today's pre-season scrimmage; Jodie was not as fortunate. In any case, the delay had made this shower possible and might even give her time to watch the pregame without her housemate. She had to make sure the DVR was working properly, didn't she?

She could practically hear Angie's voice echoing over the sound of the water: *So whipped, boi!* And, yeah. Valid.

And yet, was tuning into the pre-game a good idea?

Watching the national team these days was equal parts pleasure and torture. The good part was watching Emma and Ellie and the rest of the team kick ass on the field. The bad part was watching Emma and Ellie and the rest of the team kick ass on television rather than from the sidelines. Or, alternately, being out on the field herself.

Sometimes she thought it might have been better never to have been part of the national team player pool. This morning, for example, she'd awakened early and lay in the dark imagining Emma and their mutual friends waking up in their hotel near Denver. She could picture every step of their Game Day routine, from Ellie's habitual raw egg smoothie and Phoebe's post-breakfast hot tub soak to Gabe's mid-day meditation circle and Angie and Lisa's pre-game dance party. Could picture, too, her Arsenal teammates on the other side of the Atlantic, lacing up their boots to take the pitch for practice under the lights.

If the national team had never called, if she hadn't been invited to December or January camp, would she have been out on that London pitch? Probably. She certainly wouldn't have been lying alone on the futon in Ellie and Jodie's guest room waiting for a morning text from Emma. She wouldn't have been psyching herself up for a scrimmage with another new team, steeling herself to interact with teammates already bonded from the weeks of pre-season she had missed during Champions League.

Closing her eyes, she lifted her face to the shower spray, trying to drum out the doubt rising inside her anew. Had she made the right call? Had leaving her safe, comfortable footballer's life in London been worth it? She and Emma were finally together, but they'd barely seen each other since January, and the next few months wouldn't be much better. Would their relationship last the NWSL season? And if it did, could it survive what might be years of Emma playing on the national team without her? Her growing friendship with Ellie was something to appreciate, but even now Jamie sometimes struggled with the sense that she'd let down the national team captain—her *idol*, for eff's sake—at the end of January camp.

She tried to imagine herself attending friendlies as a fan, tried to picture herself at the World Cup next summer in a Blakeley jersey, cheering Emma and Ellie and their other friends on from the stands. She would do it, of course she would. But she couldn't pretend doing so wouldn't kill her inside a little more each match. She'd come *so freaking close* to making the national team, and maybe that really was worse than never having had a real shot at all.

Sighing, she reached for the coconut body wash and began scouring the Oregon mud from her skin. No going back now, she reminded herself. No Mulligans in real life, as one of her college coaches had liked to say. No choice but to kick off the covers each morning and get on with it. She would give the Thorns her everything, leave it all on the field as usual. After all, she was a professional, and expending effort was a huge part of the vocation that, despite the attendant ups and downs, she loved more than almost anything else. Her pro soccer career, she'd always known, was temporary. Some day she would view these years as some of the best of her life.

Maybe. Depending on how this and future seasons turned out. Right now her team's future—and that of the NWSL itself—was still a blank dry eraser board.

She stayed under the spray longer than was polite, given her goal of not running up Ellie and Jodie's water bill while living in their basement. But it was hard to pull herself away even on days when she wasn't chilled to the bone. One of the things she loved about being back in the US was the water pressure. In London, the city's ancient pipes had been infamously treacherous, and coin-operated hot water heaters in rental properties could be inconvenient, to say the least. More than once she'd run out of hot water and had to scramble about the bedroom, dripping soap everywhere while searching for a spare 50p coin. Not so here. Like Jamie's parents, Ellie and Jodie kept their water heater turned up high. There was almost always hot water to spare.

Finally, with visions of Emma slide-tackling Chinese strikers dancing in her head, she shut off the water. As she was toweling off, she heard floorboards creak overhead— Jodie was back! She raced through her post-shower routine and tugged on the first dry clothes she saw, practically sprinting upstairs until she remembered how slippery the wood floors were especially when all you had on your feet was a pair of fluffy fleece socks. She'd rather not imagine the humiliation of having to admit she'd injured herself while sprinting to watch Emma play on TV. Slowing midway up the stairs, she checked to make sure the person currently moving about the home's main level truly was her housemate before picking up her pace again and sliding sideways into the kitchen.

"Holy shit!" Jodie shrieked, hand on her chest. "Jamie! Don't do that!"

"Sorry," she said, biting back a smile.

"I can tell." She turned away and then spun back. "Wait. The game's taping, right?"

"Duh. I texted you like half an hour ago." She bounced on the balls of her feet a couple of times. "Want to watch?"

"Obviously. But can I change and get some food first?"

She sighed dramatically. "I guess..."

"Goof," Jodie said, but Jamie thought she could relate.

While Jodie changed, Jamie set about warming up leftover Thai food for them both. In a surprisingly short time the other woman was back, hair released from its tight bun, contacts replaced by glasses, the blazer and trousers she'd worn earlier swapped out for a pair of Ellie's old national team sweats. What hadn't changed was the T-shirt she'd paired with the blazer, a black crewneck that proclaimed, "Wild Feminist."

"I need to get me one of those," Jamie said, nodding at the tee.

"I think that could be arranged—*if* you agree to post photo receipts on Instagram and Twitter, that is."

Jodie was a PR rep for a homegrown Portland clothing label and often brought home freebies from the office and semi-monthly "fashion networking events"—nights when she met her friends from different design houses for drinks and the pleasure of trading swag.

"Done," Jamie said, and slurped up a pad thai noodle that had wriggled free from its container.

"Sweet!" Jodie reached for her phone and began typing away one-handed, a skill Jamie had never mastered herself.

Wait. Had she just unwittingly agreed to become— what did Ellie and Angie call it—"a brand ambassador" to Jodie's company? Not like she could have picked a better clothing company to align herself with. One of the founders of the label was a lesbian, and the clothes were mostly gender-neutral but designed to fit the female body. Maybe someday if she ever made more than minimum wage, Jamie would drop some cash at the flagship store downtown. In the meantime, freebies in exchange for "photo receipts" would work.

Plates piled high with noodles and fried rice, the two women moved to the couch in the living room, glasses of wine within reach on the coffee table. As soon as they were settled, Jamie hit play. Jodie liked the commentary, too, but they still managed to chat about their days as the pre-game unfolded with an analysis of what the team's disastrous showing in the Algarve Cup might mean for World Cup qualifying in October.

At one point, the commentator paused before saying, "Actually, we were a little concerned earlier on before the match. There was, uh—"

Out of the corner of her eye, Jamie noticed Jodie sit

upright, staring at the TV. Then as the British commentator continued on about the threatening weather system that had since subsided, Jodie relaxed, a not-so-subtle sigh audible over the crowd noise blaring from the surround sound speakers.

"What was that?" Jamie asked, eyes no longer fixed on the screen.

"What was what?" Jodie kept her own gaze resolutely elsewhere.

"That," Jamie said, waving her fork at her housemate. "You looked crazy nervous for a second there."

"No I didn't. You're imagining things, Rook."

Jamie wanted to tell her that only soccer players could call her that, but since she was presently sitting on Jodie and Ellie's couch eating off of their plates, drinking their wine, and watching their television, she figured Jodie should be allowed to call her whatever she wanted.

This was the first time Jamie had watched a national team match with Ellie's future wife, and she wasn't sure what to expect from the other woman. It soon became clear that even though she worked in fashion, Jodie loved soccer. She was nearly as rowdy as Ellie was during Premier League matches, jumping up groaning, hands on her head, whenever the US missed a shot on goal or gave up a fifty-fifty ball. No one's vitriol for poor refereeing decisions could truly rival Ellie's, but Jodie came close.

Unfortunately, there were plenty of opportunities for hands on heads in this game. Throughout the first half, the US missed chance after chance, even shooting wide of an empty net. Twice. Finally, five minutes before half-time, Maddie buried a shot from the top of the eighteen. Instead of jumping around in celebration, Jamie and Jodie simply high-fived and shook their heads. China was ranked sixteenth in the world to the US's number one. The score should be higher after forty minutes.

As Jamie fast-forwarded through half-time, Jodie made a disgusted sound. "Now I understand why they bombed out of the Algarve. That was the most uninspired half I've seen in a while."

"What I don't get is O'Brien starting over Lisa, and Gabe and Jenny mysteriously absent. Speaking of, are you *sure* Ellie's not hurt?"

When the line-up had posted before kick-off with only one of the team captains starting, Jodie had seemed as surprised as Jamie. Ellie hadn't said anything about being hurt, nor had she texted Jodie about being benched.

"Maybe Craig wants to go in a different direction," Jodie said now, shrugging.

Jamie winced. It was too soon for her to hear the phrase Craig had used when he cut her from the program. Possibly it would always be too soon.

They agreed to skip halftime coverage since it was bound to be more of the British guy and his broadcast partner, a former national team player, talking about the plethora of missed scoring opportunities and the team's current downward spiral. Nobody needed to hear yet again how long it had been since The Greatest Generation (as Steph Miller sarcastically referred to them) had won a World Cup for the US.

The second half was just beginning when Jodie's cell phone rang.

"Pause it, will you? It's her."

For a brief moment Jamie couldn't work out why Emma had called Jodie, and then her brain caught up. Her as in *Ellie*.

"Don't tell me the score," Jodie said into her phone. "We're still watching. But how are you? You started the second half!"

She listened, eyes going wide, and Jamie zeroed in on the conversation. "Craig," she clearly heard Ellie say over the tinny speakers. Also "the federation" and "meeting" more than once.

"Right in the middle of the road trip?" Jodie asked, her face still registering shock.

Jamie shifted closer, but Jodie must have twigged what she was up to because she stood and headed for the kitchen. "She is?" she asked, lowering her voice. "Well, that's something, isn't it?"

Jamie stared unseeingly at the TV screen, frozen on a close-up of Maddie preparing to take a throw-in. What the hell was going on with the national team? And why hadn't she heard from Emma?

"I won't," Jodie said, her back to Jamie. "Okay. I love you, Rachel. Everything will work out... Me too. Call me later."

She hung up and stood motionless in the kitchen for a minute, one hand on her hip.

"Is everything okay?" Jamie asked, breaking the tense silence. "Is it Emma? She didn't get hurt, did she?"

"No." Jodie was frowning as she turned back to the living room. "Not as far as I know. There's team drama going on, that's all. Let's watch the second half, okay?"

Jamie hit play and chewed on a fingernail, only half paying attention to the game. It was no secret there was occasional drama on the national team; they were athletes living in the public eye. But this sounded like unusual levels of turmoil. Did it have anything to do with the fight over turf fields at the World Cup? Had someone said something to the media they shouldn't have? Or—and here her heart fell—had a member of the team or staff been arrested? The women's team had always been significantly less prone to scandal than the men's, but that didn't mean everyone in the organization was squeaky clean.

Briefly she considered checking social media for any mention of a scandal, but then she realized she would see the score. Besides, in the months since #Blakewell had exploded, she'd been slowly weaning herself off Twitter and Instagram and had found that the less time she spent online, the happier she was. Her mentions this year had taken a turn for the ugly, as she'd known they might if she attracted a wider following. She'd turned off direct messaging and muted her notifications, but Tumblr was the only place online she felt safe anymore, mostly because there was nothing in her ultra-generic profile that could be tied to her. To avoid the homophobic, transphobic, and misogynistic creeps trolling the Internet in droves, she'd followed Ellie's advice and created private Facebook and Instagram accounts. She'd even asked her family and friends to unfollow her athlete profiles so that they wouldn't artificially inflate her follower numbers. In reality she was trying to protect them from the seedier side of the Internet—assuming such a thing was even possible.

As Jodie typed on her phone beside her, screen tilted away, Jamie drafted a quick text to Emma. "Still watching the game. Not the best team performance I've ever seen, but you're awesome as ever."

She waited five minutes. When no response was forthcoming, she texted again. "You okay? Let me know when you get a chance."

Her phone dinged. "I'm mtng rn. Call u ltr!"

The plot thickened. Emma almost never used text shorthand. *Aargh….* Once again, not being on the national team blew.

When her phone rang a few minutes later, Emma's picture flashing on the screen, Jamie headed downstairs.

"Do you want me to pause it?" Jodie called after her.

"No!" she hollered back. She had a feeling Emma was about to tell her something far more interesting than the outcome of the match. "Hey," she added into the phone, dropping onto the futon in the guest room. "What's up?"

"A lot." Emma's voice was hushed, or maybe it was

just the cold Jamie knew she was fighting. "I can't talk long. It's insane here. Barry and Rob fired Craig. He isn't even going to fly to San Diego with us tomorrow."

And that... was not at all what Jamie had been expecting. It did, however, explain what Rob Muñoz and Barry Winchester, the president and general secretary of US Soccer, were doing in Colorado. They'd showed up at the beginning of training camp, bringing with them what Ellie and Emma had both deemed a weird vibe.

"Did you hear me?" Emma asked.

"Yeah, I heard you." Jamie rose from the bed and crossed to the daylight basement window where she placed her free hand on the glass, letting the coolness penetrate her palm. "How's the team? How are you?"

"I think we're all in shock. A rep told us on the bus that Rob and Barry wanted to meet with us, but most of us assumed it had something to do with qualifying. Even Ellie and Phoebe didn't know, although they did say the federation had checked in with them after the Algarve."

As Ellie's housemate, Jamie could imagine how that meeting had gone. "Did they offer a reason?"

"Rob says it's an issue of culture. Apparently the federation has decided his coaching style isn't a good fit for the team. You should have seen Craig, Jamie. He was nothing but classy. I can't believe he's out. We've gone eighteen and two under him. Two losses, that's it, and they fire him!"

Jamie wanted to feel bad for Craig, she really did. In theory she even succeeded. But in reality, she stared at her faint reflection in the window and gave a fist pump. Craig Anderson, the man who had convinced her to give up her European football career and then promptly squashed her national team dreams, was out. The coach who hadn't believed in her enough had been cut himself, and now she might have another shot at making a future roster. The door wasn't exactly open, but it wasn't as firmly closed as it had been even a few hours earlier.

She schooled her tone and said softly, "I'm sorry, Em." Because as much as she was secretly thrilled by the news, she had an idea what it must be doing to the team.

Voices sounded in the background. "I have to go. I'll call you later, okay? Oh, and check your email. I swear it wasn't planned."

Before Jamie could ask what she meant, the line went dead. She lowered her phone and looked out the window, focusing on the yellow-orange lights of the city in the distance. No wonder Ellie had called Jodie freaking out. The World Cup was only a little over a year away. To fire a national team coach at this point in the cycle was almost unheard of. In fact, as far as she knew, it *was* unheard of.

The floorboards creaked overhead again and she heard Jodie call, "There's a goal! Do you want to see the replay?"

"Yes!" she shouted, and raced back upstairs.

They didn't talk about it. Jodie kept watching the game as if nothing had happened while Jamie divided her attention between the television and her iPad. Sure enough, Emma, Angie, and Ellie had all sent her emails before the game with identical subject lines: "The Theory of Marginal Gains." Each message contained a PDF attachment—a handout from that morning's mental training session. Reflexively Jamie started to angle her screen away from Jodie, but then she stopped. Sharing training materials with someone who had been in and out of the player pool was allowed. Sharing details of a coach's firing before anyone outside of the federation knew, on the other hand, not so much.

The handout, titled "Sir David Brailsford and the Theory of Marginal Gains," wasn't long. Jamie skimmed the text and before going back to read through again more slowly. The gist was that in 2010, cycling coach David Brailsford had been given the GM position at newly formed Team Sky and tasked with a goal no British rider had achieved previously: to win a Tour de France title. As Jamie well remembered—her English girlfriend's family had fully copped to being "a bit nutty" about cycling—Brailsford had accomplished this goal in 2012 when Team Sky's leader Bradley Wiggins became the first British cyclist to win the Tour. Wiggo's teammate, Chris Froome, came in second that summer and then, in a turn of events that had sent Clare's family "over the moon," had won the Tour himself the following year. Not only that, but with Brailsford at the helm, the British cycling team had cleaned up at the 2012 Summer Olympics.

According to the article, Brailsford's formula for success hinged on what he called "the aggregation of marginal gains." Basically, he believed that if Team Sky could improve certain areas of performance by as little as one percent each, those gains would eventually add up. He started with predictable targets: fitness, diet, and bike and rider aerodynamics. But then—and this was what set him apart from other team managers—he applied his philosophy of improvement to other, seemingly unrelated areas. Like finding the most comfortable pillows to bring on the road, or discovering the best way to avoid infection and illness while on tour. His team, clearly, had flourished under this approach.

Jamie leaned back, considering the implications. Sleep comfort and immune system health were crucial to any professional athlete's career, so it made sense that Brailsford had concentrated his attention on those areas. What else might he have selected for his program? And, more to the point, was it possible that an aggregation of custom-tailored marginal gains might help *her* stay healthy and earn another shot at the pool? Her national team buddies obviously thought so.

She was about to turn off her iPad, but then almost of her own volition, her fingers brought up her Twitter app. Biting her lip, she searched on the USWNT hashtag. They'd won the game, she discovered—not a given but also not surprising. But that wasn't why the hashtag was trending. She narrowed in on a headline from ESPN: "Craig Anderson fired from US women's national soccer team; Jo Nichols to serve as interim coach."

Jo Nichols, who had selected Jamie to the U-16 national team and made her a starter on the U-23 squad. The same Jo Nichols who, as interim head coach between Marty and Craig, had given Jamie her first cap with the senior side. She was the reason Jamie was in the pool, the reason she'd ever seen a lick of playing time, and now she was back at the helm of the senior national team.

*It doesn't mean anything,* Jamie told herself, tamping down the sudden surge of excitement that threatened to buoy her off the couch. Jo was only the temporary coach while the federation searched for someone to replace Craig permanently. Even if she called Jamie up again, it didn't mean she would make a single roster. Still, an interim coach who had always believed in her was better than one who hadn't. As she scrolled through Twitter, restless energy made her legs jump and her teeth all but chatter. The gloom and angst she'd started the day with was long gone now, replaced by—oh, her stupid, naïve heart—hope.

Jamie closed the cover on her iPad. *Control what you can,* she reminded herself as she refocused on the television screen in time to see Emma pick the pocket of a Chinese striker and send the ball up the field to Maddie. *Let the rest go.*

Easier said than done.

\*　　\*　　\*

Emma pocketed her phone and ducked back into the conference room, sucking hard on a cough drop. It had been a busy evening. After Rob and Barry dropped their bombshell, Craig had come in to say goodbye and wish the team well. She still couldn't believe that he had thanked them, the players who had played so poorly that they'd cost him his job. Emma was sure she hadn't been the only one in the room who'd had a hard time meeting his gaze as he walked out. Bottom line: Their performance under his leadership was the reason he'd been fired.

After the door had closed behind Craig, there had been a moment of silence. Then the players had begun to talk amongst themselves until Ellie held up a hand. "Let's take a break," she'd said, voice calm and commanding, "and come back in five ready to talk this through."

Their five minutes now up, the room was once again vibrating with discordant energy. This wasn't how the national team was usually informed about coaching changes. In Emma's experience, any major alteration to the program had come at the end of a World Cup or after an Olympics, tournaments with high pressure and expectations. Maybe that was why the tension in the room felt worse than she had seen since the '07 World Cup—because Craig's firing had come so unexpectedly, and now no one was sure what was going to happen moving forward.

On the one hand were Craig's supporters, like Rebecca Perry: "Not a good fit for the culture?" she said, voice rising above the others. "That's ridiculous. It's not like they weren't familiar with his coaching style before they offered him the position."

On the other were his detractors, like Steph Miller: "Seventh place, you guys. Not only that but we gave up five goals in one game. Against *Denmark*!"

The debate didn't last long. Soon Ellie was holding up her hand again and saying in that same firm voice, "Guys, I think we're getting off-course here. The decision has been made and it's out of our hands. At this point I think we need to concentrate on moving forward."

"Before we move forward, I for one would like to know why this happened the way it did," Ryan Dierdorf said, arms folded stubbornly across her chest. "Why do it in the middle of a road trip? Why not wait until Wednesday?"

"Because after Wednesday we all leave for our pro teams and don't see each other again for another month," Phoebe said. "I think they wanted to give us time to get used to the idea while we're still together. Maybe they actually learned something from what happened with Jeff in '07."

"I thought you guys knew ahead of time with him," Ryan said.

"Define ahead of time." Phoebe waved a hand. "Anyway, that was different. We all knew he wasn't long for this world after what happened in China."

Other than Phoebe, Ellie and Steph were the only remaining starters from the 2007 World Cup squad that had seen its championship dreams in China squashed by Brazil. In the days and weeks that followed the humiliating 4-0 loss in the semifinals—a game that had featured an own goal *and* a red card ejection for the US side—the players had argued bitterly amongst themselves in a feud that created a division between veterans and newer players. The loss and ensuing drama had cost head coach Jeff Bradbury his position a year before the Olympics. Emma, the youngest player on the roster, had tried to keep her head down and stay out of the inter-squad blame fest that became the Great National Team Meltdown of '07, as she and Maddie had come to call it.

Talk about a bad fit—Bradbury had coached the team to be harsh, blunt, and defensive both on and off the field, just as he'd been as a semi-pro player before becoming a coach. Unlike the national team's previous head coaches, he didn't understand how to motivate female players, relying on intimidation and pressure to achieve the results he wanted. Bradbury was a screamer, and wielded his power in a way that actively discouraged creativity and bold performances. The players used to joke before practice about who he would pick to crush that day, but dark humor did little to diminish the stress and anxiety they felt playing for him. Like most of her teammates, Emma had been relieved when Jeff Bradbury got fired.

Craig had been the polar opposite, which might have been the problem. He'd been quiet and observant and so willing to experiment with personnel and line-ups that Emma sometimes wondered if he even had a long term strategy in mind. Marty Sinclair, the coach who led the team in the years between these two very different men, had achieved positive results with an approach the players ate up. She had treated them like professionals and equals, offering them a say in the team's direction while still retaining ultimate control. She had worked *with* them, firm but respectful, and the team had thrived under her leadership.

What they needed, Emma thought now, was another Marty. She wasn't sure the federation agreed, though.

Ellie chimed in again. "I don't think there's any great conspiracy here, guys. You heard Rob: The Algarve result was a symptom of a larger, systemic issue, and they were still discussing what to do up until this morning. Today's game only further underscored the poor fit."

The game hadn't been that bad, had it? But then Emma remembered the frustration of watching as shot after shot sailed wide of the goal, as the Chinese keeper saved the few that were on frame, as one set piece after another failed to yield the desired result. They had played like a team that was the opposite of possessed. Dispossessed? The double entendre seemed fitting.

"Do you believe what Rob said?" Steph asked, face neutral. She had made no secret of her dislike of Craig's coaching style and, especially, his tendency to play untried newbies over more experienced players. But at the same time, she'd said more than once that she didn't trust the federation as far as she could throw it.

"Do you?" Phoebe asked. "How many people here believe even half of what comes out of Rob and Barry's mouths?"

Emma frowned as the assembled players exchanged weighted glances. That wasn't the point at all, and as a leader of this squad, Phoebe should know that. Before Emma could find a diplomatic way of saying as much, Jenny Latham spoke up.

"I don't think that's the question we should be asking right now. The question we need to ask ourselves is what we can do to help support the next coach. Because ladies, in case you hadn't noticed, World Cup qualifying is six months away, and I for one would prefer to avoid a repeat of 2010."

A collective groan made a short lap of the room. Forget losing to Japan in Frankfurt in the '11 finals. They almost hadn't even made it to Germany after being upset by Mexico—*Mexico!*—during the 2010 CONCACAF qualifiers. Marty used to say they took the scenic route to the '11 World Cup, and she wasn't kidding. After falling to Mexico at CONCACAFs, the team had played a two-leg series against Italy to determine who would win the sixteenth and final berth in Germany. While they had managed to defeat Italy on goals by Ellie and Jenny Latham, it had been one of the tenser moments in Emma's national team career.

"Good point, Jen." Ellie looked around the room. "What was it that Marty said right before the second game against Italy? That the glass was half-full? Well, it's half-full again, friends. A new coach brings change, but maybe it's needed change. Whatever played into the decision, Craig is out. It's up to us to decide how to respond."

That was all well and good to say, Emma thought later that night as she headed toward the ice machine on her hallway. But in reality, they had little control over their working conditions. While the players' union did its best with what they were given, and current contracted players had it better than any previous generation of women, ultimately the decisions that impacted them most were out of their hands. Emma knew firsthand that FIFA's attitude toward women's soccer—namely, that female players did not deserve equal treatment or equal pay—had found willing support among the upper echelons of US Soccer, a nonprofit that refused to be transparent with the millions earned every year by its marketing arm. That lack of transparency and tendency to misrepresent its motives and intent meant that the players— both male and female—ended up second-guessing major decisions like the one that had been handed down tonight.

As was often the case during training camp, the ice machine was empty, a state of affairs that always made Emma think of Jamie and their first fateful meeting in a Southern California hotel ten years earlier. A wave of longing passed over her, so intense that tears pricked her eyes. She was tired, a bone-deep weariness that arose from this stupid cold she'd been fighting all week; from the federation's political mind games; from constant travel and what felt like almost too much soccer. Through hard work and sacrifice, she had achieved her childhood dreams and was living the life she'd always wanted. But sometimes, even so, the thought wriggled into her mind that maybe the grass was greener. Maybe she would be happier living a lower-key life in Seattle like Dani, with a commute that didn't require passports or landing gear. Intellectually she knew that if she crossed the fence and settled in the opposite field, she would miss her current life desperately. Besides, she would still be the same person. What was the quote? "Wherever you go, there you are." Even so, she couldn't help wondering.

She was sick of all the going, going, goneness of her life. She wanted to rest, to take a day off of training here and there, to live a full week without having to think about soccer. But if she did that, she could put in jeopardy the goal she'd spent so much of her life working toward. Then again, was being a professional soccer player worth the constant emotional and physical stress? Was it worth being apart from the person she'd come to care about most? Jamie's image appeared in her mind again, and she remembered her first thought after Rob's announcement had sunk in: With Craig out, Jamie might have another shot at the team, especially with her former youth coach at the helm.

Ellie and Phoebe believed that Jo Nichols might be offered the opportunity to lead the team on more than an interim basis, just as she had after Marty left. The question was, would her answer be different this time? Since Emma had been out with a burst appendix at the end of 2012, she hadn't spent much time around the former national team star turned coaching prodigy. She did know, however, that Jo understood female athletes as well as the politics of the international game. And that she had a soft spot for Jamie, or so it seemed.

Time, Emma supposed, would tell. For now, she'd better find some ice or her ankles—and Ellie's back—were going to hate her tomorrow.

Emma glanced around Jo Nichols's hotel room, bemused to see a younger player who had cried a few days earlier at the news of Craig's firing now giggling and wrestling a teammate for a Hershey bar. It was Wednesday, their third night in San Diego, and Jo had invited the team to her room for bonding over s'mores and *Despicable Me*, her son's favorite movie. The following day they would meet China in a rematch of the previous weekend's game, only with a new coach at the helm.

Emma never slept well in hotels, but the night Rob and Barry had made their pronouncement, she'd experienced more difficulty than usual shutting off her brain. Ellie and Maddie had said they'd slept fitfully too, and even Angie had dark circles under her eyes on the way to the airport the following morning. On the flight to San Diego, most of the players had spoken in hushed tones, their usual smiles and friendly jibes conspicuously absent. How could the federation throw the program into such turmoil so close to qualifiers? Whoever took over was going to have to work some major magic in a very short period of time, they'd agreed.

Now, only a few days later, the mood on the team was lighter. Despite what had happened in Colorado, training in San Diego had been positive. It helped that most of the players had played previously for Jo or otherwise knew her from her long tenure at US Soccer. But also, maybe Rob and Barry had been right, more than one person had whispered at breakfast or on the team bus. Maybe Craig hadn't been a good fit for the program.

Either way, the game the following evening, "the first in the Jo Nichols Era," as Ellie kept referring to it, would be interesting.

"It's not her era if she isn't named head coach," Emma pointed out after she and Ellie had successfully smuggled a plate of s'mores back to their room.

"She will be," Ellie said confidently, licking marshmallow from one thumb while the other moved rapidly over her phone's screen—texting Jodie, no doubt.

On the flight to California, Ellie had admitted that she'd picked Emma as her roommate for the trip in the interests of synchronicity: They were sharing a room on the road while their girlfriends were sharing space back at home. Ellie loved synchronicity. Emma did too, if she was being honest. She picked up her own phone and scrolled through her private Instagram feed, smiling at the short video the Thorns had posted of Jamie and one of her teammates practicing slide tackles on a rainy field, water spraying every which way.

Unfortunately, she made the mistake of skimming the comments. Public figures, especially those of the female persuasion, should never read comments on the Internet. Scratch that. Human beings should never read the comments.

"What's with the frown?" Ellie asked, plopping down on the bed beside her and gazing over her shoulder. "That video is awesome. What, are you afraid your girl is going to get hurt?"

"I'm always afraid she's going to get hurt."

"Good point." Her eyes honed in on the small screen. "Oh. I see."

"I thought people your age needed reading glasses," Angie commented as she barged into the room, Maddie in her wake.

"Hey, shortie." Ellie winked at Maddie. "Red."

"Her hair isn't red," Angie huffed and dropped onto the empty bed, reaching immediately for a s'more and the TV remote.

Ellie gazed at Maddie, pretending to be shocked. "You mean your dye job is upstairs *and* downstairs?"

Emma bit back a smile as Angie stared between the two veterans, mind clearly working. How the younger woman could still be so gullible after this long was a mystery.

Maddie rolled her eyes at Ellie and patted Angie's thigh as she sat down beside her. "She's pulling your leg, sweetie. Seriously," she added as she too stole a s'more, "what are you guys looking at?"

"Instagram comments," Ellie admitted.

"Dude!" Angie's eyes remained glued to the muted television. "You never read the comments."

"I know. It was just a slip." Emma closed her Instagram app.

"Let me guess." Maddie paused to swallow a large bite. "More assholes asking why men are allowed on the women's national team?"

US Soccer had posted a video of Ellie leading the team off the bus before Sunday's match, and as usual, a mob of trolls had commented on her gender identity.

Ellie rescued the paper plate from the bedside table before their visitors could steal more s'mores and handed it to Emma for safekeeping. "In the NWSL, actually. Jamie's in their crosshairs this time."

"Fuckers," Angie announced.

"Bastards," Emma agreed forcefully, or as forcefully as she could manage with the delectable blend of chocolate, graham, and marshmallow melting in her mouth.

"How is the other half of your hashtag, Blake?" Angie asked.

"Good. Oh, she told me to tell you she likes your new 'ship name."

Angie's forehead creased. "What new 'ship name?"

"You know—Nowang?" she replied, purposely mis-rhyming Angie's last name with *rang*.

Angie's mouth dropped. "That's not our 'ship name!"

"Have you not checked Tumblr lately?" Emma asked.

Angie pulled her phone from the pocket of her black Nike hoodie, almost dropping it in her haste.

"Babe, she's effing with you again," Maddie said, placing her hand over Angie's. "Although in my opinion, Nowang sounds better than Wangvak. That just sounds like a vacuum company."

Emma and Ellie exchanged a look. It really did.

Angie shook her head. "No thanks. I'd rather sound like a Chinese manufacturer than a 1950s housewife. I mean, come on, *Madgeline*? I'm not even sure how you pronounce that one."

"I don't know," Maddie said, pushing up the sleeves of her own Nike hoodie—also black. "I think it sounds romantic. You know, like Brangelina."

Angie started to make a face and then stopped. "Huh. Angelina Jolie *is* hot. Plus she's a known bisexual."

"You two do realize that matching outfits aren't required," Emma put in, snuggling deeper into her wool sweater. Ellie liked to sleep cold. Emma had teased her about hot flashes, but alas, the age jokes hadn't had any effect on their room's temperature.

The couple on the other bed exchanged a secretive glance that wasn't remotely secretive.

"You must not have read the woman-loving-woman manual recently," Maddie said, and moved to place a resounding kiss on her girlfriend's lips.

"Whatever." Emma kept her eyes firmly on the television as she said, "Hand over the remote, Ange."

"Yeah," Ellie added, holding out her hand between the two beds. "No way you get the remote. Also, lips unlocked if you want to stay."

"You're just jealous because your girlfriends are together," Angie said smugly, tossing the remote at her.

The truth of this statement didn't prevent Emma and Ellie from glaring at her.

"You mean currently in the same household, *right?*" Ellie asked, her voice pitched lower than usual.

"Well, I didn't mean *together* together. Gross!"

Ellie nudged the TV volume up slightly. While SportsCenter showed highlights from the evening's baseball games, the four friends discussed the afternoon training session and, inevitably, the coaching situation.

"I don't know," Maddie said. "Call me paranoid, but in my darker moments I can't help wondering if they fired Craig because of the turf issue. Like, what if the federation is trying to sabotage our chances next year by chucking our coach this close to CONCACAFs?"

Emma and Ellie exchanged another look, considerably less amused this time.

"You don't sound paranoid," Emma admitted. "Ellie and I said the same thing. The fact is, if we win the World Cup next year, we're going to be in a significantly better position to renegotiate the CBA."

"When does the MOU expire again?" Angie asked.

"A year from December."

"So six months after we WIN the effing World Cup, baby!"

"Yeah, boy!" Ellie held her hand up between the beds for Angie to high five.

As a younger player who didn't regularly start, Angie wasn't as involved in talks with the federation about collective bargaining agreements (CBAs) or memos of understanding (MOUs). Only contracted players in positions of leadership and prestige typically took on the business of negotiating. Players whose status was less guaranteed were given a chance to voice their opinions on all matters that affected them, but they weren't asked to stick out their necks and potentially risk their careers.

"Still, sabotaging us would be a fairly egregious case of cutting off their noses to spite their faces," Ellie said. "I have to believe that, for the most part, they want us to succeed."

"It's the least part that worries me," Maddie said. "How many women are in positions of leadership in US Soccer? Not that many. The federation is barely better than FIFA when it comes to issues of equality. In fact, maybe they're worse. At least FIFA isn't willfully violating the Equal Pay Act."

"Besides," Angie added, "everyone knows how salty US Soccer is that we're more successful than the men's team—including the male players themselves."

"Not all of them," Maddie qualified.

Angie stared at her. "Did you just 'not all men' me?"

"Christ, I did. Sorry, babe."

"It's okay. Sometimes it's hard to resist our default cultural programming." As all eyes in the room snapped to her, Angie shrugged. "What? Max and I used to room together on the twenty-threes. I'm a nerd by association."

Emma forced herself not to sigh like a moody teenager at the mention of her absent girlfriend. It was a little ridiculous how much she missed having Jamie at camp. Being apart from Sam and Will had been difficult too, but it had felt like part of the job, a necessary evil to achieve her career goals. With Jamie, it was different. Jamie could—*should*—be here in this room with them, dishing out the teasing jabs and smiling her adorable smile. She should be getting ready to suit up for tomorrow's friendly in sunny SoCal, not slide tackling her club teammates in the rain a thousand miles away.

"You okay?" Ellie asked, nudging her.

"Yep." Emma bit her lip. "Well, no. How do you and Jodie do it?"

"It's hard, Emma, I'm not gonna lie. Sometimes I'm not sure we'll make it. You know how high the divorce rates are for athletes. We're on the road what, an average of 260 days out of the year? That's seventy percent of the time. But it's worth it for me."

"Okay, but *how* do you make it work?"

"FaceTime." She shrugged, broad shoulders moving against Emma's. "You get comfortable with sex mediated through a small screen pretty quickly—assuming you haven't already?"

Emma felt her cheeks flush. Stupid Scandinavian prudishness.

Predictably, Angie perked up at the mention of sex. "You guys sharing Skype tips over there? Can't say I miss that."

"Me either," Maddie said, and then whispered something in Angie's ear.

Angie shot off the bed. "Gotta go! Later taters."

Laughing, Maddie followed her.

"Make good choices!" Ellie bellowed after their retreating figures. As the door slammed behind them, she pointed the remote at the television. "Want to watch something? I have enough Sheraton points to pay for a movie every night for the next three and a half years."

Emma didn't ask if she would still be playing in three and a half years. That question was better left to reporters. "Same here."

"I'll let you pick up the tab if you really want."

"Glad someone will."

Ellie started scrolling through the pay-per-view options. "Yeah, I've noticed your girl's got some pride. That's a good thing, Em."

"I know. I just wish she'd let me treat her more."

"She's still starting out. You and I have been doing this for so long that we don't remember what it's like to live month to month."

In truth, Emma had never had to live like that. Her parents had been better off than most of her friends' parents growing up, and that was saying something since they'd lived in one of Seattle's wealthier suburbs. Jamie's parents weren't hurting by any means, but they couldn't give her the down payment for a condo. Or maybe they could, but they wouldn't. They believed the struggle made any eventual success more rewarding, according to Jamie.

"But I could help," Emma said. "I *want* to help."

What she meant was that selfishly, she wanted Jamie to have her own apartment in Portland so that when the Reign's bye week came around, they wouldn't have to spend it hanging around other people. Ellie and Jodie were among her closest friends, but Emma wanted Jamie all to herself.

"Be patient," Ellie said. "Jo Nichols is a huge Jamie Maxwell fan. I would bet my Kegerator she'll give her another shot—and you know how much I love my Kegerator." She coughed out a laugh. "Hey, check out this porno title: *Bend Her Like Beckham.*"

"What?" Emma's gaze shot to the screen, and then she shoved Ellie sideways as she saw the movie menu paused on an image of Olaf, the snowman from *Frozen*. "Jackass! I can't believe Maddie told you about that."

"You should have seen your face. But what do you say—*Frozen?*"

Emma shrugged. "Why not?"

They sang along, because of course they knew all the words to "the first Disney princess movie to critique the love-at-first-sight trope!" they exclaimed, laughing as they quoted Jamie. Then they sighed because yeah, they missed their girlfriends. But even so, the movie was light and fun with a touch of darkness and a compelling message about love and sisterhood—exactly what they needed the night before the first friendly in the Jo Nichols era.

Later, as she slipped under the covers and reached for her eyeshade and ear plugs, Emma wondered if Ellie knew more than she was saying. Had Jo already accepted the position? Was US Soccer waiting to make the announcement out of some (albeit small) gesture of respect toward Craig? And what had Ellie and Phoebe known about Craig's firing, for that matter?

*It's up to us to decide how to respond*, Ellie had said at the team meeting Sunday night. Again, that wasn't entirely true, Emma thought as she lay in bed, the sound of Ellie's low snoring muffled by her ear plugs. They may be in charge of their own mental resilience, but ultimately the team's direction—from lineup decisions to strategic formations—was guided by the coaching staff. And if their next head coach was indeed going to be Jo Nichols, Emma's future with the national program suddenly felt less assured than it had only a week ago.

During down time the last few days, she'd Googled Jo and discovered that she was known for favoring defenders who possessed the ability—and desire—to score. As a youth coach, she had developed a reputation for turning strikers into outside backs, whether the player welcomed the change or not. At Virginia, where she'd coached for the last decade, she'd emphasized the importance of building offensive opportunities as a unit. More than once she'd said in interviews that there was no room in her program for "one-dimensional" players: those who only scored or defended. Jo prized well-rounded athletes who could create as well as destroy.

Despite her father's one-time contention that she could be the next Mia Hamm, Emma knew herself. She was a defender, period. While she could help start the offense and even got off an assist every once in a while, she was no more a finisher than Phoebe was. She was a center back and that was enough for her. It had been enough for Marty and Craig, too. Both former coaches had told her that they believed without reserve in her ability to organize a strong defense. Would Jo Nichols feel the same way?

Emma shifted under the sheets and decided to distract herself from things she couldn't control by picturing Jamie asleep in her boy shorts and tank top a thousand miles up the coast. One good thing had come out of the team's turmoil—as Emma had thought previously and Ellie had confirmed, Jo was a fan of Jamie's. She had discovered her as a teenager, and while she may not have been able to convince Jamie to leave the West Coast for college, she had started her in nearly every U-16 match and, later, most U-23 matches as well. Not that Emma had noticed. Well, okay, *maybe* she had. But she didn't have to be embarrassed by that fact anymore, did she? It wasn't creepy if the pining was mutual; it was simply a case of star-crossed love.

Whatever happened with her own playing time under the eventual new coaching staff, she would appreciate any opportunity for her relationship with Jamie to be less star-crossed and more favored by the soccer gods. Because while she might not believe in the power of such deities herself, Jamie certainly did.

# CHAPTER THREE

Jamie flicked her sweaty hair off her forehead. God, she needed a haircut. But that would have to wait. Right now she had a throw-in to take.

The game was almost over, but the fourteen thousand-plus fans at Providence Park were still on the edge of their seats. Portland had been knocking steadily on Seattle's goal since half-time. Neither team had broken through, however, and the score remained a scoreless tie.

A diagonal run in the center caught her eye, and she turned her body quickly, whipping the ball over her head into the path of her teammate Isabela. The Brazilian international drove toward Seattle's central defense while Jamie trailed in a supporting position. As she watched, Emma closed the space, eyes focused on the ball despite Isabela's shoulder dips and half-steps.

*Damn it*, Jamie thought as Emma coolly stripped the Brazilian player. Also, *nice*, because that was her girl.

She stepped up to intercept Emma, but she didn't get the chance. Isabela, clearly frustrated, slide-tackled Emma from behind, getting mostly player. Emma slammed to the ground as the ball caromed, and even though Jamie knew the whistle had shrieked, even though she could hear the Thorns fans whistling derisively at the referee's call, all she could see was Emma sprawled awkwardly on the turf.

*Get up*, she thought. *Get up!*

She needn't have worried. Emma popped up, spun around, and took a few steps toward Isabela, emanating barely controlled fury. Or, you know, not at all controlled fury, Jamie amended as Emma's momentum carried her into the Brazilian player's body space. Isabela immediately clutched her face and went down, rolling around as if she had been head-butted Zinedine Zidane-style. Jamie huffed inwardly as she reached her teammate. Acting classes had to be a required part of the Brazilian training regimen.

Before anything else could come of it, Jamie grabbed Isabela under both armpits and hauled her to her feet. "Knock it the fuck off," she hissed, pretending to brush off her teammate's jersey.

Isabela shot her an irritated glare, but at that moment the referee stopped before them, hand on his pocket. Isabela received her yellow card for the tackle; Emma got hers for retaliation. That was one of the first rules Jamie had learned as a young player: Officials might not always catch the initial foul, but they rarely missed a retaliation.

Emma stalked away, and Jamie forced her gaze from her retreating figure. If Ellie had been playing, no doubt she would have smacked Jamie upside the head for checking out her hot girlfriend in the middle of the game. But the Thorns captain and leading scorer was currently on the bench, resting up after a national team friendly in Winnipeg two days earlier. A game Emma had played in, Jamie might add.

*Game going on here, Maxwell*, she reminded herself as she jogged back into position for the free kick. *Focus, idiot.*

Avery Jones, Seattle's starting keeper and Phoebe's longtime back-up, waved her team up the field for the kick. Jamie was still jogging backwards when the ball sailed into the Thorns defensive end with pinpoint accuracy, straight onto the foot of the Reign's captain and leading scorer, British international Megan Davies. A Thorns defender stripped her and started to clear the ball, but Davies quickly recovered, stole the ball back, and one-touched it to an overlapping midfielder. Jamie sprinted toward goal, but she was too far away and it was too late, anyway. With a beautiful first touch, the Reign player nudged the ball past Greta, Portland's Swedish keeper, and slotted it coolly into the empty net.

Seattle's small but vocal fan contingent burst into cheers while Portland's fans, still angry over the foul call against Isabela, whistled their displeasure. Jamie stood in the middle of the field, hands on her hips, watching as the Seattle players mobbed Davies and the midfielder. She checked the clock. One minute left in regulation time. *Christ.* They had been so freaking close.

There would be stoppage time, she thought, turning toward the center circle. The game wasn't over yet.

The next few minutes were frenetic, with Portland redoubling their offensive efforts and Avery continuing to make mind-boggling saves to keep Seattle on top. The officials awarded three minutes of stoppage time, and the game went end to end for most of that time. Jamie had a late shot tipped over the crossbar, and a teammate's header on the subsequent corner kick narrowly missed the frame. Avery floated the resulting goal kick well into Portland's defensive end. As the Thorns center back brought the ball down, Jamie heard it: the three shrill whistle tweets that signaled the end of the game.

That was it. Coming into today's game, their first match-up of the 2014 season, Seattle and Portland had been the only undefeated teams left in the league. Now Seattle alone could claim that title.

A fact that Emma didn't rub in too much at the bar that night.

It was their second night in a row together—a rare

occurrence—and despite the fact that Emma's team had beaten hers, Jamie felt warm and happy squished onto the bench of a picnic table at the back of a brew pub a short walk from the stadium. With Emma on one side and Ellie on the other, a lager shanty on the table before her, she couldn't help thinking of the last night of January camp when she and Emma had smiled into each other's eyes and held hands under the table.

Kind of like they were doing now.

"Ah, I see now why you defend the other team," Isabela said from the other side of the table, lips twisted in a smirk. Freshly showered and coiffed, she barely resembled her on-field persona. "I didn't realize *this* was the Blake of whom everyone speaks."

"Oh. Well, yeah, this is Emma. Emma, this is Isabela."

"We already know one another, Maximillian," Isabela said, employing her nickname of choice for Jamie.

Of course they weren't strangers. They must have come up against each other a dozen times or more at Olympics and World Cups, in friendlies and not-so-friendly grudge matches. Now that Jamie thought about it, that was probably why Emma had gone from zero to red-card-angry so quickly earlier. Isabela had broken Tina Baker's foot a few years back in a spiteful slide tackle much like the one she had executed tonight.

"We know each other," Emma agreed, and tilted her head in a gesture that Jamie recognized as one of her frostier glares. "*Isa.*"

"*Emma.*"

The stare-off continued until Ellie said, "So, Isa, are the rumors true? I hear Marisol's considering leaving Tyresö to join the NWSL."

Marisol was Brazil's star player of the last decade, with no fewer than four FIFA World Player of the Year awards to her name. But for all her brilliance and renown, she had never won gold in an Olympics or World Cup.

"Don't believe everything you hear." Isa tipped her glass at Ellie. "For example, it is almost unfathomable that you are giving up the single life in order to settle down."

Like Jenny Latham, Ellie had a bit of a reputation in the soccer world. Unlike Jenny, who supposedly fell toward the hetero end of the Kinsey scale, Ellie's conquests had been strictly girl-on-girl. And geez, Emma had told Jamie, had there been a lot of girls before Jodie.

Ellie shrugged. "What can I say? Everyone has to grow up sometime."

"I am not certain I agree," Isa said. "But the woman who can tame you must be fierce indeed."

"She is," Ellie said, the smile she reserved for Jodie and newborn babies softening her features.

"Why isn't she here tonight?" Megan Davies put in from beside Isa, her street clothes and make-up also on point, as Angie would have said.

"She had to fly to New York for work."

"What does she do?"

As the conversation moved on to significant others and their careers of choice, Jamie felt Emma lean into her side and murmur, "How much longer are we staying?"

She glanced at Emma, noting her girlfriend's narrowed eyes and the way she touched her tongue to her lips. And, right. *Okay.*

Jamie rose abruptly, nearly tipping Emma over, and tossed a few bills on the table. "It's been fun, kids."

Isa lifted a sculpted eyebrow. "Better things to do with your time, Maximillian?"

"Well, actually, yes." Jamie hoped she wasn't preening too much, but it was hard not to, given who she was dating.

At her side, Emma tilted her own eyebrow at the Brazilian. "Nice game, ladies. Better luck next time. You'll need it."

Before the boos and hoots could reach a crescendo, Jamie grabbed Emma's hand and pulled her away, laughter and the occasional whistle following them.

"I didn't mean to make you ditch your friends," Emma said as they left the bar.

"I can hang out with those guys anytime. You, on the other hand…" She trailed off, checking outside for rain before zipping up her fleece and tugging her baseball cap lower.

"I know exactly what you mean." Emma shrugged into her puffy vest and stepped out onto the sidewalk, where groups of people had gathered to share cigarettes and certain other smoking products.

Jamie moved past quickly, amazed as ever by the boldness of anyone who smoked weed in public in a state where its use was still illegal. They couldn't all have medical marijuana cards, could they? But this was the Pearl District, where hipster restaurants and microbreweries attracted liberal, wealthy patrons—the Oregonians most likely to support women's soccer, gay marriage, and the legalization of recreational drugs.

The rain began when they were halfway back to the stadium. Laughing, Emma linked their hands and tugged her along the wet streets back to the players' lot. Soon they were shivering in the front seat of Jamie's hatchback, defroster blasting as they exchanged smiles on their way back to Ellie's house. For once it would be just the two of them at home.

It didn't take long to reach Ellie's street. Heart racing in anticipation, Jamie parked out front and led Emma inside. Emma's lips were on hers the second she closed the front door, and Jamie returned the kiss feverishly, backing Emma towards the stairway. They paused long enough to make it downstairs safely before Jamie guided Emma toward her bedroom, hands and lips wandering as they stripped off each other's clothes. This coming together was different from the night before, when they had kissed almost shyly at first, relearning each other's bodies. Tonight the energy flaring between them was bolder, more demanding.

Emma pushed her back on the bed and finished shimmying out of her skinny jeans before reaching for Jamie's belt buckle. "May I?" she asked, voice low, smile sly.

"Yes." Jamie gazed up at her, taking in the lovely sight of Emma in boy briefs and a lacy push-up bra. The contrast in underwear choice, she decided, summed her up perfectly.

And then Emma's hands were on her belt buckle and her lips were on Jamie's neck, and the briefs and bra? They weren't necessary at all.

"I can't believe I have to go home today," Emma said, her breath warm on Jamie's shoulder.

Jamie trailed her hand up Emma's arm, scratching her skin lightly and feeling her shiver. "You don't, though, do you?"

"Does that mean you're planning to hold me hostage in your basement lair?"

"Hello, it's a *daylight* basement lair. And no, I'm saying we could hang out today and you could leave tomorrow morning and still be back in time for practice..."

She hesitated. "I have to lift, and I was going to run a few drills, too."

Jamie grinned at her, turning on all the charm she could muster. "Then I guess it's a good thing I happen to know an excellent soccer academy. I bet they'd even let you train for free in exchange for a bit of publicity."

"Jamie..." Emma propped herself up, brow creased.

"What?"

"You know what. If a video gets out of us training together, it could break our little corner of the Internet."

"And that's bad because...?"

"Because you could still make the national team. You know how the federation feels about players dating each other."

"Hasn't stopped Maddie and Angie."

That was an understatement. More than once Angie's New Jersey-based trainer had posted videos of them running a scoring drill while wearing each other's USWNT shorts, the numbers clear as day. Angie played for Sky Blue in Jersey and Maddie played for the Washington Spirit outside DC, but the two hundred-plus miles between them hadn't prevented them from working out together semi-regularly.

"They've already got contracts," Emma pointed out, her hand splayed against Jamie's ribs. "Are these new?" she added, caressing her abs.

"Improved, anyway." She flexed, smiling as Emma hummed in appreciation. That sound made all the hard work worth it in a way that even leading the assist column in the NWSL couldn't. "See? I'm telling you, babe, the guys at Next Level know what they're doing."

Emma pushed the sheet away and scooted down her body. "If I stay, it definitely won't be for the guys at Next Level." And then she dipped her head and began lazily kissing her way across Jamie's mid-section.

Jamie stared up at the paint swirls on the bedroom ceiling, sighing in contentment. Being together in real life definitely kicked Skype's cyber-booty. She could get used to waking up like this. Or, she could if they ever lived in the same city. For now, she would take Emma when she could get her. She started to laugh at her own pun, but then Emma's head dipped lower and she gasped instead, bunching the sheets in one fist while thoughts of puns and the Internet skittered away.

The scent of breakfast cooking finally lured them out

of Jamie's room.

"Holy shit, you're both alive," Ellie commented, expertly flipping a pancake as they took seats at the kitchen island, their hair still wet from the shower. "I wasn't sure from the sounds I heard down there."

"You should talk," Jamie blustered, pretending she didn't feel her face turning red. "Not like you and Jodie don't do the same thing!"

"Well, I hardly think they do the *same* things, babe," Emma said.

She'd pulled on Jamie's Stanford T-shirt and her old 49ers cap before trekking upstairs, and now Ellie grunted as she reached for her phone. "Wait until the Seattle fans see you flaunting your loyalty to the Niners, Blake."

"Hey!" Emma hid behind Jamie. "No cameras, Ellison!"

Ellie set her phone back on the counter. "Fine. No need to get your panties in a bunch."

Jamie decided not to inform her that the likelihood of that happening was significantly reduced by the fact that Emma wasn't currently wearing underwear.

"So what do you two have planned today?" Ellie scooped scrambled eggs and pancakes onto a trio of plates and slid them across the island. "Or do you have to head home, Em?"

"This one here has invited me to stay," Emma admitted, spooning a generous helping of cut fruit onto her plate. "Assuming that's okay with you?"

Ellie nodded as she drowned her eggs in hot sauce. "I told you guys, you're welcome as long as you like. Both of you."

"You're a good egg," Emma said. "Even if you do play for the second-best team in the Pacific Northwest."

"Second-best? Pretty sure the fans would disagree with

you on that one."

Jamie shoved food in her mouth as the other two traded insults. She appreciated Ellie's generosity, she did, but it was hard to have to depend on the kindness of others. Whenever Jamie apologized for mooching off Ellie, she would launch into her own stories of starting out back when Americans were still high on the '99 World Cup and WUSA was the first fully professional women's soccer league in the world.

"Pay it forward and it's all good," she'd told Jamie more than once, tsk-tsking whenever Jamie hunched her shoulders and replied darkly, "Assuming I get the chance."

Sometimes Jamie wished she had Ellie's faith in her. Emma's, too, while she was at it.

"Wait," Ellie said suddenly. "Does that mean you're coming to train with us?"

Emma shrugged. "I might scout out the competition. Although after the game yesterday, I'm not sure that's necessary."

"I have two words for you: Defending champs. Besides, if I had played, you know the result would have been different."

"Oh, is that right?" Emma drawled. "I'm fairly confident I could have shut you down too, Ellison. As usual."

"Sure, Blake."

"Why weren't you playing, again? *I* managed to and I went a full ninety against Canada."

As Ellie blustered a response, Jamie's attention grew fuzzy. Sometimes in moments like this, her reality still felt unreal. She was living with Rachel Ellison, one of the greatest players of all time, and dating Emma Blakeley, the woman she had been half in love with for most of her adult life, and here they all were having Sunday brunch together in Ellie's beautiful new kitchen in her beautiful new house overlooking an almost sunny Portland. And yes, she was technically living "off" Ellie instead of "with," and maybe she and Emma only saw each other in person rarely, but the fact remained that her life was pretty great even without a spot on the national team.

Almost as if Jamie had conjured it, Ellie's phone rang, caller ID blinking "US Soccer." Ellie grabbed it and walked into the living room, where Jamie heard her say, "Hey Fitzy... Yep, I got the email. Thanks for the heads-up. When will the announcement go out?... Got it... See you next month. Oh, and give Eli a high five from me."

Jamie glanced at Emma, whose eyebrows had risen. Fitzy was Carrie Fitzsimmons, the USWNT manager, Eli her first grader who, like Steph Miller's son Brodie, had grown up around the team. In fact, Eli and Brodie were best buds and often gave their parents heart attacks with their on- and off-field capers. Eli's worship for the players was equal opportunity for the most part, but he admired Ellie especially because, he said, he'd been named after her. Obviously.

"What was that about?" Emma asked as Ellie reclaimed her spot at the island.

"Captain's business," she said cryptically, and took a large bite of a Nutella-smeared pancake. She claimed she'd picked up the habit years before while playing pro soccer in Sweden, and now that Amazon would deliver the jumbo size right to her door, she planned never again to go without.

Before Emma could press further, Jamie's phone rang. She stared at the name blinking up at her: *US Soccer.* "Oh my god. OH MY GOD!"

"Well?" Emma said. "Are you going to answer it?"

Jamie hit talk and spun away from the island. "Hello?"

"Hi, Jamie?"

Jo Nichols. Jo Nichols, former star striker and current head coach of the US Women's National Team—*interim*, she reminded herself—was calling her.

"Yes. Hi." She jogged downstairs to her bedroom,

careful not to trip despite the anxiety and hope cluttering her nervous system.

"Jo Nichols here. Do you have a minute to chat?"

"Absolutely." She dropped onto the edge of her bed, ignoring the tangled sheets and other signs of her morning activities with Emma. Who was a contracted player on the national team. Who was officially her girlfriend, and unofficially off-limits to other contracted players.

Good thing Jamie wasn't a contracted player.

"So I've been making the rounds of the NWSL the past few weeks," Jo started, "and I'm calling because I saw you play against Seattle last night."

"You did?" How had she not known Jo Nichols was in the crowd? Probably because with more than ten thousand screaming soccer fans, it would be easy enough for a lone forty-something woman to blend into the crowd.

"I did, and I wanted to tell you that I'm very encouraged by what I saw."

"You are?" Okay, time to sound less like an idiot and more like a confident, professional athlete. "I mean, thanks. I've been working on fitness this summer, and I think it's helped my game as well as made me more injury-proof."

*Injury-proof?* She smacked her own forehead, but quietly so the sound wouldn't reverberate through the phone. *Nice, Maxwell. Real smooth.*

"I'm glad to hear that because I wanted to discuss your future on the national team."

Jamie gulped. "Yes, ma'am?"

"I'm about to tell you something that will be official as of tomorrow, so can I depend on you not to call ESPN as soon as we hang up?"

"Of course! I don't have their number, if that helps."

Jo laughed. "Good to know. The thing is, I'm about to be named the new permanent coach of the senior side. The reason I'm telling you this is that I want you to know why I'm not inviting you to any of the remaining friendlies this summer."

And just like that, Jamie's heart sank. What the actual fuck? She'd already been kicked out of the pool by Craig and his minions. Why did Jo Nichols feel the need to double down?

Before she could spiral too far into despair, Jo added, "Wait. Let's back up. I think I started in the wrong place. What I want you to take away from this conversation is that despite what happened in the past, you have a shot at making my team. As you know, I've watched you grow and develop over the years, Jamie, into a talented, smart, inspiring young woman who would be a valuable asset to the program—*if* you can stay healthy. I think it's fair to say that's been your Achilles heel since college."

"Yeah, that's fair," Jamie agreed.

"If it helps, I fully believe you're one of those people who can push through and come out the other side stronger. It's just a matter of getting yourself on the right track."

Jamie nodded even though Jo couldn't see her. "Ellie hooked me up with her trainer here in Portland, and I'm already seeing some great results. I know injury comes down to luck sometimes, but I'm trying to do everything I can to make sure I'm more resilient. And faster, because if they can't catch me, they can't hurt me, right?"

She'd meant it as a joke, but she winced as the silence lengthened. Maybe Jo Nichols didn't have room for a sense of humor under the weight of the mantle she had agreed to assume. Maybe coaching the number one in the world—

"I see you still have your positive outlook," Jo said. Jamie couldn't be sure, but it sounded like she might be smiling.

"Well, as my grandfather used to say, sometimes you've

got to laugh or else you'll cry."

Had either of her grandfathers ever said such a thing? Shoshanna, her former therapist, definitely had, but Jamie wasn't about to tell Jo Nichols that. In any case, someone's grandfather somewhere had undoubtedly said it.

"Isn't that the truth," Jo agreed. "Here's the bottom line, Jamie. We have a few more friendlies this summer, but I'm using those to get a sense of the existing roster. In September, after the pro season ends, I'm planning to bring in a wider pool for a two-week residency camp. If you can continue at your current level through the end of the NWSL season, I'd like to invite you to that camp.

"This isn't a promise," she added, her tone cautionary. "As you know, plenty of things can change in a matter of months. But I wanted you to know that the door isn't closed on the World Cup for you. Your future with the national team is in your hands, kiddo. Understand?"

"Yes, ma'am, I understand. Thank you so much for the opportunity."

"It isn't an opportunity yet. More like a dangling carrot."

"Good thing I like carrots," Jamie said, and then face-palmed for the second time.

"Good thing," Jo said, a smile in her voice once again. "Now, is Blake there?"

"Um…" Jamie stood up and glanced around the room as if Emma might be hiding nearby. "I don't…"

"It's not a trick question," Jo said. "She texted Fitzy that she was at Ellie's, so I'm wondering if she still is. You are living with Rachel Ellison currently, aren't you? That's the address we have on file."

"Oh! Yes. Right. Emma—Blake was upstairs a minute ago. Should I go check?" Jamie started up the stairs, taking them two at a time.

"If you don't mind. It's been nice talking to you again, Jamie. I look forward to more conversations in the near future."

"Me, too, Coach!"

A moment later she burst into the kitchen and practically threw her phone at Emma. "Jo Nichols wants to talk to you."

Emma frowned for a second before accepting the phone. "Hi, Jo. What's up?" She walked away, headed for the living room, and it was all Jamie could do to keep from following her.

"So?" Ellie asked.

"What?" Jamie tore her gaze away from Emma, who was standing near the picture window in the living room.

"So what did Jo say?"

Jamie dropped back onto her stool and picked up her fork. "She said she's the new head co—oh, shit!" She clapped her free hand over her mouth.

Ellie's shoulders shook from her nearly silent laughter. "Max, it's fine. I already knew."

"Oh, thank god. She told me not to tell ESPN."

"Last I checked, I'm not ESPN."

"Right. Yeah." Somehow managing to block out the sound of Emma's voice, she relayed her conversation with Jo. She'd just recounted the dangling carrot comment (Jo's, definitely, not her own ridiculous reply) when Emma came back in and set her phone on the counter.

"So?" Emma asked, her expectant face a mirror of Ellie's earlier expression.

Jamie wanted to tell her about the newly reopened door, but what came out was, "Did she tell you we can't date?"

Emma blinked at her. "What? No. She wanted to chat about the team."

66

Jamie noted that Emma didn't give away Jo's newly official status. Maybe she thought that blatantly ignoring the terms of her contract in front of the team captain would be rude.

"It's okay. She knows," Ellie told Emma. "Fitzy said Jo is calling everyone today to let them know she's replacing Craig permanently. Or, I guess not *permanently*, but until the federation someday forces her out, too."

Jamie wanted to pause on that—hadn't Marty Sinclair resigned of her own free will?—but Emma was still waiting. She repeated her conversation with the USWNT's new head coach, once again leaving out her excessive use of "ma'am" and her unfortunate "I like carrots" comment. Most people liked carrots. Besides, it was supposed to be a metaphor.

Emma was smiling broadly even before she finished. "See? I told you the door wasn't closed for good."

"You told her that?" Ellie asked. "What a coincidence—so did I. You should listen to your elders, kid."

"Says the old lady who couldn't play two games in one week..." Jamie ducked as Ellie chucked a grape at her.

"I can't help that I got sick on the flight!"

Emma coughed an unsubtle "Bullshit," and Jamie grinned at her, elation expanding inside her chest. Emma Blakeley was her girlfriend, Rachel Ellison was her housemate, her pro team was over .500, and Jo Nichols had called to dangle a giant, metaphorical carrot in front of her. Wait—did that make her the rabbit in this scenario? Was that how Jo Nichols saw her, as a cuddly, fluffy bunny? Whatever. No need to read too much into the national team coach's word choice. Life was good, friends were good, love was good. And so was Nutella. You didn't have to be a genius—or a resident of Western Europe—to know that.

"Pass me the Nutella," she said, interrupting her once and future teammates' bickering.

"Yes, *ma'am*," Emma said, and winked.

Damn it.

\*     \*     \*

Emma settled into her seat overlooking the Sea-Tac tarmac and took out her headphones, eyelids already drooping. While it was true she hadn't gotten enough sleep the previous night, her current state of exhaustion was related more to her hectic schedule than to a single night's lack of rest. Since facing Jamie's team in Portland the previous month, the Reign had gone on to play five games in four weeks—three at home, one in Kansas City, and one in New Jersey. Today was the official start to the Reign's bye week, but instead of visiting Jamie in Portland, Emma was on her way to Tampa for the first of two international friendlies against France. From Florida, the national team would travel to Connecticut for game number two, and then Emma and Avery would rejoin the Reign in Western New York for a match against the Flash before finally—*finally*—returning to Seattle to play Sky Blue at home.

She opened her message app and typed, "I made it!"

"Whew!" Jamie replied. "Or should I say bummer?"

"Definitely bummer. Miss you already."

"I know. Me too…"

"Where are you?" she typed.

"Almost back at yours."

"*Wish you were*—" Emma deleted the words and tried again. "Have a good couple of days off."

"I will. Thanks for letting me crash here. Text me when you land."

Before she could answer, a group text alert sounded.

"Gee, thanks for including me, guys," Dani's text to both of them read.

"You were driving!" Emma typed back. "Anyway, you know I'll miss you most of all."

"Liar."

"I resemble that."

"OMG you are such a dork," Dani sent.

Jamie replied all with a laughing face and a string of hearts. Then the jet's door closed and a flight attendant informed the passengers that it was time to switch their portable devices to airplane mode.

"Gotta go, gals."

"Hate to tell you, but only one of us is your gal pal," Dani texted. Then, "Love you, Blake. Safe travels."

"Love you too. Both of you." She typed a blowing kiss emoji, and they each returned it.

How cool was it that Dani and Jamie got along, she thought, closing her message app as the plane slowly rolled away from the gate. She wasn't sure why, given how different they were. But ever since Dani and her brothers had come to Jamie's rescue against Justin, Emma's bullying ex, they'd only had good things to say about each other. What was the line from that movie with Sandra Bullock and Keanu Reeves? "Relationships that start under intense circumstances never last." Fortunately, that didn't appear to be true of Jamie and Dani's friendship.

Damn it, why had her brain gone and dredged up *Speed*, a movie about an explosive device hidden on a city bus? Emma rested her head against the tiny airplane window and closed her eyes, turning up her calming New Age playlist. She really didn't like flying. Probably, then, she should find another job. Except that most of the time she loved her job, especially when the teams she was on kept winning. Under Jo's leadership the national team seemed to be regaining its form, while in Seattle the Reign hadn't lost a single match.

The same couldn't be said for Portland. The night before, after an embarrassing 5-0 home loss to Western New York, Jamie had called Emma and asked if she could come see her off. Emma, who had made peace with the idea that she wouldn't see Jamie before she left, jumped at the request even though she and Dani had planned to grab brunch this morning. Dani gallantly offered to reschedule, but Jamie had been adamant that they not cancel because of her. They'd met Dani at the Five Spot as planned, Jamie apologizing for crashing the meal and Dani telling her to knock it off as she tugged her into an affectionate hug. After demolishing omelets and french toast, they'd lingered over coffee and extra plates of fresh fruit so long that Emma had nearly missed her flight—and yes, maybe that hadn't been an entirely unconscious ploy on her part. Now, as the plane taxied down the runway, she cursed Dani for getting her to Sea-Tac on time.

The plane lurched as the ground fell away, but Emma doggedly kept her eyes shut. While she disliked flying in general, she especially hated take-off. She couldn't believe she had passed up a non-stop flight for one that connected in Houston, but the non-stop had left before nine AM, thereby violating the rules she'd established to prevent her travel commitments from disrupting her sleep. Then again, her dedication to a good night's sleep had become more flexible lately. Since the NWSL season had started, she and Jamie had taken turns driving late at night or early in the morning to be together. Otherwise they would only see each other when their teams faced off in league play—three times during the four-month season, to be exact.

It had been Jamie's turn to come see her last night, but even so, she was grateful that her girlfriend was willing to make the long drive for not even twelve hours together. Admittedly, her "sweet digs" might be part of the draw. Jamie had asked if she could stay in Seattle for an extra night or two to regroup from her club's recent losses—two in a row with a total scoring differential of one to nine. Emma liked the idea of Jamie sleeping in her bed, watching movies on her television, drinking the red Gatorade Emma kept on hand for her.

Speaking of hands... Eyes still closed, she smiled,

thinking of the activities she'd initiated shortly after Jamie had arrived the night before—to distract her from her team's recent failures, of course.

"But it's late," Jamie had said, pulling back from the kiss.

And it had been. Emma, however, was still keyed up from her own match that night, a commanding 3-1 win over Chicago. Besides: "We can sleep when we're dead."

Hopefully that wouldn't happen today, Emma thought now as the plane shuddered in mid-air. She chanced a look out the window only to the see the familiar hulk of Mt. Rainier approaching. The usual worry popped into her mind: Would they have the necessary altitude to clear the fourteen thousand foot behemoth? She closed her eyes again and tucked her cheek into her travel pillow. If she was lucky, she hadn't jinxed herself and would wake up from any in-flight naps.

And if she didn't, she wouldn't know the difference, would she?

Later, she wished she'd kept sleeping. No, that wasn't quite accurate. She wished she had taken the early morning flight because then she wouldn't be sitting in Houston considering chucking her phone across the gate during her regrettable hour and a half layover. If she'd flown out at seven-thirty that morning, she would already be in Tampa now. More importantly, the teenage fan who'd asked for a selfie with her in line at Sea-Tac security wouldn't have taken, let alone posted, a video of her and Jamie hugging goodbye, their brief cheek kiss fortunately—*fortunately*—obscured by the shoulder of a man who stepped in front of the illicit videographer at precisely the right moment. But she hadn't taken the earlier flight, and now she was sitting in another airport terminal watching another WoSo fan meltdown over Blakewell.

At least Ellie wouldn't kill her this time. She and Jamie were in a committed relationship, and things like this were bound to happen. They couldn't be on guard all the time. Her Twitter mentions were the distressing part. Unlike other social media platforms that offered a variety of privacy options, Twitter was public. As such, it contained multitudes of anonymous males who hid behind their keyboards and lashed out at any woman they perceived as a threat. Tumblr, on the other hand, was mostly LGBTQ+ kids squeeing. Even if they could sometimes get a tad obsessive, their adoration came from a generally good place.

A grammatically challenged tweet from FootballFan24_7, a brand new account with no profile photo and zero followers, attracted her attention: "That wanna-be man better keep it's hands off my girl if it knows whats good for It!!" The tweet might be another example of the usual homophobic trolling Jamie and other masculine-identified female athletes experienced, but for Emma, the invocation of "*my girl*" set it apart from the litany of "gaaaaay" and "fucking dykes" and "I just threw up in my mouth" comments. Whoever the guy on the other side of the screen was, his sense of entitlement reminded her way too much of the man who had gone after her and Sam.

She hesitated briefly before clicking "Report Tweet." She maneuvered through the form, vacillating between "Someone on Twitter is being abusive" and "Someone on Twitter is sending me violent threats." But the violence in the tweet was implied, and besides, Jamie was the target, not her. *Jamie was the target…* Damn it. She should have known better than to let Jamie walk her to security. They should have said their goodbyes in the car, or better yet at home that morning before breakfast.

She bent over her phone, finger hovering above the screen. The general consensus on social media was that if you ignored and reported the harasser, they would lose interest once they realized you wouldn't engage. That hadn't proven to be the case with the man who had fixated on her during her time in Boston. Instead of losing interest, he'd only doubled up on attempts to get her to meet him in person. But it wasn't until after a photo circulated of Sam in a Blakeley jersey hugging her after the World Cup quarterfinals that his tweets had turned threatening.

At least he'd never progressed to real life stalking like the guy Maddie had gone out with a few times only to discover he had a literal shrine to her in his apartment. In Emma's case, there had been no online mentions of her home address, no private photos of her or Sam they couldn't trace, no strange men following them about their daily lives. The harassment was vicious, but it had followed the pattern of most online attacks and remained virtual.

Emma exited out of Twitter without submitting the abuse report and slumped back in the airport chair, glancing around surreptitiously. She hated when the feeling of being tracked online carried over into real life. Her phone buzzed and she flinched, checking the screen through one barely open eye. It wasn't Twitter this time; Jamie had texted. Had she seen the tweet? But no, she was simply saying hello. And sending a photo of... Emma gasped and turned her phone face down, relieved that no one was sitting close enough to have seen her girlfriend's naked pic. She tilted the screen up carefully. Well, not entirely naked. She was wearing Emma's national team shorts, the American flag standing out against the white of the kit, her arms folded across her chest hiding various and sundry private parts. Atop her head was a USWNT hat on backwards, the American flag (again) vivid above her grin.

"Hi from Seattle!" the caption read, and Emma realized Jamie must have set her iPad up in her condo's living room because there, in the corner, was a slice of window that revealed the Space Needle. The other option was that Dani was still there, and... no. Jamie and Dani were comfortable with each other, but not *that* comfortable.

"Love the view," she typed back.

"Well, good. 'Cause I love you!"

They texted until Emma had to board her second and final flight of the day. On the plane, the last thing she did before setting her phone to airplane mode was return to Twitter and submit the abuse report form. She couldn't do nothing. For Jamie's sake, if not her own, she had to stay on top of the situation so that this time it didn't blow up in her face.

An image of a hydra popped into her mind: cut off one head and another two would grow in its place. That should be the default icon for Twitter users—a hydra, not the little blank egg.

She turned on her music and closed her eyes. One take-off down, one to go. *Boo yah.*


Emma stared at the laptop, struggling to focus both on the game clips flashing across the screen and on what Jo Nichols and Melanie Beckett were saying. It was the first day of training in Florida, but instead of heading out into the sultry mid-June heat, the coaches had set up one-on-one meetings with each player. Emma's meeting was one of the first. While relieved not to be outside under the Florida sun, she hadn't been sure what to expect when she walked into the conference room. Video review definitely hadn't been at the top of her list.

Jo had had a US Soccer staff member assemble clips of Emma from recent matches, and now the coaches were breaking down her role in the team's offensive transition. Or lack thereof, to hear Jo talk. Again and again she pointed out opportunities where Emma's passes out of pressure could have been better weighted or more accurate, where she could have gotten forward during the run of play, where she had chosen to hang back instead of getting involved in a set piece.

*I'm not a scorer,* Emma thought, glancing at Melanie,

Craig's defensive coach who Jo had opted to keep on staff. But the assistant was nodding as if she agreed with Jo. As if being one of the best defenders in the world was no longer enough.

Maybe it wasn't.

"You've been a valuable member of this team for eight years," Jo said when the tape ended, "and none of us see that changing anytime soon. However, and I don't think this will come as a surprise, no one's position on this team is safe. Everyone is going to have to work to fit into the system I'm asking you to play. I need you to stretch yourself, Emma, to get outside of your comfort zone."

Jo was right. What she was saying wasn't a surprise. But even so, Emma felt herself tense at the coach's next words: "What that means is that I want you to figure out how you can contribute offensively. Is it taking a more involved role in building the attack out of our defensive third? Getting into the box during set pieces? We need a more disciplined, efficient approach to defense as we gear up for the World Cup. The international game is evolving quickly. My goal is to move this team away from traditional long ball and toward a more technically savvy style. We can't rely on what worked in the past, Emma. Failing to grow has left us stagnant, and I plan to change that."

What she said sounded good. Great, even. Emma just wasn't sure whether such a major shift in playing style could be achieved in a year, especially so close to the World Cup. But team strategy was out of her hands. Her job—what she'd signed on for—required that she nod and say, "All right. I'll think about it."

"I need you to do more than think about it," Jo said. "Between now and the end of the pro season, I'm challenging you to find ways to stretch yourself with the Reign. And then I want you to bring those expanded roles, whatever they end up being, to residency camp this fall. Can you do that?"

Emma hesitated, because honestly, the request was a bit amorphous. Was Jo asking her to score for the Reign, or would she settle for a handful of assists?

"I can try," she said finally.

"Good. That's all I'm asking, Emma," Jo said, rising and offering her hand.

Emma rose and clasped the older woman's hand, noting her firm grip and her encouraging gaze. Then she nodded at Mel and left the conference room.

In the hall, Maddie looked up from her phone. "How did it go?"

Emma kept her voice low as she highlighted the takeaways from her meeting: "Video review, new playing style, and fitting into her technically savvy system. Oh, and no one's position is safe."

"Sounds about right," Maddie said as she pushed away from the wall. "See you at lunch?"

"Yeah. Good luck."

"I don't need luck," she said confidently, and squared her shoulders before knocking on the closed door.

That made one of them. Emma knew that she was a good defender, but Jo's challenge had unnerved her. No one had demanded she learn a new skill in a long time, possibly since college. And while she knew the test would be good for her in theory, she wasn't sure how it would go in reality.

As she headed toward the elevator bank, Emma toyed with the end of her ponytail. The federation reviewed national team contracts twice a year, and for the first time in a long time, her upcoming renewal didn't feel automatic. For once, it felt like her position truly was on the line—maybe because her coach had told her it was.

Wouldn't it be funny if Jamie made the World Cup roster and she didn't? Well, not funny so much as terrible, awful, no-good... Maybe the vending machine near the exercise room had Hershey's bars. A little chocolate would go a long way right about now.

She was almost to the vending alcove when reason raised its anti-candy head. With her individual meeting complete, she was expected to attend the afternoon fitness training—outside, in the sort of heat and humidity that routinely brought many a Pacific Northwesterner to her knees. Emma sighed. She missed Seattle already, and she'd been in Tampa for less than a day.

As she rode the elevator to her floor, her mind returned to Jamie. Text app open, she loaded the photo of Jamie in shorts, baseball cap, and little else, the Space Needle visible behind her. Immediately the knot in Emma's stomach loosened.

"I miss you," she texted, adding a quick selfie with her face screwed into an exaggerated pout.

She was almost to her room when her phone buzzed. "I miss you too," Jamie had written back, accompanied by a photo of her lying on Emma's couch reading on her iPad, a half-empty bottle of red Gatorade on a coaster on the nearby coffee table.

She had used a coaster. Without even having to be told.

"I love you!" she typed.

The reply was immediate: "I love you, too!"

Who needed chocolate, Emma thought as she entered her hotel room. She had Jamie, and that was more than enough.

# CHAPTER FOUR

"Damn, you *are* cut," Meg said, holding Jamie at arm's length for a big sister once-over.

"She literally gets paid to work out," Todd, Jamie's brother-in-law, said, waiting for his turn to hug her.

"I know that." Meg smacked him in the shoulder. "But no wonder the national team wants you back, Jamester. You're a freaking machine, aren't you?"

"That's the idea," Jamie said, and followed her sister and Todd out to short-term parking.

The view outside the Salt Lake City airport—mountains dusted with the winter's first snow—wasn't entirely unfamiliar. Meg and Todd had been in graduate school for what felt like forever to Jamie; she had a hunch it felt even longer to them. The land of Mormons wasn't their style, as they insisted each time the topic came up. But their program was good and the state capital had plentiful pockets of non-straight, non-white, non-Mormon residents. For the most part, they were insulated from the city's Latter Day Saints community, Meg claimed, or else she and Todd wouldn't have lasted this long in Utah.

The drive from the airport took a while, mostly because

Meg and Todd's rental house was relatively far from the freeway. Meg rode with her body almost completely turned toward the back seat as Todd drove them along the surface streets, busy on a Tuesday evening at rush hour.

"So?" Meg prodded. "How did the season end up going?"

"We ended up third in the league and made the playoffs—"

Meg made an impatient sound. "No, dummy, for *you*, not your team."

Jamie shrugged at her sister ultra-casually. "Well, I was named Player of the Week three times, Player of the Month once, *and* I made the NWSL Best XI, so…" Normally she didn't brag about herself, but their parents had always encouraged them to use positive self-talk. This, she figured, counted. "Oh, and most importantly? I didn't get injured!"

At the beginning of the summer, Ellie's trainer had suggested she cross-train at a martial arts academy in Beaverton. After three months of kick-boxing and tai chi—which Angie called the old person's martial art: "I will defend myself only if you hit me verrry slooowly"—she could feel the difference in her timing and flexibility. Her mental focus had improved, too, probably because as her instructor often said, tai chi was basically meditation in motion.

That was one reason Shoshanna, her old therapist, had recommended Jamie study martial arts back in high school: to strengthen her mental and emotional acuity. They'd been discussing the rage attack—like a panic attack, but angry—that Emma's ex-boyfriend's aggression had triggered, and Shoshanna had explained that when it came to trauma, some people retreat into themselves and become more passive while others grow angrier over time. With some martial arts training, Shoshanna had thought she might feel more empowered and less personally vulnerable even as she learned to channel her anger in a socially acceptable manner. Ten years later, Jamie wished she had taken her therapist's advice to heart sooner.

"Way to go," Meg said, and held out her hand for a high five. "Now that your first season back is in the books, do you think leaving London was the right decision?"

Jamie considered the question. "A couple of months ago, I wasn't sure. But now? I'm here, and Emma is too, or she will be soon, anyway. So yeah, I think it was the right decision."

Technically Jamie didn't have to be in Sandy, a suburb of Salt Lake, until Friday, but she'd decided to come to Utah a few days early to spend time with Meg. With training camp taking place in her sister's current home city, it had been too good of an opportunity to pass up. In the five years Meg and Todd had lived in Salt Lake, Jamie had only managed to visit them one other time, and that had been before she'd begun her European football adventure.

"You'll have to tell me more about this marginal gains theory," Meg said. "Maybe it can help me finish my dissertation sometime before the pending zombie apocalypse."

"Pending? I didn't know the status had been upgraded."

"That's because you live in Portland, not Stepfordville." Meg gestured to the neat houses that lined the broad avenue where they were currently stuck in stop-and-go traffic.

"Hey, now," Jamie said, "I heard that Salt Lake is increasingly queer-friendly."

Meg's eyebrows shot up, disappearing beneath her newly acquired razor-straight bangs. "Where on god's green earth did you hear that?"

"Reddit."

"Oh, Jamie, my sweet summer child…"

In a practiced little-sister move, Jamie leaned forward and flicked Meg's arm.

"Ow! Brute." Meg turned in her seat, flouncing as much as one could while restrained by a seat belt, and faced resolutely forward.

"Baby."

Meg only folded her arms and ignored her.

It was funny, Jamie thought as the mountains drew slowly nearer, that here they were in their mid-to-late twenties and they still had the same exact bickering matches. Sisters. Couldn't live with them, which in their case was actually too bad.

Meg and Todd's house was a cute brick bungalow sandwiched between apartment buildings across the street from a café where they said they spent more time than money because the excellent coffee was the only menu item they could afford. The house was small, but it had a guest room, covered patio, small back yard, and—Meg's favorite feature—a porch swing. The basement where the washer and dryer resided was dark and dank, but it wasn't nearly as creepy as the laundry room at their old apartment building, Todd pointed out.

"Definitely a win," he and Meg said in unison.

Jamie hid a smile. It always cracked her up when her band-geek sister and brother-in-law whipped out the sports metaphors.

After the home tour, Jamie stowed her carry-on and soccer duffel in the guest room and then got cleaned up in the tiny tiled bathroom that had nearly made Meg turn down the rental two years earlier. Now that she was here, Jamie could see why. Every surface in the room was covered in tile and grout that, as Meg had moaned more than once since moving in, was a complete and utter bitch to keep clean.

She dried her hands on a dark red towel that matched the modern art shower curtain and emerged into the narrow hall that led from the bedrooms to the living area. The murmur of voices reached her from the kitchen, accompanied as ever by music.

"What are we listening to tonight?" she asked as she stepped into the brightly lit kitchen.

Her sister and Todd were at the counter preparing a spinach salad and a pre-cooked tuna-quinoa casserole. Jamie had blanched at the meal description, but Meg had insisted it was both tasty and packed with protein.

Meg stared pointedly at Jamie over the top of her glasses. "I don't know. What *are* we listening to, James?"

She screwed up her eyes. "Let's see. That's a pentatonic scale, isn't it? So, Chinese folk?"

"Well done," Meg said approvingly.

When your sibling was a doctoral candidate in music, you tended to pick up a few things. Same with having an athlete sibling—Meg knew more about soccer than she'd ever wanted to.

The casserole ended up being good, Jamie had to admit. Not just significantly better than some of Meg's other pescatarian experiments, but so delicious that Jamie had thirds while Todd watched wide-eyed.

"Sorry," she said around a bite. "I've only had a protein bar and some pretzels since noon."

Meg's head tilted. "Why didn't you pack more food for the flight?"

"Um…" Jamie bit her lip. How to explain why she'd ended up packing last minute for residency camp? It wasn't like she had lacked prep time. Her pro season had ended with a loss to Kansas City in the semifinals ten days earlier. After that, she'd headed up to Seattle to hang out with Emma before the NWSL championship match that the Reign had hosted on Sunday. She still couldn't believe they'd lost. They'd been at home *and* they'd had the best record of anyone in the league, with only two losses the entire season.

Their second loss had come at Portland in the last regular season match, a victory for the Thorns that Jamie supposed she could live with.

With nothing to keep her in Seattle after the finals, Emma had come back to Portland with Jamie. Ellie and Jodie were in LA for a quick post-season getaway, leaving them the house all to themselves. Instead of packing, they'd spent the last day and a half watching movies and eating take-out as Jamie did her best to distract Emma from her angst over losing to Phoebe Banks and Jenny Latham's team. While Jamie couldn't wait to get to residency camp, Emma hadn't exactly been thrilled at the idea of two weeks with Jenny and Phoebe lording the win over her.

Meg lifted an eyebrow at her hesitation. "Emma was with you, wasn't she?"

"Maybe. Whatever." She felt her ears heating up and tossed a sliced carrot at her sister.

"Hey!" Meg gave her their mother's withering parental glare. "This is a classy house. We do not throw carrots here."

Todd lifted a spinach leaf dripping with balsamic vinaigrette. "What about leafy greens?"

"Those are fine," Meg said, and sipped more wine.

"Classical, maybe, but classy?" Jamie shook her head. "Not a chance."

"A music pun—nicely done." Meg nodded sagely, her tone approving.

Jamie rolled her eyes. Meg had been mothering her practically since the day she'd been born, according to their parents. Personally, Jamie hoped there would be a mini-Meg or mini-Todd running around sooner rather than later. Not only did she want a chance to be the fun aunt, but it would be nice to have her big sister's maternal energy concentrated on someone who needed it.

After dinner, they did the dishes together like in the old days, Jamie washing and Meg drying. Todd had offered to clean up so that they could have sister time together, but they'd looked at him like he was crazy. Doing the dishes was the ultimate act of nostalgia for the Maxwell sisters, who had grown up hearing their parents inform guests that they didn't need to buy a dishwasher because they already had two. Naturally, they'd purchased an electric dishwasher as soon as Jamie left for college.

"My bad," Todd said, and wisely retreated from the kitchen. A moment later, Jamie heard piano music drifting in from the living room, upbeat modern classical to accompany their kitchen clean-up.

As they washed and dried, Jamie asked her sister about Salt Lake and the university, her dissertation progress and Todd's doctoral committee. They discussed their parents' health and well-being—their dad's blood pressure was increasingly worrisome while their mom's arthritis was making painting and sculpting a challenge. Meg told her about Todd's parents, too, who were a bit older and in the process of deciding which of Todd's older brothers to move closer to after retirement. Todd's parents still didn't understand how he could have picked music school over dental school. Everyone in his nuclear family worked either as dentists, hygienists, or dental assistants. Except one sister-in-law. As an orthodontist, she was considered almost as much of an outlier as he was.

Kitchen cleaned, Jamie and her sister joined Todd at the small, upright piano Meg had found on Craigslist. It wasn't fancy by any means, but they kept it tuned. Todd was one of those people who could play multiple instruments by ear. This talent made him good to have at a holiday party, as Meg often joked.

"Pick a tune, any tune," he said to Jamie now, riffing up and down the major scales.

"Um, 'Rude'?" she said, offering up the song that had inexplicably been stuck in her head for weeks now.

Meg and Todd stared at her from the piano bench.

"You know," she added, "why you gotta be so rude, don't you know I'm human too?"

Meg covered her ears, laughing. "Stop, please! I forgot that you're tone deaf."

"I am not tone deaf!" Jamie protested for at least the eighty-seventh time in her life.

"Sure, Jan," her sister said. She glanced at Todd. "What do you say?"

"I think I know the tune, but you'll have to help with the rest."

Google gave them the lyrics, and soon they were singing and laughing their way through the pop song about a slacker musician whose girlfriend's father refuses to approve their marriage. When they reached the end, Todd launched into background music and told the story of how he had asked the senior Maxwells for Meg's hand. Jamie had heard the story multiple times, but it never got old listening to Todd describe the way their parents had reacted—their mom jumping out of her seat and flinging herself into his arms while their dad watched, tears (of joy, Todd insisted) shining in his eyes.

This time, though, the story left a slightly sour taste in Jamie's mouth. Lately any talk of weddings or engagements only served to remind her of her own persistent second class citizenship. In May, a federal district court decision had made gay marriage legal in Oregon. But for the rest of the country, a hodge-podge of state and regional laws both for and against same-sex marriage still existed. More than a year had passed since the US Supreme Court had invalidated the Defense of Marriage Act (yay!) while simultaneously refusing to rule on the legality of state prohibitions against gay marriage (boo!). At this point, several cases seeking a decision on the Constitutional right of same-sex couples to marry were on their way to the highest court in the land, but no one could predict when—or even if—SCOTUS would agree to hear them.

When she was younger, the lack of federal recognition of her relationship status had bothered her more on a theoretical level. But she was in her mid-twenties now, and everyone around her was getting married and starting families. When—if—she did get gay-married, she didn't want to have to worry that if she and her future wife crossed state lines (say, for a soccer game), their marriage might not be recognized if one of them were to get injured and require hospitalization. If and when she and her future wife (okay, *Emma*) started a family, she didn't want the possibility of their children not being considered hers because they didn't share genetic material. Her sister and Todd didn't have to worry about any of those things. The older they got, the more Jamie became aware of the gap in their experiences.

They sang a few more songs, Jamie muddling through the lyrics as best she could, enchanted as ever by her sister's alto harmonizing with Todd's baritone notes. Then, reluctantly, Todd tore himself away from the piano to plan for the following morning's classes.

"Do you have to work, too?" Jamie asked Meg, but her sister was already topping off their wine mugs (*so* classy, Jamie had teased) and tugging her outside to the front porch swing where they could spy on neighbors and strangers alike.

"There's always more work to do," Meg said as they settled on the swing side-by-side, chains rattling noisily. "But I don't get to see my baby sister all that often. Oh! Speaking of babies, did you hear about Becca and Rhea?"

Becca was Meg's best friend from high school, Rhea her wife of only a few years. "They're having a baby already?" she asked, mildly shocked by the news.

"Two, actually." Meg grinned. "They're having twins!"

"Holy crap! When are they due?"

"In March, but possibly sooner since twins are full term

at thirty-seven weeks. Who knew."

"Wow." Jamie tried and failed to imagine Becca pregnant with one child, let alone two. "How's she doing?"

"She's a nervous wreck. Rhea's handling it well, though, considering she has two human beings gestating inside her body."

"Wait, Rhea is carrying the babies?" She was the slightly more masculine of the pair, so Jamie had assumed that Becca would be the baby mama if and when the time came—for no other reason than heterosexism, she realized belatedly. Awesome.

"Yes," Meg said, letting the heterosexist assumption slide by unchecked. Jamie peered at her sister, noting the faraway look in her eyes, the slight smile lurking around her lips.

"Wait." She turned to face Meg more squarely. "Do you and Todd have news on the baby front?"

"What? No." But her protest was feeble at best.

"Oh my god, you do! Should you even be drinking?"

Meg laughed and held her mug of wine out of Jamie's reach. "It's fine. We're only talking about timing at this point. Like, should we wait until we both have jobs? Or start trying when only one of us has a job? Ideally we would find a spousal hire, but what about tenure?"

"I hear it's never the right time to have a baby. You just have to do it."

Meg eyed her curiously. "Who did you hear that from?"

"Ellie. Although it isn't true in her case. If she and Jodie decided to have a baby before the World Cup, quite a few people would have something to say about it."

"Oh. I thought maybe you were talking about Emma."

"Emma?" Jamie blinked at her sister. "We haven't even been together for a year."

"I know, but wasn't that one of the reasons you and

Clare split up? I thought maybe you and Emma would have talked, you know, to make sure you're on the same page."

"I already knew from forever ago that she wanted kids," she said dismissively.

Her sister stared at her. "And yet you're still together."

Jamie peered back. "Obviously."

"I thought you didn't want kids. If you're changing your mind to be with her..."

"What? I never said that."

"You said the thought of being a parent terrified you," Meg insisted, "and that you and Clare broke up because she wanted to get married and have kids."

"I meant she wanted to start a family right *away*. And yeah, the idea of being a parent does terrify me. But just because something's scary doesn't mean it's not worth doing. I'm legitimately worried I'm going to get cut again at the end of this camp. Jo is bringing in twenty-nine players, and only twenty will be selected to the qualifying roster in October. But even with the odds so clearly not in my favor, I wouldn't miss this camp for anything."

Her phone decided to beep at that moment, and she glanced at the screen, smiling as she saw the photo Emma had sent her. She was seated on her bed with her laundry in giant piles around her. Talk about terrifying—post-season catch-up could be a bitch.

Meg rolled her eyes indulgently as Jamie sent back heart emojis. Then Jamie set her phone to selfie mode and posed beside her sister. "Say cheese." Meg obliged, and Jamie sent the photo to Emma with the caption, "Wish you were here!"

Immediately the reply came back: "Me too!!! And not only because I'm currently surrounded by dirty clothes. Tell Meg hi. Can't wait to see you soon!"

Jamie knew her smile was loopy as she typed back, "I can't wait either. Love you!!!!!" But she couldn't find it in herself to care.

"Looks like things are going well with you two," her sister commented.

Jamie nodded and tucked her phone back in her hoodie pocket. "They are. Not perfect, but good."

"No relationship is perfect. I imagine being apart all the time can't be easy."

"It's not," she admitted.

"Want to tell me about it?"

Disarmed by her sister's lack of sarcasm, Jamie found herself opening up, explaining to Meg the challenges of long distance dating while playing on rival pro teams. The inequality of having one be on the national team and the other not wasn't exactly easy to manage, either.

"But in general, we're good. Solid," she added. And they were. So much so that sometimes she couldn't help wondering when the other shoe would drop. "I've never dated someone I was such good friends with before we got together. Emma and I have actual history, and while sometimes that's not a good thing, most of the time it is."

"You two have definitely known each other a long time," Meg said. "You both want kids and your relationship is going well. Does that mean you could see yourself settling down and starting a family with her?"

Jamie gulped hard. *When you put it like that...* But then she remembered Emma's hand beneath hers all those months ago on the last night of January camp, Tina's baby spinning and kicking inside her mother's abdomen and her own flash of longing, quickly stifled, to see Emma similarly glowing. She remembered babysitting that same baby with Emma in March, the calm and joy she'd felt in the newborn infant's—and Emma's—presence. She remembered Emma explaining oxytocin to her, and the peace of dozing on the couch with Emma beside her, both of their arms wrapped around the sleeping child.

"Yeah," she said finally, feeling the same dopey smile as before stretch across her face. "I can. After the World Cup, of course. And the Olympics."

"Of course," Meg said, but her tone was affectionate. "You two and your crazy obsession with soccer…"

"Says the pot to the kettle."

"People have been making and studying music for millennia, I'll have you know."

"The same goes for the game of soccer."

"I don't think that's true at all."

"Yeah, but you don't *know* that it isn't."

"I may not, but you know who will?" She held up her phone, eyes challenging as she said, "Siri, when was soccer invented?"

Jamie waited, smirking, because she already knew the answer. Sure enough, Siri reported that while England had invented modern football, a similar game was first played in ancient China—two thousand years earlier.

"Told you so."

"Whatever." Meg tossed her hair, apparently forgetting that she had chopped it to chin-length. "Anyway, back to the issue at hand."

"Which is…?"

"Emma. Mom and Dad will be here next week for the game against Mexico. Will you be bringing your girlfriend to any family get-togethers?"

"Absolutely." Then she paused. Was that a question she needed to ask Emma? Was it too early in the relationship to assume she would attend family events? Emma already knew her parents and had hung out with them in California after January camp. She already knew Meg, too. The only Maxwell family member she hadn't met was Todd, and he was technically a Kirschoff.

"Want to do a big dinner out?" Meg asked. "I know a

great place. Mom and Dad will want to treat us, I'm sure."

Jamie elbowed her. "Is that grad speak for you can't afford a fancy restaurant *and* the rent on this house, so let's get M & D to foot the bill?"

"Maybe," Meg said, holding her mug in both hands.

"Sounds good to me. I make less in a year than you do, so…"

"Seriously? Freaking sexism. Speaking of which, what's happening with the turf issue? Did Emma and the other players file their lawsuit?"

"Not yet," Jamie said, and then stopped herself, remembering belatedly that she wasn't supposed to know details of the lawsuit planned against FIFA and the Canadian Soccer Association. But when you lived with the lead player on the case and dated another player who was nearly as involved, certain information was bound to come your way. Like, for example, that the players didn't have high expectations for the lawsuit but were pushing ahead anyway because it felt like the right thing to do.

Meg, she knew, faced her own gender discrimination battles. Todd's research was higher profile than hers, and he was already being courted by a number of universities on both coasts. They were hoping for a spousal hire, where they would both be employed by the same university. But if Meg were to be hired mainly because one of the schools wanted Todd, she worried that their careers—and therefore their marriage—would start off on uneven footing. What would that mean about her standing in a career she'd chosen before she ever met him? Would her career always be secondary, and if so, what would that mean to their plans to raise a family together?

But they didn't have to solve the world's problems—or even their own—that night, a fact for which Jamie was grateful as they finished off the bottle of wine and watched the Utah sky darken.

Her cell buzzed long after she and Meg had said goodnight, after she'd used the tiny tile bathroom and gone through her nighttime tai chi routine. She'd already slipped between the guest futon's sheets and was getting settled on the noticeably hard bed when her phone signaled an incoming video call from Emma. Smiling, Jamie hit accept and propped the phone up on the knee that allowed her to display her good angle.

Emma always got irritated when she said that. "Every angle is a good angle," she would insist. But Jamie wasn't completely ignorant of the crap said online about her physical appearance. Just because she identified as genderqueer didn't mean she wasn't vain. In fact, it probably meant she was more insecure about her looks than the average cisgender person.

"Hi!" she said as Emma's face flickered into focus. Her hair was up in a messy bun and her face was make-up free. This was Jamie's favorite Emma—the casual, unencumbered version she allowed few people outside of her teammates and family to see.

"Hi yourself," Emma said, face softening into a smile. "It's good to see you."

"You, too. I miss you."

"I miss you too, sweetie."

They discussed their days, Jamie describing the time with her sister and Emma detailing her cleaning/packing progress. She didn't have that much to do, a situation Jamie knew was only made worse by the fact that US Soccer was enforcing a mandatory weekend off for Seattle and Kansas City players. Because they'd competed in the NWSL championship match the previous weekend, they weren't allowed to participate in the first few days of residency camp. It was part of the federation's strategy to combat burnout, a very real issue for athletes who played an average of ten months out of every calendar year.

"Why don't you go to that spa you like for a couple of days?" Jamie suggested. "The one on the island with the natural springs hot tubs. That would be relaxing, wouldn't it?"

"Actually," Emma said, eyebrows lifting, "that's a good idea. It's September, so they should have some openings. And since I can't come early and hang out with you..."

Jamie almost asked her if she was sure about that, but managed to catch herself. No need to make Emma feel worse than she already did about missing the beginning of camp. "I wish. But speaking of hanging out, you know how my parents will be here?"

"Yeah. I'm excited to see them again."

"Excited enough to spend some time with the whole Maxwell-Kirschoff clan?" Jamie asked, squinting hopefully into her phone's camera.

Emma's smile was subtle, but it was definitely there. "I'd like that. But are you sure you want me tagging along? I know you guys don't get much family time..."

"Are you kidding? You have no idea how much my parents are looking forward to seeing you." Jamie wasn't sure if she should be gratified or peeved that her parents seemed more excited about the chance to see Emma than they were about Jamie's call-up.

"Oh. Well, good," Emma said. "My mom feels the same way about seeing you. I'm sure she'll make it to a game soon now that you're—" She broke off. "Sorry."

"It's okay," Jamie said, even though her stomach was twisting up again, undoing all the good relaxation work she'd achieved through tai chi. The next two weeks could determine if she was destined to be just another player in the pool who might have been. Fewer than 200 players in history had suited up in red, white, and blue, and she knew that to be among that number was impressive. Still, for her, it wasn't enough.

Taking a breath, she pushed away her ever-present fears. "Anyway, I'm glad you want to hang out with everyone," she said. "My sister was thinking we could all go out to dinner next week."

"Dinner? With your whole family?" When Jamie nodded, Emma sighed. "Dang it—now I'm going to have to figure out how to fit a decent outfit in my luggage, aren't I? And shoes, too."

"Yep," Jamie said. "Sorry not sorry."

"Jerk."

"You know you love me."

"That, I do."

They talked about random topics they'd saved up for each other until, somehow, it was past midnight and more yawning was being done than actual speaking.

"Sweet dreams," Emma said, starting their customary sign-off.

"Sweet dreams to you too. Love you."

"Love you more." She stuck out her tongue, and then the call suddenly ended.

Laughing, Jamie texted, "Love you most!" before plugging her phone into the charger on the bedside table. Emma always wanted to have the last word. Occasionally Jamie even let her.

She picked up her iPad, a birthday present from her parents a couple of years back, and navigated to Archive of Our Own (AO3), the open source nonprofit website where fan fiction authors posted their works. Reading some angsty fluff about imaginary people would definitely help her forget the feeling of not knowing what her future held. That was the wonderful thing about fan fiction—authors created fictional settings where, for the most part, homophobia didn't exist and gender and sexual fluidity was the norm.

Due to the uber-rosy alternate realities it offered, fan

fiction was slowly and steadily ruining Jamie's appetite for mainstream literature and movies. Fortunately, there were independent queer presses and film production companies putting out more and more works. It would feel good to spend money on those—once she earned enough to have spending money. For now, free femslash works on the Internet would do nicely.

Slouching lower, she clicked a tag and began to scroll through, open to wherever tonight's reading experience would take her.

Once camp started, Jamie discovered she didn't mind Emma's absence too terribly. Without her gorgeous soccer-playing girlfriend's presence to distract her, she could bond with her teammates, focus on her coaches, and concentrate on making her body perform at its absolute best. Meals and bedtime were less complicated, too, a fact she especially appreciated since Britt, her closest friend for the past three years, had been invited to residency camp to fill the fourth goalkeeper spot. Jo and the rest of the national team coaching staff had been impressed by her season with the Washington Spirit, who she'd helped propel from dead last in the league the previous year to a winning season and a spot in this year's playoffs.

When she arrived from DC the first day of camp, Britt tried to wave off Jamie and Angie's enthusiasm at "getting the band back together." Fourth string wasn't anything to be that excited about, she maintained, but they were having none of it. Fourth was significantly better than fifth, sixth, or seventh, and besides, the World Cup roster had room for three keepers. In her current spot, she was only one slot away from a chance to play in her first major tournament for the senior side.

Having Britt and Angie in the same place again, however, meant relearning how her supposed best friends liked to gang up on her. Whenever those two got together, the practical jokes weren't far behind. That was why Jamie was kicking herself after breakfast Saturday morning for going back to her room all innocent and unsuspecting, only to have the bejesus scared out of her by Angie and Britt lying in wait inside. They filmed the whole thing, the bastards, and put her blood-curdling shriek on Instagram later that day, choosing to edit out the part where she tackled Angie and gave her a revenge wedgie.

"You poor thing," Emma texted that night, only just returned from her island getaway.

Jamie almost wrote back, "*Come save me!*" But then she remembered how annoyed Emma was about her enforced absence from the start of camp, and sent instead, "Still arriving tomorrow night?"

"Yep," Emma replied, even the single word managing to sound testy.

"Sweet. See you soon!!!!!" She added a variety of emojis, smiling when Emma sent back a string of hearts.

Jamie missed her, as ever, and couldn't wait to see her. As ever. Still, she was nervous about balancing their relationship with the demands of national team training. The last time they'd been at residency camp together, they'd barely been friends. Now they were significantly more, and she wasn't sure what to expect.

After a quick dinner with the team the following night, she headed up to the room she was sharing with another newbie, Jessica North from, ironically, the deep south. Jamie wasn't sure if it was a social experiment or a cruel joke, but sharing a hotel room with someone who had posted a Bible passage about sinners on Instagram the day the Supreme Court invalidated DOMA was not her idea of a comfortable situation. There were a few other Christian players on the team who studied the Bible together, but they ascribed to the "love everybody in Jesus's name" school of religious thought. Jess, on the other hand, seemed sketchy when it came to anyone with different beliefs. Jamie wasn't sure who was being hazed—the out, gender nonconforming lesbian, or the fundamentalist social conservative.

Fortunately, Jess was out when she reached their room. The other girl was freakishly prudish around Jamie, which made her feel awkward as hell. She didn't want to catch sight of Jess's naked body any more than Jess wanted her to, and yet she'd felt guilty when it had happened. How did straight women do that? How did they make you feel like the pervert when they were the ones fixating on pervy notions?

Despite the fact that the room was currently empty—Jamie checked and double-checked this time, even after leaving Britt and Angie at dinner with the rest of the team—she still brought her clothes with her to shower. Better to risk slightly damp clothing than to stroll naked out of the bathroom to find Jess and her God Squad friends glaring at her over their Bibles.

Except, again, Jess would presumably be the only God Squad member glaring. Rebecca was one of Jamie's oldest friends on the team, Emily Shorter (who at 5'2" was, indeed, the shortest member of the squad) gave off quite the queer vibe herself, and Jordan Van Brueggen, who played for the Thorns, had posted a very nice Instagram message with her boyfriend about love and acceptance on Pride weekend. Those three didn't act homophobic because they were actual Christians. You know, people who follow Jesus's teachings? Jess could stand to learn a thing or two from them.

After a brief shower, Jamie dressed in jeans, a flannel shirt, and a baseball cap and headed out, wallet and keycards—hers and Emma's—tucked into her back pocket. She checked her phone on the elevator to the lobby. Crap. Emma's flight had arrived ten minutes early.

"I'm driving as fast as I can," Meg said a few minutes later, hands fixed firmly on the steering wheel at ten and two. She had volunteered to help pick up Emma, though now Jamie was questioning the wisdom of accepting that offer since her sister refused to drive over the speed limit.

"For eff's sake," Jamie muttered. "It's a suggestion, not a hard and fast limit. You're not going to get a ticket for going five over."

"A suggestion doesn't have the power to raise my insurance rates," Meg said. "Do you have any idea how expensive it is to share a car with a man under the age of thirty?"

"Nope," Jamie said, thanking her lucky stars as she did most days that she had been born so utterly gay.

Despite Jamie's exhortations, her sister insisted on adhering to the speed limit the entire way to the airport. Fortunately, Emma texted that she was still waiting for her luggage when they arrived, so they parked in short-term and headed to baggage claim. Somehow Meg spotted her first across the cavernous room.

"Emma!" she exclaimed, pulling her into a hug when they reached her. "Holy hell, girl, it's been too long."

"Hi Meg." Emma smiled at Jamie over her sister's shoulder.

And just like that, Jamie wondered why she had worried about distractions. She felt stronger, calmer, smarter somehow when Emma was around—basically, a better version of herself both on and off the field.

"How was the flight?" she asked as she gave Emma a brief hug. After the last Twitter meltdown back in June, she'd been careful not to linger too long when she touched Emma in public. But damn if she was going to give up doing so altogether.

"Fine," Emma said. "How about you two? Did you get some quality time together?"

"We did," Meg said. "Hopefully now we'll get some with you, too."

The baggage carousel beeped in warning, and soon they

were chatting about Utah's weather and Washington's San Juan Islands as they watched for Emma's luggage in the circling masses. Jamie was first to catch a glimpse of the navy blue bag, familiar now from the sheer amount of time they'd spent on the road since January. Slipping through the crowd, she grabbed the suitcase from the conveyor belt.

"Your luggage, milady," she said as she returned, adding a bow for good measure.

"So chivalrous," Emma commented, her mouth quirking.

"Oh my god, you guys are too cute." Meg sighed, the sound uncharacteristically sappy. "Can I just say I'm glad you two idiots finally realized you belong together?"

Jamie stared at her sister in surprise, a sentiment that grew exponentially as Emma reached for her bag, her lips ghosting over Jamie's cheek so fleetingly it almost felt like an accident.

"So am I," she said, and Jamie could only nod in agreement.

The drive back to the hotel felt considerably faster than the outbound trip, but that was likely only Jamie's mind warping time since Meg kept the old Subaru Legacy at or under the speed limit again. Jamie didn't mind the snail's pace as much as she settled back in her seat and listened to her sister chat up her girlfriend as if they had been best friends forever. Emma fit so easily into her life. Jamie and Clare had never been that well-matched, and while Laurie, her college girlfriend, had been awesome, she didn't care much about soccer. Also, she could be a bit—well, *preachy* at times when it came to her admittedly admirable ideals.

When they reached the hotel, Emma suddenly shifted gears as she sometimes did, becoming more or less business-like as she thanked Meg for the ride. With a quick glance around the driveway and an almost curt nod to Jamie, she hurried inside, wheeled suitcase trailing behind her.

"Is it me, or was that sort of abrupt?" Meg asked as Jamie gave her a quick hug and shouldered Emma's carry-on.

"I know. Sorry. People on this team can be weird." This was a fact she'd learned in her daily life with Ellie and Emma. The weirdness was usually justified, but there it was.

"I'll take your word for it. Have fun tonight," Meg added, smirking as she climbed back in the car.

"Shut up," Jamie called after her, laughing as Meg flipped her off through the open window.

Emma was waiting near the elevator, restless hands belying her neutral expression.

"You okay?" Jamie asked as she pushed the up button.

"Fine. Just, a couple of fans posted the hotel's location online, so…"

"So you're hoping they aren't lurking in the shadows?" She meant it as a joke.

Emma pushed the already-lit button. "Something like that."

The elevator opened and they stepped aboard. During the short ride to the second floor, Jamie held herself carefully separate, worried that if she started kissing Emma now, she wouldn't want to stop. She had no idea when they might get a chance to be alone; she only knew they would make it happen somehow. Angie and Maddie clearly managed. If things got truly desperate, Jamie could always ask them for tips.

On the second floor, she led Emma down the hallway to the room she would be sharing with Maddie. The door was propped open, so she knocked once and walked in, relieved to see that Maddie and Angie were decent. Angie was practically in Maddie's lap as they watched TV, but on the plus side they were fully clothed and not actively making out.

"Blake!" Maddie set Angie aside and rose to give her roommate an enthusiastic hug. "You're here, thank god. Camp isn't the same without you. Oh, and sorry about the finals."

Jamie suppressed a wince as she lowered Emma's duffel onto the currently unoccupied bed. Emma had been clear that the less said about the previous weekend, the better. Maddie, however, was not one to sweep losses—or emotions, according to Emma—under the rug to be ignored. More was the pity.

Emma's eyes flickered but she only said, "Thanks."

"How was your flight?" Angie asked from the bed.

"Average to middling." Emma placed her suitcase on a metal stand near the dresser, and then she yawned in a way that Jamie thought might even be genuine. "It's good to see you guys, but I'm not sure how much longer I'm going to last."

"We can take a hint," Maddie said. "Right, honey?"

"Right, sugar muffin." Angie winked at Jamie as she rose.

"Please tell me you do not actually call her that," Jamie said, making herself comfortable on the other bed.

"She doesn't."

"I totally do."

"You guys have a couple of hours until curfew," Maddie said, tugging Angie with her to the door. "Use your time wisely." And with that, they were gone, the sound of their laughter echoing down the hallway.

"Christ." Emma shook her head as she stepped out of her tennis shoes. "Tell me they won't be like that forever."

"Ooh, babe, I don't think I can do that."

Emma touched her cheek affectionately and then headed toward the bathroom. "I'll be right back. Save my spot?"

"You got it."

While Emma used the bathroom, Jamie turned off the

TV and gazed about the hotel room, a mirror image of hers and Jessica's. Maddie had left the metal security latch wedged into the outer door, and Jamie left her comfy spot on the bed to remove it, shutting the door all the way. Emma seemed tired and slightly rattled, so Jamie doubted they would do more than cuddle, but it would still be nice to cuddle in private.

The toilet flushed and the water ran, and then Emma reappeared from the bathroom. "Hi," she said softly, and dropped onto the bed to nestle into Jamie's waiting arms.

"Hi," she replied, feeling her muscles relax at the feel of Emma burrowing against her side, the familiar scent of her body wash, the sound of her contented sigh. "I missed you."

"I missed you too."

Jamie hesitated. "Are you okay?"

"Fine."

"Was there turbulence?"

"Uh-huh."

Jamie didn't push, simply carded her fingers gently through Emma's loose curls. She had learned that she couldn't force Emma to open up, and attempting to do so would only cause an even deeper withdrawal. Since they had started dating, Jamie had become increasingly aware of the separate personas Emma wielded against the world. When they were alone or with Dani or other trusted friends, Emma was open, soft, affectionate. But around someone she didn't know—or didn't like, as was the case with Jamie's teammate Isabela—she drew into herself, but so subtly Jamie almost didn't notice. Then there was soccer Emma. On the field she was almost all business, calm and controlled and in charge—until someone took her out or fouled one of her teammates. Then the fire that she only rarely displayed would blaze out before being quickly extinguished.

In her arms, she felt Emma soften. "The flight was fine. It was just hard not being at camp when I knew you were here."

Jamie's fingers stilled. "I know what you mean. Sucks, doesn't it?"

"It really does."

"Well, I'm glad we're both here now."

"Me too." Emma kissed her cheek and then settled back against her. "It was fun seeing Meg."

"Hope you don't mind I let her be part of the welcoming committee. She was excited to see you."

"She was?"

"I told you, she thinks you're awesome. Spoiler alert— so do I."

"I should hope so," Emma said, her voice all haughty.

"Hey! You're supposed to say I'm awesome too." Jamie tickled her, feeling Emma's squeal of laughter vibrate against her chest as she squirmed away.

"Stop it, Jamie! I'm serious!"

She relented, and they settled back together, chatting idly about camp, Meg's house, Britt's arrival, and Emma's weekend in the San Juans. Jamie didn't have anything new to report. The good thing about modern technology was that even when they were apart, it never felt like Emma was that far away. Training camp didn't swallow them whole the way it used to when they were teenagers. Now there were cell phones with unlimited text and talk plans, cameras, email, and other apps that let them maintain the illusion of proximity from a thousand miles away.

That said, nothing beat the power of touch, Jamie thought, trying to memorize how it felt to have Emma pressed against her, their breath rising and falling in unconscious rhythm, her arm around Emma's shoulders, Emma's arm around her waist. This was what she had been missing since Tuesday morning when she'd forced herself to leave Emma and fly to Utah. This was what she needed to keep her grounded and centered at residency camp, where she was literally fighting for her soccer life. She needed Emma.

But was the same true for Emma? Jamie couldn't be entirely sure, but she could hope. Maxwells were good at that.

She woke up, her arms around a still-dozing Emma, to the sound of cooing: "Come on cute girls, it's almost curfew."

Maddie's touch on her arm was remarkably gentle, and Jamie blinked up at her sleepily, surprised to see the fondness in her expression. Emma wasn't the only one with split person—er, multiple personas.

"Come on," Maddie said again, moving away as Emma finally stirred. "Let's get you home safe, Max."

Jamie unfolded herself from the bed, missing Emma already. Maddie gave them a moment alone at the door, and Jamie gathered Emma into her arms one last time. "This sucks," she said again, burying her face in her hair.

"Completely," Emma agreed, hugging her so tightly that it almost hurt. Then she let go. "See you tomorrow, bean pole."

Jamie was so tired from double sessions and the emotions of the day that the only comeback she could think of was, "See ya, grammar nazi."

"I love you," Emma added as she opened the hotel room door and pushed her gently into the hallway, fingertips lingering on her chest.

"I love you too," Jamie murmured back. Then she forced a smile and turned away, heading back to her room where her hostile, Bible-banging roommate was no doubt awaiting her return with bated breath.

Could be worse, she told herself as she strode down the hotel corridor. Because, usually, it could.

# CHAPTER FIVE

"What the hell?" Maddie demanded, her eyes fixed on the team captains. "Did you guys know about this 'personal relationship management' crap?"

Beside her on the double bed of their hotel room, Emma slid her arm around her friend's shoulders. She'd been there when Maddie had been outed to her family by a college assistant coach who didn't approve of her "chosen lifestyle." Her parents had not reacted well, and if she hadn't been at UNC on scholarship, she might have had to drop out.

"We knew," Phoebe admitted. "In fact, we helped draft the policy."

"You what?" Angie, who had been leaning against the wall near the bathroom, straightened. "This is bullshit. I'm out."

"Ange…" Maddie said.

"Don't." Angie held up her hand. "Wouldn't want to get turned in or anything."

"Wang," Ellie tried, "come on. Let's talk this through."

But Angie only flashed her a wounded look before stalking to the door.

When Britt followed, Emma caught Jamie's eye,

gesturing subtly toward the hallway. *You go after her; I'll stay here.* Jamie hesitated only a moment. Then she nodded and went after her friends.

Emma and Maddie's room had become an impromptu—and crowded—meeting space following the team conference Jo had called to describe the new coaching staff's expectations. Dedicating a full training session to setting revised expectations was a fairly common practice any time the national team underwent a "regime change," as Steph referred to it. But what had taken place in the hotel conference room that afternoon had been neither common nor, Emma couldn't help feeling, fair.

The first slide in Jo's PowerPoint had sent whispers cascading across the room: "PERSONAL RELATIONSHIP MANAGEMENT." Things had gone downhill from there, with straight players glancing worriedly at their queer teammates as Jo explained the team's new policy regarding interpersonal conflict among US Soccer and National Training Center employees and players.

"Let me be clear," Jo had said, hands on her hips at the front of the conference room. "This is not about who on this team may or may not be involved with each other. The policy we're implementing applies to the conduct of every single member of this team, including the coaching and support staff.

"But"—and there was always a but, Emma had thought cynically—"any discussion of personal relationships on the national team must include talking openly about intra-team dating."

She'd gone on to say that in the past, relationships between teammates had been ignored or even frowned upon, approaches that she believed fostered a climate of secrecy, dishonesty, and fear. The new relationship management policy she and her staff were implementing was meant to encourage responsibility and maturity, from coaches and players alike.

So far all it had done, Emma thought now, tightening her grip on Maddie, was create conflict within the team.

"You heard Jo," Phoebe said, eyes flicking between the two of them. "This isn't about you guys. It's about anyone who has any kind of conflict with anyone else in the federation. Most places of business have rules about appropriate work behavior. That's all this is."

Maddie snorted. "My sisters and their friends have boned more dudes at their places of work than I can name *while at work*, so don't give me that bullshit. Hetero relationships did not spawn this policy. Homo ones did."

"That may be true," Jenny Latham put in. "And you're right, it does sort of feel like the coaches are singling out the lesbians and bi women on the team. But let's be honest. If you guys weren't as professional as we all know you are, you and Angie could become a major distraction." Her eyes flicked to Emma, who braced for a mention of the Tori Parker debacle. "You and Jamie, too. Not to be blunt, but me boning a dude doesn't have the same potential to cause rifts on this team."

"Unless you picked someone's boyfriend or husband to hook up with," Gabe pointed out.

"Like Bancroft did," Phoebe agreed, nodding. "From what I've heard, he's a big part of the reason for the personal conduct clause in player contracts."

Scott Bancroft, a star striker on the men's team back in the '90s, had been abruptly cut from the pool before the 1998 men's World Cup. Rumor had it that he was having an affair with one of his teammate's wives—a rumor that had, a dozen years later, been confirmed by multiple sources. Not only had Bancroft broken the athlete code, he had also shown a flagrant disregard of team and federation policy. He was a brilliant player, but after cheating with his teammate's wife, he'd never played another game in a US uniform.

"As if any of us would do that," Jenny said. "The point

is, this policy could be a good thing. It's acknowledging your guys' relationships instead of pretending they don't exist or, worse, banning them outright. Isn't that a step forward?"

Emma considered her question. On the one hand, the policy felt like increased scrutiny that, frankly, she didn't need. But at the same time, Jenny wasn't wrong. Intra-team relationships did carry the potential for increased drama within the team. While Emma did not subscribe to the melodramatic and blatantly sexist claim that managing emotions on female sports teams was difficult, she didn't mind acknowledging that women traditionally dealt with conflict less directly than men did. Maybe Jo simply wanted to keep ahead of any potential trouble.

The coach's comments at the outset of the meeting had appeared to reflect that intent: "I recognize that talking about personal relationships is new for this team," she'd said, face partially illuminated by the light from the projector. "But we're all adults here, and by now most of us understand that how we interact with each other can be the key to the emotional-social success of a team—or, as we saw in the aftermath of the 2007 World Cup, the cause of dissolution and chaos."

According to the handout the coaches had distributed, the new policy was meant to apply to any situation where players might have interpersonal conflict, be it relationship-related (romantic or non-romantic), religious, or political in nature. Basically, Jo wanted the team to have a set of guidelines that would help them navigate any interaction that could adversely impact team unity.

As conversation continued around her, Emma smoothed out the sheet on her lap, rereading the rules: "(1) All staff and players are to behave professionally toward each other and toward any romantic partner on team time, including during practice, competition, team meetings, team travel, overnight hotel stays, locker room visits, and training and weight room activities. (2) Any team member who becomes romantically involved with a US Soccer/NTC athlete or other employee is expected to maintain focus on their role as a team member when on team time. (3) All US Soccer players and staff are expected to avoid PDA and exclusivity/cliquishness during travel, meals, team meetings, practice, warm-up, etc. And (4) under no circumstances is interpersonal conflict to be brought into the locker room or onto the field."

It all sounded good, Emma thought, tuning back into the room. It just felt—uncertain somehow, like it might be a federation tactic to police the lesbian and bisexual members of the team. Still, if it was Jo's policy, Emma supposed it made sense that she would want to start her first residency camp on a consistent note.

"She's right about one thing anyway," Maddie said from beside her, her voice less hostile. "We *are* all professionals, and we won't let any personal drama affect the team. Look at Gabe and Ellie," she added, gesturing to the co-captain and her ex. "Their break-up didn't impact their play or the team at all."

"That's exactly right," Emma put in, adding her voice for the first time. "We're professional enough that we won't let our relationship drama affect the team any more than the rest of you do. I was around in 2007, and I can tell you that I have no intention of doing anything that might set this team on the road to implosion. I want to win next year as much as the rest of you."

"Fuck, yeah," Maddie said, and held up her hand for Emma to high-five.

"Then you guys don't have anything to worry about, do you?" Jenny quipped as the crack of their hands echoed through the room.

"Personally," Emma added, "I think you guys are just jealous that we get to spend so much team time with our 'romantic partners.'" She added air quotes at the end, mocking the policy's terminology.

"Why do you think I haven't had a long-term relationship since 2007?" Jenny asked.

"Aw, poor baby," Maddie said.

Lisa threw a pillow at her. "Nice empathy, 708er."

"Whatever, Cheesehead," Maddie shot back.

Jenny raised her eyebrows at Emma, who shrugged back. Maddie and Lisa's Midwestern rivalry was a mystery to the rest of the team because, after all, weren't Wisconsin and Illinois basically the same state?

The conversation devolved into the woes of long-distance dating, and soon the tension in the room noticeably waned. Until Jamie and Britt returned with a slightly sheepish Angie between them.

"Sorry," she mumbled to the group at large.

Maddie crossed to her side and gave her hand a squeeze. Then she stared around the room, mouth set in a firm line. "Does anyone here have a problem with me hugging my girlfriend? Because if you do, I suggest you leave my room right now."

Not that it mattered, but no one seemed to mind.

"They're on our side," Emma heard Maddie murmur as she pulled Angie into a hug. "As long as we don't fuck this up."

"Gee, no pressure or anything." Angie rested her head on Maddie's shoulder and shot a smile around the room. "I never doubted y'all for a second."

"Liar," Gabe said, and everyone laughed.

"Actually," Ellie said to Phoebe, "I'm wondering if maybe we should ask Jo to tweak the policy. This team is nothing if not handsy. Saying that only certain teammates get to hug or otherwise express affection does feel a bit Big Brotherish, if you ask me. What do you think?"

Phoebe wasn't one to engage in group hugs or movie

night cuddling with the rest of the team. Still, she shrugged. "You have a point. If she's committed to treating people like adults, I think she has to be prepared to allow us all to decide for ourselves where to draw the line. Half the time I walk into a hotel room and find five people curled up on a bed like a litter of puppies, braiding each other's hair. Limiting that would be the opposite of her intent."

Her stated intent, anyway. Emma knew that people who had played for Jo at Virginia or on one of the youth national teams almost uniformly adored her. But she hadn't had enough experience with the former national team player to feel like she knew her. She liked her, liked how down-to-earth and open she was, appreciated how she didn't appear to play games. She even admired the way Jo parented her pre-teen son, and her husband seemed like a good guy, too. Her family would be joining her in Utah at some point—though they would not, the players understood, be staying in Jo's room. Apparently she wanted to demonstrate that she planned to abide by her own policy.

The team cleared out eventually, everyone off to do the usual pastimes at camp in the brief periods of downtime they were allowed—sleep, talk to parents/friends/partners, check email, shower, soak in warm or cool baths. After a brief negotiation, Maddie and Angie went back to Angie and Britt's room to talk while Emma and Jamie sat down on her bed cross-legged, facing each other.

"This is so strange," Jamie said, toying with the top of her low athletic socks. Her hotel uniform of shorts and a lightweight sweatshirt made Emma shiver just looking at her. "I've played for Jo before, and I didn't see any of this coming."

"Neither did I. But Jenny had a good point earlier," Emma told her.

"What was that?"

As she relayed the part of the conversation Jamie had

missed, Emma had to actively work to keep from touching her. But was that necessary? They were alone in her room with the door locked, and Maddie wouldn't come in without texting first. Players weren't really considered to be on team time twenty-four-seven at training camp, were they? It was unrealistic to think they could spend weeks in a hotel together without engaging in any form of physical affection. The team had been in residency at the NTC in Carson for a month before the 2011 World Cup, and would likely be again next summer. Did Jo truly believe that people who were in a romantic relationship could spend four weeks around each other without ever touching? That they *should* refrain from such contact? Doing so would be emotional *and* physical torture, and certainly wouldn't make anyone else near them happy, either.

Except maybe a homophobe like Jessica North.

Downstairs, when Jo had opened the floor to questions, North had raised her hand and asked, "Does this mean you want us to report anyone who violates the policy?"

A ripple of reaction had passed over the room, and Emma might have felt vindicated by the hostility being channeled North's way if she hadn't been too busy fuming. The athlete code was so strong that Emma, like pretty much everyone else she knew, had kept a variety of secrets over the years for teammates she didn't even necessarily like, from drug and alcohol abuse to risky sexual behavior. Many of these activities had violated the personal conduct terms of their contracts, but unless their behavior threatened the team or others, that was a line you didn't cross. Making sure they got the help they needed, absolutely, but ratting them out to the federation? No way. Loyalty on a team was almost as important as fitness, because without trust, what kind of cohesion could you hope to have?

Emma had been relieved when Jo answered, her voice hard, "This policy is intended to encourage honesty and open communication among team members, and to avoid unproductive conflict. As I said before, we're all adults here. If you personally witness something that you feel crosses a line, I would hope you would address it with your teammate first, same as with any other conflict."

Mel, the defensive coach, had stepped forward then to hammer home the importance of transparency and productive conflict resolution, not uncommon discussion topics in Emma's experience with the senior national team. Conflict was a fact of life, especially when you had twenty-plus people routinely competing for eleven starting spots on the number one team in the world. If you didn't know how to play well with others, then you didn't belong at this level. That was why players like North rarely lasted long. Team chemistry was an actual thing, and players who were intolerant or outright bigoted about race, sexuality, or anything else caused more problems than they were worth.

"Do you think Jo will report any intra-team relationships to the federation?" Jamie asked now. "Like, is this policy really her idea, or could it be an old school witch hunt?"

"I don't have any idea," Emma admitted. "You know her better than I do."

"I'd like to think she meant what she said, but I don't know if I do."

"I guess we'll see."

"I guess so." Jamie hesitated, staring down at her socks again, fingers tracing the black Nike swoosh sewn into the white cotton. "We could always take a break, you know. If you wanted, I mean."

Emma tried to hide her sharp intake of breath, but she suspected she'd failed when Jamie's gaze shot up and locked on hers. "I... Is that what *you* want?"

"No, of course it isn't. But I know what this team means to you, how important next year is. I would never want to do anything to jeopardize that."

"Oh, Jamie," Emma said, her breath returning, "you don't. Just the opposite—you make it better. You make *me* better. The way you play the game reminds me how much I love it, too. Besides, with you here, there's no way we can lose. I don't think you understand how good you are, sweetie."

The term of endearment slipped out. Emma wasn't normally a pet name kind of person. She could count on one hand how many times she'd called Sam anything other than her first or last name; same with Will, her other ex. But Jamie was smiling at her now, eyes crinkling at the corners, and Emma found she didn't mind how sappy she sounded.

"Thanks," Jamie said, voice soft. "You always have such faith in me."

"That's part of the deal, isn't it?" Emma pressed her forehead against her girlfriend's. "I'm your anchor, remember?"

"Yeah," she said, breath gentle on Emma's lips. "I remember."

And if they kissed there in the privacy of Emma's hotel room, it wasn't anyone's business but their own.


"Funny," Jenny said, smirking at her. "You didn't have any problem hitting the crossbar a couple of weeks ago."

Emma took a deep breath, willing away the urge to slap her longtime friend. *It's only a game*, she told herself, not believing the platitude for an instant.

"But that's how posts are, right?" Jamie put in, patting Emma's shoulder as she stepped up to take her turn. "Easier to hit when you're not aiming for one."

And then she proceeded to hit the crossbar in question seven out of ten tries, easily defeating Jenny and claiming the title of USWNT Crossbar Queen.

Emma could have hugged her—but then she realized

she wasn't technically allowed to. Instead she contented herself with a smile at her victorious girlfriend and an overly sweet, "Shoot, and you were so close to winning!" to a visibly irritated Jenny.

It was Thursday, two days before the upcoming friendly against Mexico, and the coaches had announced that they were changing things up in the afternoon session. Instead of the endless drills and half-field scrimmages pitting offense against defense, practice would consist of games and challenges: taking penalty kicks blindfolded, scoring from the corner, hitting the crossbar, playing soccer tennis, and—one of the team's old favorites—competing in the piggyback challenge. So far Emma hadn't performed particularly well at any of these tasks, but after the past few days, that no longer surprised her.

She had come to Utah the previous week already off-kilter, the loss in the NWSL finals against Kansas City was still shadowing her. But it was more than that one loss. Ever since Tampa, she'd felt off. Jo's insistence that playing defense was no longer enough had made her doubt herself on the field for the first time in recent memory. Her college coach had taught his players that breaking down the other team's attack was equally important as building an attack, and Emma had embraced his philosophy. As the sign on his door read, "Offense wins games; defense wins championships."

Or loses them.

On the day of the finals, Emma had attempted to ignore the voice of self-doubt whispering away in the back of her head. But the voice grew stronger during the first half when she banged a shot off the crossbar, and grew to a cacophony at the end of regulation when she mistimed a tackle and was called for a foul outside the box. With two minutes left in regulation, Jenny Latham bent the ball around Seattle's wall and into the far corner netting. That goal had won the game for Kansas City, and while Jenny and her teammates celebrated, Emma hadn't been able to resist checking for Jo in the stands.

She'd found her near midfield jotting notes in an old-school notepad. "CUT BLAKELEY," she'd imagined one of the notes read, though the likelihood of Jo doing so wasn't very high. "BENCH BLAKELEY" had a better chance. By giving up the foul that led to Jenny's goal, Emma had lost the championship for Seattle. She wasn't the only one who thought so, either. Her Twitter mentions the next day were mostly positive, but while the fans chose to emphasize the broader picture—*It was a great run! You played so well all season!-*—Emma could read between the lines.

Soccer wasn't the only factor in her current crisis of confidence. Her Twitter troll had grown bolder over the summer, hinting at plans to contact her in real life. He hadn't crossed any lines, at least not yet, but that didn't stop Emma from worrying. On several occasions now, she'd been outside the stadium or her training academy when she'd suddenly become aware of the prickly sensation of being watched. More than likely it was nothing, but each time it happened she grew a little less secure.

Normally at camp she felt safe. The team had its own security, and the hotels they stayed in promised to safeguard their identities. But not only had some kid from Salt Lake stalked Maddie and Angie's arrival and posted a photo of them entering the team hotel, there was the new relationship policy to worry about. She and Jamie, already so vulnerable being themselves out in the world, now had to regulate their behavior when they were with the team, too. Truthfully, they already did, so she supposed it wasn't much of a change. It had simply felt safer when everyone pretended not to know. Like the players who partied too hard in the off season or made other questionable choices off the field, she'd assumed the couples on the team had free rein to live their lives as long as they weren't hurting anyone.

The thing about assumptions, Emma reminded herself, is that *they make an **ass** out of yo**u** and **me***. Check.

"Are we still on with my family tonight?" Jamie asked as they walked away from the crossbar station.

Honestly, Emma wanted nothing more than to hide out in the hotel with their friends and watch silly movies she'd seen a dozen times. But they wouldn't have another opportunity to spend time with Jamie's family anytime soon, and besides, she'd already committed.

"Can't wait," she said, nudging Jamie with her shoulder. "Now let's go kick some soccer tennis ass."

"We are so going to clean up, aren't we?"

"Damn straight."

"Or not."

Emma only shook her head and smiled as she kept on moving toward the next challenge. National team camp really was better with Jamie. Good thing Jo Nichols appeared to share that sentiment.


The restaurant Jamie's sister had picked was airy and open with a patio warmed by heat lamps. The afternoon's temperature had hovered in the low 70s—perfect soccer weather—but the evenings in Salt Lake cooled down quickly. Emma, for one, appreciated the heat lamp at the center of their table. She was also grateful for the secluded feel of the enclosed patio, with its potted plants, a fountain, and fairy lights. She and Jamie had considered asking Meg if they could do take-out at her and Todd's house, but Jamie's sister had been so excited about a night out with their parents footing the bill that they had decided to let her and Todd choose the evening's entertainment.

"So, Emma," Jamie's dad said after their server had brought their drinks, "how have you been? You had an excellent season in Seattle, even if Portland did manage to best you in that last match."

"Yeah, it was a good season," she agreed, and cleared

her throat slightly. *Chill, Blakeley*, she told herself. It was ridiculous to be nervous. She had known Jamie's parents practically forever, and after a rocky first meeting, they had been nothing but kind to her. Of course, she hadn't been sleeping with their daughter then. Even back in January, she and Jamie had been little more than friends. Now they were so much more, and everyone sitting around this table knew it.

"Who would have thunk it all those years ago?" Jamie's mother said. "The two of you making your way in the world as professional soccer players. We've certainly come a long way, haven't we?"

"Absolutely," Emma agreed. "But there's still a ways to go in terms of equity and inclusion."

Meg snorted. "I can't believe those boneheads at FIFA are making you guys play on turf next year."

"I know, right?" Todd added. "They would never make men's teams play on artificial surfaces."

And with that single comment, Jamie's brother-in-law won her over.

They decided to share a taster platter while they waited for their entrées, and Emma was surprised at how easily the conversation flowed. It was like she was a teenager again visiting Jamie and her family at the beginning of a year that would prove desperately difficult before it ended. And yet, thank the soccer gods they weren't those clueless, soon-to-be heartbroken teens anymore.

It wasn't long before Meg brought up that first visit: "Do you remember how you scared off that group of bullies at Jamie's game?"

"Of course." If only it was as simple now to deal with asshole boys and men…

"What are you talking about?" Jamie asked.

At the time, Emma had convinced Meg not to tell her sister what had happened. She knew how easy it was to tune out crowd sounds when you were playing, and if Jamie hadn't realized she was being heckled, Emma hadn't wanted to be the one to clue her in.

"Oh my god, you should have seen her," Meg said now, and launched into an enthusiastic retelling of how Emma had silenced the hecklers by commenting on the size of their genitals. Emma saw Jamie's father blink down at the table even as his wife let out a short, startled laugh.

"I didn't actually say anything about their, *you know*. I…" Emma trailed off as she realized that making a crude gesture might be equally as vulgar in Jamie's parents' minds. Why had Meg needed to bring up the only story in their shared history that contained a reference to male genitalia?

"That's right," Meg said. "You just did this."

As Meg supplied the crude gesture in question, Emma considered the pros and cons of excusing herself from the table—and never returning.

"Wow. My hero, I think?" Jamie bit her lip to keep from laughing, a battle she soon lost. "I can't believe you never told me that!"

"It's not exactly one of my prouder moments," Emma groused.

Still laughing, Jamie reached for her hand across the table. Before she could catch herself, Emma flinched away. Jamie changed courses smoothly, picking up her water glass as if that had been her intent all along, but Emma saw Meg exchange a look with her mother. Fantastic. Now they thought she was a closet case making Jamie pretend they weren't together in public. And, okay, maybe it seemed like that from the outside, but… Well. Maybe she really was.

At least Jamie didn't seem upset. If anything, she was squinting at Emma like *she'd* been the one to screw up. All at once Emma wanted to tell her the truth about why Sam had left, to explain about the Twitter troll who might in fact be the same man with a renewed fixation. She wanted to tell her about the police station in Boston and the afternoon she had spent recently filling out online abuse reports, worrying the entire time about the reaction she might be triggering. But while revealing the truth would make Emma feel better, what would it do to Jamie?

Better to stay quiet for now and avoid the public eye. Once Jamie was on the team—or not, although that wasn't a possibility Emma was willing to entertain—there would be plenty of time to clue her in to the shady side of dating Emma Blakeley, longtime USWNT player and veteran sociopath attractor.

Jamie's dad intervened in the conversation and introduced the less personal topic of the upcoming CONCACAF tournament. After a moment, Emma recovered her equilibrium and joined in. She could always talk about soccer. As Jamie described the potential hurdles facing the team at World Cup qualifying, Emma thought that was something else she and her girlfriend had in common.

*Girlfriend.* She took in the bright, caring people who had made Jamie who she was, people Emma had known and cared about for more than a decade now, and she felt her shoulders relax and the nearly omnipresent worry slip away. This was good. They were good, and as Jamie had said, her parents clearly supported their relationship. It was one thing to hear your girlfriend say her family loved you, but it was another to spend an evening with those same people and feel for yourself their affection and respect.

Except Meg. Jamie's sister, who had been one of their biggest champions from the start, according to Jamie, was still watching her with a slight frown even as the conversation moved on.

They lingered over coffee and dessert well into the night, tables turning over around them as they stayed where they were in the center of the fairy-lit patio. Emma was warm and comfortable and a tiny bit tipsy from the glass of wine she had ordered, an uncommon treat during training camp. Typically she cut out alcohol the week before a match, but life was short, and the wine had helped dull her nerves. At last, after their second server of the night checked in on them again, Jamie's parents paid the bill over their children's insincere protests.

"You know, Sarah," Todd said as Jamie's mother signed the credit card receipt, "your children may have taken their leftist upbringing too much to heart, since neither values money all that much."

Meg laughed. "Says the pot. You should be a partner in a dental practice by now, and instead you're a poor, starving music student married to a fellow starving music student."

"True," Todd agreed, and slid his arm around her shoulders.

In Emma's family, meanwhile, the emphasis had been on being of service to others, service that in her dad's case happened to include a lucrative patent and a large life insurance policy.

"Speak for yourself," Jamie said. "I'm on track to make more than twenty-five thousand dollars this year. That's right, twenty-five big ones. I know you're all jealous."

Her parents laughed, but their smiles seemed resigned as if to say yes, they had indeed raised their daughters to prize personal happiness more than individual wealth.

Emma hated to hear Jamie putting herself down, though, even as a joke. "Just wait," she said. "Once we win the World Cup, you'll have a dozen different sponsors banging down your door." She didn't mention that if they failed to win gold, as the team had done in each of the three previous World Cups, millions of dollars' worth of sponsorships would quietly dry up.

Jamie's smile lost its self-deprecating edge, and she held Emma's eyes as she nodded. "Once we win the World Cup."

They almost managed a clean getaway. Jamie's parents had paid, everyone had shrugged into their jackets, and Emma was laughing at something Meg had said when she saw it: the familiar visage of a nervous teenager. Or three nervous teenagers. As she watched, the shortest of the three linked her arms through her friends' and tugged them forward.

"Excuse me," she said determinedly, her voice wobbling slightly. "Are you Emma Blakeley?"

Emma could feel Jamie's family watching as she sighed inwardly and stepped forward, lapsing into her professional persona with ease. "I am. Are you soccer players?"

The conversation went the way it usually did. The girls were in town with their club team from Boise to watch the national team play on Saturday. They were huge fans—they recognized Jamie too—and how amazing that it was actually them! At this restaurant! Tonight! Emma smiled and nodded, but she couldn't help wishing they would cut to the chase.

Finally, the middle girl asked, "Could we get a picture with both of you?"

Before Emma could politely decline, Jamie said, "Sure. Right, Blake?"

"Right," she said, and prepared to pose, careful not to stand near her girlfriend.

When they'd finished, Emma held out a hand. "Would you mind not posting those photos online? We're out with family tonight," she explained, waving toward the Maxwells.

The girls agreed but seemed disappointed. To improve the odds of their compliance, Emma offered to get some of the other players to take selfies with them after the match on Saturday. As they walked away happier than they'd been a minute earlier, Emma sighed inwardly. Crisis averted. She hoped.

Jamie waited until the three girls were out of ear shot to ask, "What was that about?"

"I was just feeling selfish," Emma lied. She resisted the urge to slip her arm through Jamie's, settling for an elbow to the ribs instead. "Come on. We have a curfew to keep."

"It's like two hours away," Jamie pointed out. But she followed her lead, as she nearly always did.

In the parking lot behind the building, Meg and Todd announced that, rather than squish into the back seat of the rental car like earlier, they'd decided to walk the half mile home.

"It's a nice night," Meg said. "Besides, it'll wake us up for all the planning and reading we failed to do before dinner. Right, T?"

Todd slapped her upraised hand. "Right, M."

During the round of family hugs that followed, Todd bent his head and told Emma that he was psyched to have another non-Berkeleyite in the family, particularly one as awesome as she was. Touched, Emma almost didn't notice that Meg was murmuring urgently to Jamie, her eyes flicking to Emma more than once.

While the sisters were thus engaged, Jamie's dad singled Emma out and said, "Can I have a word?"

Startled, she nodded.

"I just wanted to say that I'm online a lot, and if you ever need advice or assistance, I hope you'll reach out."

Emma squinted up at him, trying to figure out what, exactly, he was getting at.

"Also, if Jamie should ever need help of any type—I know therapy isn't always covered by health insurance—my cell number is on the back." He handed her his business card.

"Is this about Twitter?" she asked as she tucked the card into her purse.

"Yes," he admitted.

"We have a general rule on the national team," she told him. "Never read the comments. Also, what happens online almost always stays online."

"Thanks, Emma. I'll try to keep that in mind."

And then Meg was at her side to say goodnight, her

hug noticeably less warm than it had been at the airport. Emma couldn't blame her. Meg had always had Jamie's back, and she always would. As someone else who loved Jamie, Emma could appreciate that.

"Great to see you," Emma said, squeezing Meg's shoulders before stepping back.

"You too," Meg said, her brow still furrowed.

Emma let Jamie usher her into the back seat of the waiting sedan, where they fastened their seatbelts and linked hands, waving to Meg and Todd until they were out of sight.

"That was such a nice dinner," Jamie's mother said, turning around in the passenger seat to smile back at them. Her eyes flicked over their joined hands and away again. Emma flashed to the night she and Jamie had met, to the elevator ride they'd shared with their parents, disapproval wafting off her father and Jamie's mother in equal amounts. But Emma was no longer a confused teenager. She hadn't been that girl in forever.

"It *was* nice," she agreed, clutching Jamie's hand more tightly and turning on her professional charm again. "Thank you so much, Mr. and Mrs. Maxwell. I had a lovely time tonight."

"It's Tim and Sarah," Jamie's dad said. "And we're glad to get this time together. I for one am happy that you two are together again after all these years. I have to say, I always hoped it would happen."

"You did?" Jamie asked, clearly nonplussed by her father's admission.

"I liked your other partners too, don't get me wrong," he said, slowing the car at a stop light. "But I always thought there was something special about the two of you."

"So did I," Emma said, scooting as close to Jamie as her seatbelt would allow and smiling into her eyes.

"Me too." Jamie grinned back at her.

"Well, I guess that makes it unanimous," Jamie's mother announced. "Because so did your sister and I."

"I'll take unanimous," Jamie said, squeezing her hand.

"Works for me," Emma agreed, and turned her head to watch out the window as the buildings and streets drifted past, the sky overhead darkening the further they got from downtown.

"You doing okay?" Jamie asked, her voice quiet.

"Better than okay. That was fun."

"I told you, you've always been a Maxwell family favorite. Which reminds me." She lowered her voice even more. "What was with my dad's cloak and dagger shtick back there?"

Emma smoothed the clasp on her purse. "He wanted to check in, make sure you were doing okay."

"And he didn't ask me because...?"

"He knows I'm a more reliable source of information. What about Meg?" she added. "I saw her talking to you. She thinks I'm a closet case, doesn't she?"

Jamie frowned. "Meg doesn't understand what it's like to live in the public eye."

Even though she'd been expecting it, Emma felt her shoulders fall. Sometimes she hated what being on the national team meant to the rest of her life.

"It's okay," Jamie insisted. "I informed her that as a straight, married woman, she doesn't get to have an opinion on how we manage our relationship. It's up to us—and, I guess, the coaches."

And the federation, and the fans, and *and AND*... Emma tightened her grip on Jamie's hand briefly, then loosened it as Jamie winced. "Sorry. I'm sorry." She exhaled a short, sharp breath of frustration. Why did it feel like everything was spiraling out of control?

"Emma," Jamie said, "it really is fine. I love my sister,

but she's a music professor who has no idea what it's like to be a team player, no clue the level of compromise and sacrifice required to do what we do. She's the one who doesn't get it."

Emma stared back at Jamie, searching for any sign that she agreed with her sister even a tiny bit. But Jamie held her gaze unflinchingly, her expression sincere. "Okay," she said at last, nodding.

When they stopped in front of the hotel, Emma checked the perimeter carefully before saying her farewells and stepping out of the car. Jamie took longer, kissing her parents and assuring them they shouldn't get out, that she and Emma had to get back to their rooms for curfew.

"If you're sure," Emma heard Jamie's mom say.

"Yes, Mom, I'm sure." Jamie gave her mother a last peck on the cheek and then exited the car with promises to text them in the morning. She followed Emma into the hotel, stopping to wave one last time at her parents.

"Christ," Jamie groaned as they finally made it into the elevator, "I forgot how exhausting they can be! Family."

"Can't live with them." She left it at that.

"Ain't that the truth." She reached over and kissed Emma's cheek, jumping back as the elevator stuttered to a stop. "Thanks again for coming to dinner."

"Thanks for inviting me," she replied, wishing the doors would magically open onto her condo hallway. But the doors opened onto their hotel floor, and they were officially on team time once again.

"See you tomorrow?" Jamie asked as Emma stopped at her room, fishing in her purse for her card key.

"See you tomorrow." Emma held her hand up for a high five, mouth twisted into a rueful smile.

Jamie caught her fingers and tugged her closer. "Love you, Blake."

"Love you too, Max." She opened the door reluctantly. "Sweet dreams."

"Sweet dreams to you too," Jamie replied in a sassy voice. And then she was strolling away down the hallway with a last flirty wink over her shoulder.

She was too much. But Emma would take her any way she could.

# CHAPTER SIX

Jamie shouldered her duffel and tugged her suitcase behind her to the Heathrow taxi line. At least it wasn't raining—definitely a plus when it came to November in England. She checked her messenger bag for the thirty-second time, making sure she had her passport. Lately she'd had nightmares about losing it and getting stuck in a foreign country where she didn't speak the language. Three guesses where that particular nightmare came from.

After a summer of crisscrossing the United States for the NWSL, the fall had felt like a rotating door of different countries: Utah in September (not a foreign nation per se, but the snow-tipped mountains and smiling blonde citizens did make it feel like Scandinavia), Poland and the UK in October, and now Switzerland and the UK again this month. If she'd made the CONCACAF roster, her October travels would have been confined to the continental United States with Emma and crew, but she had failed to make the team once again.

The news hadn't torn her up as much as she'd expected probably because Jo had told her that if the roster were larger, she would have made it. At twenty, the World Cup qualifying roster was among the smallest for an international competition, second only to the Olympics' eighteen. Jo had also informed her that her 2014 in a US jersey might not be over yet. She was a "likely candidate" for the national team's trip to Brasilia in December to play in the International Tournament of Nations—yet another foreign excursion. The coaches were taking twenty-four players to Brazil, and Jo seemed to think that Jamie had a good shot at making the cut.

Her phone beeped and she perked up as she read the text. Emma wanted to video-chat. They'd barely spoken for the last few days while Jamie was in Switzerland, and she'd missed Emma more than was probably healthy.

"Yes!" she texted back. "Please!!!"

Skype buzzed and she answered it, gazing eagerly at the pixelated view of her girlfriend on the screen. "Hi! Oh my god, hi!"

"Hi yourself," Emma said, smiling. "What's up, cutie? It's good to see your face."

"You too." Jamie scooted up in line. She was almost to the front, *finally*.

"Where are you?" Emma asked. "I thought you were supposed to be back in London already."

"I got held up at baggage claim. Can you freaking believe it? They lost my bag, the bastards. But only temporarily. Somehow it ended up on another carousel."

"What about the rest of your team?"

"They ditched me."

"Even Britt?"

"Yep. I actually can't blame her. Our flight was delayed. It's been a massively long day."

"Aw, poor baby. I wish I were there. I would totes give you a massage."

Jamie scrunched up her face. "I hate you."

"No you don't. You love me. Hey, I gotta go. Text me when you're settled and we can chat some more, okay?"

"Okay. Wait, where—"

But Emma had already blown her a kiss and ended the call.

"—are you?" she finished, and sighed. Dang it. The first time they'd video chatted in almost a week and Emma had to cut it short. Still, Jamie was holding her to their chat later. Sure, she'd be stuck in a room the size of a closet crashing at the basement apartment of one of her teammates, but she could close the door to achieve a modicum of privacy. That door had come in handy on the night of Emma's birthday a few weeks earlier when Jamie had Skyped her—naked. What were the kids calling it these days? Oh, yeah: *skexing*, AKA sex via Skype. Nowhere near as good as the real thing, but it would have to do for now.

When she reached the front of the line, she barely waited for the approaching taxi to stop before loading her gear into the back seat and climbing in after it. "Edgware," she told the driver as he pulled away from the curb, relieved when he only nodded and kept his eyes on the road. At this point she was too exhausted to even feign politeness. She imagined that if Heathrow was a regular route, the driver would be used to catatonic travelers.

She might have dozed a bit in the warm back seat that smelled of Thai food, or maybe she was technically daydreaming as she pictured Emma the last time she'd seen her. After September's residency camp ended, they'd spent the next two weeks together holed up in Emma's condo, only leaving the building to work out, buy groceries, and, occasionally, socialize with Dani or members of the Reign. It had been an amazing break from their crazy summer schedule, and had made Jamie's non-selection for qualifiers easier to handle.

They'd had such a great time together in Seattle that she'd almost invited Emma to join her in Europe after CONCACAFs. But she knew Emma was looking forward to downtime after the tournament, and besides, as a USWNT poster child and Nike-sponsored athlete, Emma had press junkets and a meeting with her agent and other Very Important Person commitments to handle in the brief off-season the federation granted.

And so, at the beginning of October, Jamie had headed to Europe with Britt, unsure how long their Champions League run would last. While the Emma and the US were narrowly winning their first World Cup qualifier against Trinidad and Tobago, Jamie and Arsenal were making up a two-goal deficit at home against their Polish opponents in the Round of Thirty-two. Jamie could barely believe it, but they'd scored three goals in twenty minutes to come from behind and win on aggregate.

Now, three weeks later, they'd once again fallen behind on the away leg, this time in the Round of Sixteen. With last night's match in Zurich ending 1-2, they would have to win their home match by two goals if they wanted to advance to Champions League Quarterfinals in March. Zurich was flying to London tomorrow and the match would take place the following day, less than seventy-two hours after the first leg. The one good thing about the quick turnaround was that they would know their fate sooner rather than later.

Her phone buzzed, a text from Britt: "Did they ever find your bag?"

Whoops. She'd promised she would text once she was on her way. "Sorry. Yes!" she typed back.

"Excellent! Come to ours for a nightcap?"

Frowning, she pondered her response. She wanted to sleep, like, badly. Realistically, though, would her temporary roommates let her? The closet she was crashing in bordered the living room of the apartment four of her Arsenal teammates were currently letting, and the odds that the others wouldn't be up past midnight watching DVRed Premier League matches were next to nil. That meant she would be up past midnight watching DVRed Premier League matches, too.

"On my way," she texted back. "See you in fifteen."

Maybe she would even give in and sleep on the couch at Britt's girlfriend's cousin's place in Camden, as they had been bugging her to do. It was a mighty comfortable couch.

"Sweet!!!!!" Britt texted.

Her exclamation point usage felt a bit excessive given they'd lost yesterday and spent today in travel hell, but then again Allie, Britt's girlfriend, had flown in from DC for the Zurich matches.

The driver accepted the trip revision without comment, and soon they were stopping in front of a nondescript terraced house on a cramped block not far from the famous Camden Market. Jamie paid for the ride, pocketed the receipt, and lugged her bags up the brick walk. Someone buzzed her in, and she headed for the flat at the rear of the building, glad Allie's cousin lived on the first floor. The last thing she wanted right now was to haul her luggage up a flight of stairs.

The flat door was slightly ajar. As she pushed her way inside she sang out wryly, "Lucy, I'm home," in a poor imitation of Ricky Ricardo. Or, more accurately, of Lorelai Gilmore doing her rendition of Ricky Ricardo. The greeting was a throwback to the days when she and Britt had shared a garden flat within spitting distance of Meadow Park, Arsenal Ladies FC's training ground.

Lizzie, Allie's cousin, waved enthusiastically at her from the kitchen while Britt and Allie avoided her eyes, seemingly frozen on the couch. Before Jamie could ask about their weirdness, she noticed a familiar purse on the coffee table. Wait. Was that Lizzie's, or could it be...?

"Surprise!" an even more familiar voice sang.

Jamie spun, dropping her bags as she discovered Emma smiling at her from just behind the door. "Oh my god! You're here!" And then she was sweeping her girlfriend into a tight hug, laughing as she twirled her around. "I can't believe you're here!"

"Believe it, babe." Emma hugged her back, lips warm against her neck.

"What are you doing in London?"

"I wanted to see you play! It's not every day your girlfriend plays in Champions League, you know."

"This is so awesome!" She set Emma down and simply stared at her, taking in her pink cheeks, sparkling eyes, honey-colored hair falling in loose waves around her shoulders. "It is so good to see you. You have no idea."

"I think I might have a slight idea," Emma said, reaching for her hand. "Come sit for a minute. Lizzie's making us tea before we head to the flat."

"The flat?" Jamie echoed, shrugging out of her jacket as Emma guided her across the room.

Emma tugged her down onto the couch, squishing in beside Allie and Britt. "I rented a place in Hampstead through the weekend."

"But my flight leaves on Thursday." Even as she said it, she realized how ridiculous she sounded.

"That's what change fees are for, silly." Emma snuggled into her side. "Assuming you want to have a European vacation with me..."

"I don't know. Twist my arm." Jamie leaned forward to regard Britt and Allie. "You knew about this, didn't you?"

Britt, whose inability to keep a secret was legendary, nodded. "And I didn't even screw it up!"

"Well done, babe," Allie said.

"Way to go," Jamie agreed, and then sighed, all of her accrued negativity from the day seeping away into the atmosphere. Just like that, she was warm and comfortable and *stationary*, Emma's body pressed into hers, the week stretching ahead a good deal brighter.

The tea kettle whistled, and Jamie watched as Britt and

Allie hopped up to make tea—and, presumably, to give them a moment.

"Good surprise?" Emma asked softly.

"The best," she said, pressing a kiss to her girlfriend's forehead. "It's funny—I almost showed up in DC for your birthday, but then I remembered how you feel about surprises."

While Emma liked showing up on other people's parents' doorsteps and announcing her intention to kiss those people, she had never been much of a fan of being surprised herself.

"I don't *dislike* surprises," Emma objected. As Jamie tilted her head, she added, "Well, maybe a little."

"Besides, you guys had your last group stage game that night, and I didn't want to distract you."

"We were playing Haiti."

"I know, but you still hadn't advanced. I was being respectful."

Emma blinked up at her. "You actually thought about flying back to the US for my birthday?"

"Well, yeah. It would have had to be quick, but I could have made it work."

"I would have loved that. Not that I didn't enjoy the care package and your scintillating sexy times dance." Emma bit her lip, but not out of appreciation. Instead, Jamie was all but certain, she was trying not to laugh.

Admittedly, Jamie's dance routine had been rough around the edges, but it had been the wee hours of the morning in London, and she had been stuck in a closet. Irony duly noted.

"Whatever. You know you want all of this," Jamie said, gesturing to her Arsenal Ladies FC sweats.

"I do," Emma agreed, as she always did. "But for the record, you're welcome to show up unannounced any time."

It was Jamie's turn to blink at her. "Promise?"

"I promise."

"Huh." Jamie looped one of Emma's curls around her finger. "I might hold you to that."

"I hope you will," Emma said, gazing up at her.

"Those are some serious heart eyes," Britt commented from the kitchen.

"I know," Allie said, and Jamie could hear the smile in her voice. "Aren't they sweet?"

They were, she thought, gazing back at Emma. No doubt about it.

"Holy shit." Jamie dropped her bags on an expensive rug and surveyed the flat, eyes wide. "This is... It's... Jesus, Emma. How much does this place cost?"

Emma waved a hand and swept past her, turning on lights as she went. "I don't remember. Dani found it for us while I was in LA."

The previous week, Emma had gone to Southern California with Jenny, Maddie, and Angie to film a Nike ad campaign that would air over the holidays. The life of an international soccer star, Jamie had teased her at the time. Taking in the luxurious flat now, she realized that the title was perhaps more fitting than she'd realized.

To the left of the entrance was a sitting room decorated with bright, modern (Jamie surmised) art pieces that likely cost more than her entire annual salary—each. That wasn't saying much, but still. She moved forward, noting two more sitting rooms off the entrance, one with brighter artwork and a large-screen television that took up most of one wall, the other decorated in more muted tones with a distinctly mature feel. Like the room you would retire to if you were a stuffy business type having a dinner party with your colleagues and their spouses. The floors throughout the flat were sanded and polished dark wood, the rugs deeply piled, the ceilings high. Bright white molding complemented light gray walls, lending a cool, tranquil air to the rooms. The light fixture in the entrance way—the foyer?—was an honest-to-god chandelier. She felt like she'd stepped onto a movie set for a modern revival of *Pride and Prejudice*, only a gayer, chicer version.

"Check this out," Emma said, grinning over her shoulder as she headed through a doorway straight ahead.

If Jamie had thought her eyes couldn't get any wider, she'd been wrong. The back half of the flat was taken up by an open-plan kitchen, dining area, and game room complete with a full-sized pool table. The exterior wall was almost entirely floor-to-ceiling windows that overlooked a spacious patio illuminated by fairy lights. Beyond the patio was—*what?* Jamie strode to the sliding doors and stared out over the spot-lit garden, surprisingly large even for this part of London.

*No. Fucking. Way.* "Is that—"

"A soccer field? In miniature, but yes." Emma's smile broadened. "But wait, there's more," she added, channeling a cheesy TV infomercial.

And indeed there was. The master bedroom off the kitchen included an en suite bathroom equipped with a glass-walled shower and a jetted tub. Down a short flight of stairs, the daylight basement offered a small cinema with comfy arm chairs arranged in stadium seating, a fitness room with weights and cardio machines, and an additional bedroom.

"Holy shit," Jamie breathed for what felt like the hundredth time as she catalogued the fitness equipment. Whoever owned this place had gone all out. She couldn't believe they rented it out to strangers, but the exorbitant rental cost probably ensured a certain level of clientele.

Back in the kitchen, Emma filled the electric kettle and set it to boil. "I asked to have it stocked with your favorites," she said, opening a tin marked *Tea* on the counter and holding it out for Jamie to survey.

Sure enough, inside were packets of English breakfast, blueberry green, and ginger turmeric tea. For some reason, that personal touch moved her more than the flat's superlative amenities.

"You are amazing," she said, and moved forward to take Emma in her arms. "I love you."

"I love you too." Emma wound her arms around Jamie's neck and reached up to kiss her lingeringly. Then she pulled back, head tilted, one eyebrow quirked. "Maybe we should give the steam shower a whirl, you know, test the water pressure?"

"Last one there's a rotten egg!" Jamie answered, tugging off her hoodie as she sprinted, laughing, toward the master bedroom.

Later, they dressed in comfy sweats and returned to the kitchen where Jamie reheated the water and Emma scrounged a pair of mugs from one of the slate gray cupboards above the sink.

"Babe," Emma said as she rifled through the tea tin, "I can't wait to see you play on Wednesday! Do you realize it'll be the first time I've ever gotten to watch you? Well, in person, anyway."

"What do you mean, in person?"

"I saw your first cap against Ireland on TV. Your second one too, although that one wasn't quite as enjoyable."

Jamie took in the information. She'd seen the replay on YouTube, the resounding crack of her ankle audible on the sideline mics, her own disturbing shriek, followed by the silence of the crowd somehow louder than anything that had come before. What must that have been like for Emma? Probably just as bad as it had been for Jamie to watch the fan video of Emma collapsing at open practice after her appendix burst.

"I didn't realize you were watching," she said.

"Well, I was." Emma wiped a few drops of water from the granite countertop. "With my mom, actually. I was staying with her for a few weeks."

"Oh, you mean after you neglected your health and had to be rushed to the hospital by ambulance? Yeah, I should hope you stayed with your mom." She shook her head, unreasonably irritated by the fact that Emma had nearly died.

"If my appendix hadn't decided to explode," Emma said, propping her elbows on the countertop and resting her chin on one hand, "we would have both been at those games. I wonder if anything would have happened between us?"

Jamie didn't bother telling her that she and Clare had still been happy at the time. It was possible it might not have mattered anyway.

"It's hard to believe that was only two years ago," she said instead. "It feels like so much has happened since then. You know?"

"Well, yeah." Emma gave her an affectionate smile. "I do."

A few minutes later they were curled up facing each other on the couch in the nearest living room, mugs cupped in hands, feet tucked under each other's bodies for warmth. They had talked, texted, or video chatted every day since the first week of October, but it simply wasn't the same as being together in real life. Despite their near-constant contact, somehow Jamie still felt like they had tons to catch up on.

For example: "Anything new to report on the lawsuit?" she asked, sipping her steaming tea.

At the beginning of October, a group of international players had filed a lawsuit against FIFA and the Canadian Soccer Association alleging gender discrimination. The suit called for grass to be installed over the turf fields selected for the World Cup, and had been brought in front of a Canadian

Human Rights Tribunal, a court that focused on mediation, as a signal that the players were seeking a workable compromise.

Emma made a face. "Don't even ask."

"Oh. Okay. Sorry," she said awkwardly.

"No, you can always ask. It's just not good news."

"What's going on?"

"FIFA's attorneys are using every trick in the legal book to torpedo the case—or at least slow it down so much that it can't be decided before the World Cup. In a way, it's our own fault," she added, her hand tightening on Jamie's calf. "We admitted we had no intention of boycotting the World Cup, and since no boycott means no leverage, Amy Rupert says only one party is operating in good faith. It sure as hell isn't FIFA."

"God, they're such assholes. Why can't they do the right thing?"

"They're not going to do the right thing until someone forces them to because as far as they're concerned, we should be grateful for whatever amount of funding they grace us with." She sighed. "Ellie and I thought calling them out in front of the entire world would make them even *pretend* to listen, but nope. Our bad."

Jamie had played soccer for years in the UK, where the attitude toward female players was only a step above atrocious. But still, it was disheartening when that attitude turned into real world consequences—like forcing the best teams in the world to play a World Cup, the penultimate competition of the international game, on sub-par fields. It reminded her of how Jo Nichols had once said in an interview that her high school program had been funded because someone's parents had threatened a Title IX lawsuit, and even then the girls' team had played their matches on the JV football team's practice field, with long grass, ankle-deep holes, and no stands to speak of.

"It gets worse," Emma said, wrinkling her nose. "You know Veronica Padilla from Mexico and Sophie Durand from France?" Jamie nodded. She had faced Durand in Champions League more than once. "They dropped out of the lawsuit a few days ago because they said their national federations threatened retribution. They're not the only ones facing threats, either."

"What?" She stared at Emma, aghast. "The federations can't do that, can they?"

"Whether or not they can, they are. The good thing is that a bunch of other women have stepped forward to sign on, including twenty players from the German team."

Women footballers were badass, even if male federation officials weren't.

"Anyway," Emma added, "have you heard about the Brazil tournament?"

"Nothing definitive yet. But Ellie thinks it looks good."

"I hope so." Emma squeezed her leg. "It would suck to be apart that long, especially so close to the holidays."

Jamie's heart skipped at Emma's use of the words "together" and "holidays" in such close proximity. When it came to being in the same place at the same time, they'd been living week to week since the start. Pro athletes didn't have a long shelf life, so they'd both agreed that the game had to be their priority for now. In some ways Jamie was relieved to finally date someone whose commitment to soccer matched hers. She understood when Emma had to be away for national team duty for weeks at a time, and didn't take it personally if Emma turned down a date or even sex for more sleep or a scheduled workout.

In other ways, being with a fellow athlete was harder. With Clare, when Jamie was out of town for an away game or training with the national team, there had been someone at home keeping the refrigerator stocked and the rent paid, the mail sorted and the electric bill current. Not only that, Clare had been in the stands for every home game and many of the away ones. Before now the only time Emma had seen her play was when their NWSL teams met, and rarely had they gotten a chance to be together for more than a few stolen nights. While their current arrangement was necessary for their careers, Jamie didn't feel like she could up and ask Emma to come home with her for Thanksgiving or Christmas or—the holiday she really hoped they could spend together—New Year's.

Good thing her girlfriend didn't have that particular hang-up.

When Jamie remained quiet, Emma nudged her hip. "What about you? Still planning on Berkeley for Thanksgiving?"

"Well, yeah. It'll be my first Thanksgiving in the States in a while."

"Feel like company?" Emma gazed at her over the top of her mug, eyelashes fluttering prettily.

"You mean you?" Jamie asked.

"No, I meant my brother." She poked her leg. "Of course me. Do you think your parents would mind?"

"No!" Jamie said quickly. "I think they would love it."

"And you?"

"I think I would love it too."

"I should hope so." Emma squinted at her. "In that case, I have a proposal for you."

"Okay?" Jamie held her breath.

"I propose we stay here an extra week and fly back to California right before Thanksgiving. Because after that..." She trailed off.

After that, the national team would be headed to Brazil for most of December, with or without Jamie. And then it would be 2015, a new year that would be even busier than the current one.

"By here, do you mean this flat?" Jamie clarified.

"Yeah. With the fitness room and mini pitch, we can keep up our training. Plus this way you can show me London. I didn't get a chance to see much of the city last time I was here."

On the surface, Jamie thought, the plan sounded ideal. Showing Emma the places she'd lived and played in London would be amazing. Since they'd hung out in each other's hometowns as teenagers, this was the closest she would get to sharing unknown parts of her past with Emma. But this flat was posher than anyplace she'd ever stayed, and Emma had already laid out so much more for their relationship than Jamie could ever repay...

"I don't know, Em," she said, waving at the art-clad walls around them. "This place is—"

"—perfect for us," Emma interrupted. "I know it's a bit much, and I know you worry about money, but let me treat you. Please?" When Jamie only continued to stare at her, lips twisted uncertainly, she added, "If it helps, any spending money I have comes from the interest on my father's insurance policy. I own my condo outright, and I have a retirement fund and investments *and* I give fifteen percent of my annual salary to charity. The rest of it goes to food, travel, and training. Please, *please* let me do nice things for us? We don't get to see each other all that often, in case you hadn't noticed."

"Low blow, Blake." Jamie could feel herself weakening. It would be sort of ridiculous to let her pride come between them, wouldn't it? Wasn't this chance to be with Emma everything she'd been hoping for? Give or take an extra sitting room or two.

"Totally," Emma agreed with zero remorse. Her hand pressed warmly against Jamie's leg. "What will it be?"

Jamie sighed. "Fine, you win. You may treat me to a fancy European vacation."

"Twist your arm, huh?" Emma asked, smiling back.

"Exactly." Considering how little Emma's father had liked her, Jamie couldn't help appreciating the irony of his insurance money funding their super-gay London holiday. She sipped her tea and regarded Emma over the top of her mug. "Thank you, by the way. In case I forget to say it later."

"I'm pretty sure you already thanked me in the shower," Emma drawled, her voice simultaneously lazy and suggestive.

And suddenly even two weeks in this flat didn't feel like nearly enough time together.

*　　*　　*

Emma checked the scoreboard, knowing what she would find. The game was nearly over, and Arsenal was still only up 2-1. If they didn't score again, and soon, they would lose on aggregate goals and their Champions League run would be over in the Round of Sixteen.

"Come on, Jamie," she yelled, unable to bring herself to shout out the name of one of Manchester United's biggest rivals. There was love, and then there was football. She was here, wasn't she? That was more than she could say for most of London.

Jamie had warned her that the Women's Super League didn't draw even a fraction of the fan support that the NWSL did. Seattle's attendance this past season had averaged close to four thousand, a fifty-five percent increase over their inaugural season. Those figures were embarrassing when compared to Portland's thirteen thousand or the Sounders' forty-five thousand, but even the Reign's attendance figures dwarfed the numbers she could see in the stands at Arsenal's home pitch, which seemed smaller even than her high school stadium. What were there, 800 people here to witness a Champions League Round of Sixteen playoff match? No more than a thousand, surely.

Allie, Britt's girlfriend, grabbed Emma's arm and

pointed. Jamie was sprinting through the midfield, head up and ball at her feet, and Emma could see the play unfolding even before Jamie slotted the ball between a pair of defenders and into the path of a striker Emma recognized from the English national team. The fleet-footed woman took a touch and then blasted the ball into the corner of the net.

Emma and Allie leapt out of their seats, cheering mightily. They had done it! They had taken the lead in the two-game series. She checked the clock again. Two and a half minutes left in regulation. Now all they had to do was hold on until the referee blew the final whistle.

As Jamie jogged back to the center circle, her eyes sought out Emma in the stands.

"You got this," Emma mouthed at her, shooting her a thumbs-up.

Nodding, Jamie waved and turned away.

*That's my girl*, Emma thought, exchanging a grin with Allie. Watching Jamie play was so fun. Why hadn't she done this sooner? Oh, right. That thing called a job. Playing for club and country didn't leave much wiggle room.

Four agonizingly long minutes later, the referee blew her whistle in the standard three long tweets. Arsenal had won 3-1, and in doing so they'd stolen the round from the Swiss team and earned a spot in the quarterfinals in March.

Emma followed Allie down to the field and jumped the barrier. She would have been content to wait near the center line, but Allie took her hand and dragged her over to the home bench while the two teams shook hands. After a brief team talk with the coaches, Jamie and Britt came jogging over all pink cheeks and smiles. Britt pulled Allie into a hug, but Jamie stopped a pace away and held her hand up for a high five, eyes slightly questioning.

Emma closed the space between them and hugged her firmly. "Well done," she said into Jamie's ear before stepping back.

"Thanks." Jamie was grinning again. "We're in the quarterfinals!"

"Barely," she teased. "Allie and I almost drew blood, we were clutching each other's arms so tightly."

"It's good entertainment, right?" Jamie waved at the sparsely filled stands. "We're all about the fan experience here, obviously."

While Jamie and Britt changed out of their cleats, several of their teammates approached, greeting family and friends and grabbing assorted gear from the bench.

"Yo, Yanks, are you coming out to celebrate?" a tall woman with a nearly shaved head asked.

"Wouldn't miss it. The pub?" Britt asked as she tucked her gloves into her team bag.

"Natch. And bring your ladies," the tall woman added with a wink.

*Ladies.* With difficulty, Emma bit back a sarcastic retort. These were Jamie's friends and teammates, she reminded herself. She was only along for the ride.

A little while later they were gathered around a table in the Twelve Pins Pub's function room, where the wait staff knew the players by name. At first the conversation centered on who their competition might be in the next round of the tournament. Results from most of the other matches weren't online yet, and the draw to determine quarterfinal, semifinal, and finals match-ups wouldn't take place for another week. But with only fourteen teams still potentially alive, they could make some educated guesses. One possibility was the Lyon club. Emma glanced at Jamie. As far as she knew, Jamie hadn't been back to the French city since her trip there as a teenager. What would she do if Arsenal ended up with a Champions League match there?

Jeanie, the center striker who had all but leered at her in the stadium, picked that moment to start chatting Emma up about Seattle and the NWSL. She had known who Emma was all along, she admitted, and had merely been "jerking her chain." With half a pint of English amber in her, Emma relaxed and joked back with Jeanie and the other Arsenal players. The only touch-and-go moment came when Britt, tipsy and happy, let it slip that Emma was a United supporter. Emma quickly bought a round for the table, and the momentary flare of enmity faded away.

The celebration was raucous but short-lived, mostly because it was a week night and the majority of the team had to work in the morning. Emma huffed in frustration when Jamie told her why the party was breaking up early. Even in the UK, where soccer was the most popular sport, women players in the top league weren't paid a living salary. Meanwhile Arsenal's men side, she knew, had paid a fifteen million pound transfer fee to steal Danny Welbeck from Manchester United a couple of months earlier. Fifteen million pounds for a single player, while the women at this table earned on average, Jamie had told her, fifteen to twenty thousand pounds from their club contracts. She supposed they should be grateful that male soccer players in the US only made ten or twenty times what female players earned, rather than a thousand times more.

When most of the others had gone, Britt leaned in, her arm loose around Allie's shoulders, and said, "It's karaoke night at She. What do you say? Up for a sing-off?"

"She Soho," Jamie explained to Emma. "It's a women's bar in London."

"Oh." Emma paused, wondering if she could afford the potential exposure. Not only was there Twitter to worry about, but for years Emma's agent had counseled her to keep her sexuality to herself while she was a national team regular. From a career standpoint, she understood why he thought the closet was the better choice. He repped Ellie too, and her sponsorship deals had narrowed significantly since she'd come out a few years earlier.

"It's okay," Jamie said into the weighted silence,

offering a smile that Emma recognized as fake. Judging from her frown, Britt did too. "I'm tired, you guys. Maybe another night."

"No," Emma said, one part of her mind making itself up without telling the other, "let's go. How often are we in London?"

Jamie stared hard at her. "Are you sure? Because we don't have to."

She touched Jamie's hand. "I know. I want to. Don't you?"

"She totally does," Britt said, back to smiling. "Jamie loves karaoke, don't you?"

This was news to Emma. "You do?"

"Not as much as Britt and Allie," Jamie said. "Oh, god, maybe we *should* call it a night..."

"You know, if you're worried about being recognized," Britt said, "you could wear your hair down and maybe, I don't know, add some glasses? You know, like Supergirl?"

"Like Supergirl," Emma repeated. Was she being serious? Her face was so earnest, and at camp in Utah she had seemed like a genuine type of person.

"Britt is a comic book nerd," Jamie supplied.

"Like you're not!"

"I prefer graphic novels," she said, her tone haughty.

This was also news to Emma. She thought she might like hanging around the London version of Jamie, particularly if Britt was going to continue to dole out glimpses of the person Jamie had become in the years they'd been apart.

The siren call of karaoke could not be denied. Soon the four of them were on a train headed into the heart of the city, dark tunnels and brightly tiled stations with their distinctively rounded walls slipping past. Being underground reminded Emma of Boston. It had been easy there to hop a train to anywhere she needed to go. Seattle, meanwhile, had buses.

Emma routinely thanked the powers that be that her building (1) was only a few blocks from sushi, frozen yogurt, Trader Joe's, and Safeway; and (2) had a garage.

At the Leicester Square stop, they piled out and headed up to street level where they emerged onto the narrow, crowded streets of central London. The short walk to the bar took them past theaters and restaurants, red double decker buses and black old-fashioned taxis. Emma had spent time in London before, but she had always visited for soccer. Never had she come as a tourist; the difference was startling. Here she could walk arm-in-arm with Jamie without worrying that someone would stop her to exclaim, "Oh my god, you're the girl who made that penalty kick in the World Cup!" While making the final penalty kick that sent the US into the 2011 World Cup semifinals in Germany was one of the most memorable moments of her career, it had also made her face recognizable all over the soccer—and non-soccer—world.

A year later at the 2012 Olympics she'd made a different kind of name for herself during an epic semifinal match against Canada. When Emily Shorter, her fellow defender, slipped in the box during a corner kick and Canada's Catherine Beaumont trod purposefully on her head, leaving ugly red cleat marks across her cheek, Emma was one of the only players close enough to witness the dirty play. Instead of punching Beaumont on the spot—an automatic red card—she helped Emily to her feet and bided her time. Ten minutes later the opportunity for revenge presented itself, and she slide-tackled the Canadian midfielder so hard that Beaumont had to be stretchered off the field. The following day, ESPN showed the match highlights as an example of the opposite of the Olympic spirit. But when the interviewer asked Marty about Emma's tackle, her coach insisted that Emma had shown quite a bit of spirit in her defense of an injured teammate.

"Are you saying that you encourage your players to seek revenge?" the interviewer had pressed. "Don't get mad, get even?"

"I prefer to think of it as natural consequences," Marty had replied, her voice infused with a touch of the playfulness she was known for. "Blake's tackle was legal, whereas the foul against Shorter that the ref missed? Not at all. Blake simply sent a message to the opposing team that they had better think twice about any more funny business. I think the message was received, don't you?"

Half the time when a stranger approached her on the street or in the grocery store, they referenced either the PK in Germany or the slide tackle in London. That was actually the last time she'd been in the UK: for the Olympics. Then, she'd been sequestered for weeks, training, eating, and sleeping with the same twenty-one teammates—eighteen official plus four alternates. Now, there was only her, Jamie, and Jamie's friends, and they could do anything and be anywhere they wanted. Including a women's bar in Soho.

She clutched Jamie's arm more tightly, excited by the sheer novelty of the evening. Earlier she had watched Jamie help win a round of Champions League, and now they were going out to a gay bar. Emma had been to a few in the States, but never to one in a foreign country.

On Old Compton Street, Britt and Allie led the way to a discreet doorway that opened onto a steep set of stairs. At the bottom they entered a dimly lit room with a low ceiling that arced overhead in a half-circle, lending the space (in Emma's opinion) a claustrophobic air.

"You guys," she said as they wound past faux leather club chairs and small glass tables lit by candles. "I swear this place used to be an actual Tube station."

Britt laughed over her shoulder. "I know, right?"

Apparently Emma was the only one who found the idea of a gay bar in a bomb shelter disturbing.

They ordered drinks from the tattooed woman working the bar situated at one end of the room before following the sounds of drunken singing into the next room. Or the next *bunker*, as Emma was beginning to think of it. At least if there happened to be a terrorist attack or other disaster, they should be all good down here.

A drag king and a woman in lingerie were running karaoke. Emma felt eyes on her and Jamie as they pored over one of the song books. She was fairly certain the other patrons were checking them out because they were in a women's bar, not because anyone recognized them, and started to relax—until she remembered that she was about to sing in public. She would need to be tipsier for this, especially with Jamie in the crowd. But for once, she wouldn't have to feel guilty about drinking too much. Her next game was weeks away, and while she needed to keep up her regular work-outs, she could also afford to let her hair down a bit.

After they made their selections, they found a cocktail table to cluster around while they waited. Conversation flowed easily as they rated other singers' song choices and discussed their current home cities. The same week Jamie had moved to Portland, Britt and Allie had moved to Maryland so that Britt could play with DC's NWSL team. As a British national, Allie was in the country on a tourist visa. Fortunately, she had found work through an online tutoring company teaching English via Skype from their apartment in Germantown. With their combined income and the Champions League pay Britt was picking up on top of her NWSL salary, they were doing fairly well for themselves.

As they complained about the small town feel of Germantown—"There's a Walmart and a movie theater and that's about it!"—Emma listened enviously. She and Jamie had to fit their time together around the edges of their individual lives, all while living in different cities. Barring a fortuitous trade, she didn't see that situation changing, either. That was why they needed to enjoy moments like this one, she reminded herself, gulping down the last of her beer as the hosts called her name.

Was she drunk enough to stand up in front of a roomful of foreign lesbians (and Jamie) and sing? No. But too late to remedy the situation now.

Emma hadn't sung karaoke in years, not since a private national team party at a bar in North Carolina on what was supposed to be a victory tour after the last World Cup. She was glad she'd decided to go with her old stand-by: Pat Benatar's girl-rock anthem, "Hit Me With Your Best Shot." Her voice was shaky at first, but soon she found her rhythm, encouraged by the enthusiastic cheers from Jamie and friends and, surprisingly, a whole bunch of women she didn't know. Girl power anthems, it turned out, were popular in lesbian bars.

She was grinning and sweaty by the time Jamie came up for her turn.

"Nice song. Wasn't it on one of the mixes I sent you back in high school?"

"Maybe," Emma said, and winked at her as she handed over the mic. "Have fun!"

Jamie sang another song from the CD Emma had listened to for years until her car stereo devoured it: Gloria Gaynor's "I Will Survive." Jamie might have struggled to stay on pitch, but that didn't stop half the bar from shouting out the words with her as she strode across the stage with sure steps, her entire being screaming "survivor." Emma's heart swelled with love and her eyes filled with stupid tears, and when Jamie returned to the cocktail table, Emma swept her into a tight hug, not caring who saw. But that was the beauty of singing karaoke in a dimly lit underground bar in a foreign city. People were there to have fun, not to stalk American soccer players.

"I love you," she said into Jamie's ear. "I'm so proud we're together. You know that, don't you?"

"Same." Jamie pulled back to smile down at her. "And I love you too."

Up on stage Britt and Allie launched into a cheesy duet that had the women near them rolling their eyes. They were cute together, though, and for the second time that evening, Emma found herself envying the simplicity of their relationship.

*Maybe someday*, she thought, glancing at Jamie only to find her already gazing back, a slight smile on her lips, blue eyes hooded in the dark bar. Jamie reached for her hand, tugging her closer until their hips bumped.

"Thanks for surprising me," she said, her breath stirring the loose hair at Emma's nape.

"You're welcome." She slipped an arm around Jamie's waist and leaned against her as Britt and Allie's song reached a crescendo.

Then again, today was pretty awesome, too.

# CHAPTER SEVEN

"I have a plan," Jamie announced the following morning when Emma emerged from the master bedroom, freshly showered. "What do you say, Blake? You up for an adventure?"

Emma pursed her lips. She was fairly certain she hadn't had enough coffee for this conversation. "Depends. What kind of adventure?"

"You're just going to have to wait and see," Jamie said, gazing at her over the top of her A-Z map.

Her look was challenging, and Emma felt her temper flare. Then she tamped it down. She had crossed an ocean to surprise Jamie with an impromptu vacation. She could probably let her decide how to spend one of their too-short days together.

"Fine," she made herself reply. "Lead away."

"That killed you to say, didn't it?"

"Yes. Yes, it did."

The thing about Jamie, however, was that she apparently rivaled her friend Britt in not being able to keep a secret. By the time Allie pulled up in her cousin's Volkswagen Golf, Emma had managed to wrangle the gist of the plan out of her girlfriend: visiting the home stadiums of all six top tier Premier League clubs in London—in a single day.

"Britt convinced me to cut out the second tier," she'd admitted as they loaded her messenger bag with bottled water, protein bars, and bananas. "Otherwise we would have been hard pressed to get to all thirteen stadiums."

Six top tier soccer clubs in a city of eight and a half million (according to her Fodor's guide) was like New York City having six NBA or NFL teams. Emma couldn't even begin to imagine the viciousness of the rivalries among neighbors and coworkers throughout the city.

Jamie's itinerary had them driving in a wide circle around London, starting with Queens Park Rangers FC in the northwest and Chelsea's Stamford Bridge on the north bank of the Thames. Next they journeyed south of the Thames to Crystal Palace FC in Selhurst. From Crystal Palace they wound their way northeast to West Ham's London Stadium, Tottenham Hotspur's White Hart Lane, and finally, Arsenal's Emirates Stadium, the last stop.

Naturally, Jamie knew someone who slipped them into the Emirates Legends, a stadium tour led by a legendary Arsenal player. Their guide that afternoon was Charlie George, a long-time Gunner who had scored the winning goal in the 1971 FA Cup Final.

"He's the reason we're doing this today," Jamie confided to Emma as they followed George through the interior of the huge stadium. "The others are great too, but Charlie is a character."

This became clear over the hour-long tour as George led them past the trophy cases and through the changing rooms, providing color commentary all the while on Gunner history, the new stadium, and the current coach and players. Even Emma, a United fan, got goose bumps walking down the players' tunnel. It wasn't difficult for her to imagine the roar of sixty thousand fans. The gold medal game against

Japan at the 2012 Olympics, a rematch of the 2011 World Cup final, had drawn more than eighty thousand fans. That match, played only a few miles away at Wembley Stadium, had been one of the highlights of her national team career. So far, anyway. She was hoping that next summer would trump even their gold medal run in London—assuming she made the team. Maddie said she was ridiculous to worry. Ellie too. But Jo had been clear about her expectations, and Emma was fully aware that she hadn't met them.

With difficulty, Emma pushed her anxiety away. This vacation was supposed to be about her and Jamie, not the national team. But realistically, on a soccer tour with Jamie of the very city where only two years earlier she'd stood atop an Olympic podium, her second gold medal hanging around her neck, the national team wasn't likely to be far from her mind.

The sun had set by the time they left the Emirates and headed back to the flat, tired from the long day.

"My sister would think we're crazy for spending a vacation day like this instead of at a museum," Jamie commented as the car idled in North London traffic.

"She'd have a point, wouldn't she?" Britt said as the light turned and traffic surged forward.

Everyone laughed in rueful agreement. Emma sat content in the back seat, her hand in Jamie's as non-touristy parts of London skimmed past their windows offering varied glimpses into what regular life might be like in this foreign city. But it was familiar, too. People here ate, drank, and breathed soccer the same way she and Jamie always had, even if they called it by a different name.

Britt and Allie dropped them off back at the flat, declining an invitation to stay for an ultra-fancy dinner of cold beer and frozen pizza. They had an early flight out to DC in the morning and still needed to get packed, so after hugs all around, they headed back to Lizzie's flat, leaving Emma and Jamie on their own again.

The pizza was in the oven and Emma was checking the weather app on her phone when Jamie slid an envelope with Arsenal's logo across the kitchen counter.

"What's this?" Emma asked, frowning. Her eyes flew up to Jamie's. "Wait. Are you joking? Because if you are, Jamie Maxwell..."

"Open it and find out," she said, half-smiling.

Emma tore the flap open and gasped as a pair of red and white tickets fell into her palm: ARSENAL v MANCHESTER UNITED, BARCLAYS PREMIER LEAGUE, Saturday, 22 November 2014, Kick-Off 5:30 PM.

"You said we couldn't get tickets!" she said, her brain stuck on what she had known—or believed, anyway—to be true.

Her shrug was casual. "I called in a favor. Besides, you're not the only one who can be sneaky."

Emma dropped the tickets on the counter and flung herself at Jamie. "You're—I'm—holy *shit*, Jamie!"

"Is that a good holy shit, or...?"

Emma laughed and kissed her. "What do you think?"

When Jamie had first agreed to extend their trip, Emma had suggested they try to find tickets to the match between their favorite clubs that just happened, by wonderful coincidence, to be scheduled for the Saturday before Thanksgiving. But Jamie had told her that none of her friends had any extras, and refused to let her "blow" five hundred pounds, the going rate online for decent seats to the fixture. Emma didn't want to miss the match, but she knew Jamie was already uncomfortable with the amount of money she was spending on the flat. Reluctantly she'd agreed to watch on the big screen at the Twelve Pins, where Jamie had assured her she would still get the taste of a real English football match.

"Huh," Emma said now, arms looped around Jamie's neck. "I didn't know you had it in you."

"I didn't either," she admitted. "That envelope has been burning a hole in my freaking pocket since before the Legends Tour! Sheesh. I would make a terrible secret agent."

"Yes, my sweet, you really would." Emma kissed her again, scrunching up her nose as the timer went off.

Jamie pecked her lips and set her aside, reaching for the oven mitts. "Sorry, babe, but I need calories pronto."

"No worries. We've got time."

While Jamie checked the pizza, Emma bent her head to study the tickets again. ARSENAL v MANCHESTER UNITED. What were the odds their teams would play the one time she and Jamie were in London together? Maybe she should get on board with the whole soccer gods notion. After all, soccer was the reason they'd met, the reason they'd fallen in love the first time, the reason they were together at last.

Gods or no gods, Arsenal and United were playing and Jamie had gotten them tickets. Emma bit her lip, barely suppressing an embarrassingly non-badass squeal. She couldn't wait for the game—except she could, actually, because it would signal the approaching end of their European vacation.

Good thing it was still a week and a half away. Like she'd told Jamie, they had time.

As the days passed, filled with exercise and sex and the relaxation that comes with never having to set an alarm, Emma tried to hold onto the disparate moments as best she could, etching them into her memory before they could fade and dissolve into mere flashes of light and color. Jamie took her on touristy adventures, like visiting the British Museum and the London Tower; touring Westminster and the Churchill War Rooms, an underground complex that had housed the British government command center during World War Two; and taking a turn on the London Eye, during which she mostly kept her own eyes shut. But Jamie also showed her the gems she'd discovered during her years in the British capital: Hampstead Heath at sunrise on a clear morning; the Camden Markets on a crowded weekend day; and the statue of Boadicea against the backdrop of the Westminster Bridge at night.

There were other forms of entertainment, too—watching and rewatching the newly released *Pitch Perfect 2* trailer, for one, which contained a cameo by the Green Bay Packers that they both found hilarious. After Emma's mother texted that they shouldn't leave London without seeing a play in the city's West End, they went online and found last-minute tickets to a Shakespeare production in a famous theater near Leicester Square. The play ended up being one of the highlights of the week, they agreed, as did their pre-show dinner at a China Town restaurant where the staff seated patrons with strangers at large tables and dished out whatever the special happened to be that evening.

Another highlight also included dining with strangers. Midway through their holiday, they caught a bus to Finsbury Park for a day of volunteering with Foodcycle, the non-profit community food program where Jamie had learned to cook. There they donned the hideous hairnets the cooking managers provided and got to work peeling potatoes and mincing garlic in the Community Center's kitchen. Jamie was more skilled with a paring knife, but for once Emma didn't mind being one-upped as they worked with the rest of the team to produce a free meal for local residents out of the odds and ends that supermarkets and restaurants would otherwise have thrown away.

Once the meal was ready, they exited the kitchen only for Jamie to be swarmed by several community members who wanted to know where she'd been hiding herself. One ancient couple in particular, with matching bushy eyebrows and age spots on their heavily veined hands, clearly doted on her. Harold and Glenda invited them to dine at their table and proceeded to quiz Jamie about Champions League, her family, Oregon and the NWSL. In return she asked about their children and grandchildren, who they were only too happy to gush about. They seemed proud of her, and excited to meet Emma, too. She couldn't help being touched by the community that Jamie had managed to build for herself during her years away from home.

When they weren't exploring the city, they practiced tai chi on the deck (Jamie was teaching her), ran their favorite drills on the backyard pitch, spotted each other in the weight room, and ran sprints up Parliament Hill on nearby Hampstead Heath. Emma was used to working out alone, but *this*, she thought one morning as she and Jamie dribbled around the flat's backyard pitch practicing freestyle tricks— the pancake, the elastico, neck stalls, assorted flick-ups, and, of course, the rainbow, laughing each time the ball went awry—this she could get used to.

And then, simultaneously too soon and not soon enough, it was Saturday, their next to last day in London, AKA Game Day.

Since kick-off at the Emirates wasn't until later, they spent the morning playing small-sided pick-up at the Heath with a group of Jamie's teammates. For once it wasn't rainy or windy, and as the day wore on the temperature climbed towards sixty—a record, according to Emma's weather app.

Around three they donned their club gear and got ready to leave the flat. Emma wore her United jersey, the one Jamie had sent her all those years ago, while Jamie donned assorted Arsenal Ladies FC gear.

"You're seriously going to wear that?" Jamie asked, watching her in the dresser mirror.

"Are you kidding? It's my lucky jersey. Not that my boys need luck today, seeing as we haven't lost to you in the last fifteen matches."

"You also haven't won on the road this season, in case you haven't noticed."

"Maybe not, but our record is better than yours," she bragged, securing her hair in a ponytail.

Jamie only made a sound of disgust and turned away. She had to know her team was going to lose today. And if she didn't, she really should.

Emma dialed up a black cab on her phone, and ten minutes later they arrived at the Twelve Pins, the pub where they'd celebrated the win against the Swiss women's side the previous week.

"It's a game day tradition," Jamie said after Emma had paid the driver, "to pop into the pub for a pint."

"Nice alliteration." Emma followed her into the sprawling green and white building on the corner of a busy thoroughfare. The first time they'd come here, she'd thought it odd to find a Subway shop, a money exchange, and a kebab restaurant all in spitting distance. Now she thought the variety nicely summed up the London she was beginning to feel like she knew. "What?" she added, feeling Jamie's eyes on her.

"I like alliteration too."

"Who doesn't?"

"Plenty of people, I would assume."

She might be right.

The closing doors shut out the sounds of bus engines and truck brakes, but that didn't mean the pub's interior was quiet. It was packed, and not just with random patrons, either. Most were men and boys with the odd woman, nearly all clad in Arsenal jerseys and scarves that offered a brief history lesson on the local club. Some decades had certainly been more tasteful than others.

Jamie led her to the less jam-packed back room where they'd hung out the last time. "Max!" a chorus of voices rang out *Cheers*-style. At a nearby table, Emma recognized several of the players from Jamie's team, all in Arsenal gear. As she and Jamie approached, Emma was glad she'd worn an old UNC sweatshirt over her United jersey. No matter how warm it got in here, she doubted she would be shedding that particular layer anytime soon.

"Did you hear?" asked a dark-skinned woman whose name Emma thought was Marjorie but who everyone called The Major. "PSG next round."

Jamie nodded. "Yep. Paris in the spring. Can't say I've ever been."

Her tone was glib, but Emma remembered how relieved she'd been when the draw earlier in the week showed them facing Paris-St. Germain, not Lyon. Still, if Arsenal managed to get past the strong Paris side—Jamie had confided this was doubtful—*and* Lyon managed to beat the Swiss team they'd drawn for the quarters, Jamie might yet travel to Lyon for Champions League semis.

As Emma watched, Jamie changed the subject by asking the Major about her day job at an investment bank. That did the trick, and they discussed international economics until their teammates booed them good-naturedly and brought them back to Premier League and WSL fixtures.

It really was like the bar in *Cheers*, Emma decided. Everyone appeared to know each other, including the wait staff. A woman named Judy, who Jamie said was the owner's daughter, even pulled up a chair to chat.

"Judy, this is Emma," Jamie said.

"Aye, I know who she is." Judy eyed her shrewdly for a moment and then nodded decisively. "I'd been wondering why you didn't come back to us. Now it seems I have my answer."

Emma watched delightedly as the back of Jamie's neck reddened.

"What? No. I mean, I moved home to play in the NWSL."

Judy's eyebrows rose. "Right. 'I still have a year left on my contract,' you said. 'I'll be back,' you said."

"I *am* back," Jamie argued.

"Sure you are, Max. But not alone, are ye? Not that I blame you," she added, tipping her glass at Emma and winking.

As kick-off approached, Jamie's teammates remembered that she was a United fan and began to heckle her. Like before, Emma bought a round to quiet the discord. No doubt that was what they'd intended as they nudged each other and grinned appreciatively, magically restored to cheerful spirits.

*Jackasses*, Emma thought, shaking her head at their antics. Since they knew her loyalties, she might as well take off her sweatshirt. The back room was getting hot. Or maybe it was the beer and the rowdy company warming her up.

When Jamie handed her phone to Jeanie and asked her to snap a shot of them smiling over their shoulders, names visible on their jerseys, Emma didn't think about US Soccer or her Twitter following. She didn't think of WoSo fans or Tumblr teens until her phone blew up and she checked her notifications to find that Jamie had posted the photo of the two of them on her public Instagram account. Quickly Emma shut off her social media alerts, ignoring the ball of fear hardening in her stomach. She couldn't believe Jamie had posted the photo without asking her first. Must be the lager shanty talking. Jamie was such a lightweight—one drink and she was already pink-cheeked and twinkle-eyed.

Emma rubbed her forehead. It had been nice to be off the grid. She hadn't heard much from Twitter in weeks, not since the end of CONCACAFs. Maybe her troll wouldn't notice the photo. Either way, she told herself, it wasn't worth ruining their day over. It was a great photo of them, and the Tumblr teens at least would be happy to see more evidence of Blakewell. Besides, she was about to see United play in person! In London! With Jamie! That was what mattered, not what may or may not set off an anonymous creep presumably thousands of miles away.

The television above the bar was tuned to a Premier League review show. An hour before game time, the announcers began discussing the upcoming match at the Emirates. When an image of Roelof Peeters in his United jersey flashed across the screen, the room immediately erupted into boos and whistles. This time the heckling was decidedly serious.

"Damn," Emma commented. "Bitter much?"

Jamie snorted. "He moved to one of Arsenal's biggest rivals. Of course Gooners are going to be pissed about his lack of loyalty."

"Peeters put Arsenal on his back for what, eight seasons? And what does he have to show for it? An FA cup title? His first year with us he won a league title. Roelof's move to United was a clear case of career advancement, and you know it."

"I know nothing of the sort," Jamie said stubbornly. "He was getting older, so he moved to a team that already had a star striker. Retiring to a team where you'll be less challenged is a time-honored football tradition, and *you* know *that*."

Emma shook her head, certain that Jamie couldn't believe what she was saying. Facts were facts, and emotion couldn't change the clear fact that United was the better team, with or without Roelof Peeters.

"You're just angry because your boy jumped off your club's sinking ship."

Jamie's expression remained unaffected. "I'm not angry. You know the saying—don't get mad, get even? Well, we stole Danny from you, didn't we?"

That was actually a sore spot. Welbeck was a rising star, and the new United manager's recent decision to let him go to one of the club's biggest rivals had not been well received by the team's fan base. Still, she wasn't about to admit as much to Jamie.

163

"You're welcome to him. It's not like he's done much for you."

"It's been two months. Geez, Blake."

"*Geez*, Max."

They glared at each other, and then suddenly Jamie started laughing.

"What?" Emma asked, peeved.

"Are we really having our first fight over Arsenal and Man U?"

One part of Emma's brain prodded her to shout at Jamie that it was United, not Man U, *for eff's sake!* Fortunately, the rational part won out. "It isn't technically our first fight, is it? Wasn't there that very slight disagreement we had that led to you not speaking to me for, what, five years?"

"Oh, you mean that little quarrel over Tori Parker?" Jamie asked, and then added almost under her breath, "The whore."

It was Emma's turn to laugh, mostly in surprise. "Um, okay."

Jamie winced and pushed her pint glass away. "I'm sorry. I shouldn't have called her that. This is why I don't drink."

"Such a cheap date," Emma said, but fondly. "You know I never felt even a tenth as much for her as I do for you, right?"

Jamie glanced up from where she was practically wearing a hole in the table with her fidgeting fingertips. "You didn't?"

"No. Dani and my mom accused me of hooking up with her because I couldn't be with you."

Jamie's head tilted. "How did hooking up with her help?"

"It didn't," Emma admitted. "In hindsight, it's obvious that it could only make things worse. But we were kids then.

164

And my father's death—well, you know from personal experience that it made my decision-making less than stellar."

"You're right, we *were* kids. That's why I reacted the way I did. I wanted to be able to date other people, but as soon as I heard about you and Tori I was all, 'You are dead to me.' Talk about a double standard."

Emma smiled. "I'm glad your soccer gods waited until we grew up to bring us back together."

Jamie smiled back. "Me too. Somehow I suspect that was their plan all along."

She was adorable, and Emma wanted terribly to kiss her. Instead she segued from soccer gods into a safer topic: Manchester City's spending spree to buy the league title two out of the last three years. To her credit, Jamie didn't point out the hypocrisy of a United fan accusing another club of overspending.

Emma's anxiety over the Instagram photo slowly lessened as the tasty English beer continued to warm her from the inside out. By the time they left the pub en masse, singing Arsenal supporter songs (not her, *obviously*), Emma had nearly forgotten about the fan meltdown likely happening across the sea. It was comforting to be surrounded by a group of strong female athletes who would no doubt have her back should she need it. Jamie was family, which in their world made Emma family by extension. That was the way teams functioned, no matter what side of the Atlantic you happened to be on.

At the Emirates, they parted ways with the rest of Jamie's crew and entered a concourse that opened onto the lower tier of stands directly above the player tunnel. Emma held her breath as she and Jamie descended closer and closer to the brightly lit field, only remembering to breathe again as they stopped a handful of rows behind the home team bench. She couldn't believe these seats. They were far enough off the edge of the pitch that they could easily see over the home bench while still being close enough to practically smell the players' sweat. Or maybe it was the coaches who were sweating. A Premier League manager's hot seat was comparable to that of a national team head coach.

"So?" Jamie asked, looking rightfully pleased with herself as they settled in. "What do you think of the view?"

"It's okay," Emma said, her voice offhand. Then she added, laughing, "Oh my god, it's fantastic! How did you get these seats?"

"I told you, I called in a favor. Besides, dropping your name goes a long way in the football world, Ms. Blakeley."

Emma doubted her status as a USWNT starter had much traction in one of the top male leagues in the world, but she supposed it was possible that some people involved in the Premier League were more progressive than others.

"By the way," Jamie added, leaning closer, "you might want to keep your sweatshirt on here."

"Oh, I see how it is. Don't want to be seen with a United fan, do you?"

"No, that's not it. It's just, the supporters can get out of hand, depending on the how the game is going... Well, I guess you'll see, anyway."

The early evening was still unseasonably warm, but not warm enough that she felt compelled to strip down to her jersey. Emma figured she should take Jamie's advice and assess the crowd's mood before attracting the enmity of nearby fans. In a world full of soccer fanatics, English hooligans had a particularly brutish reputation.

It didn't take long for Emma to be glad she'd listened to Jamie. She had thought Roelof Peeters getting booed at the pub was poor sportsmanship; she'd even believed that playing in front of certain CONCACAF home crowds had taught her about the hostility a group of fans could level at the members of a rival team. But nothing had prepared her for the real-life experience of a top tier Premier League crowd. It was one thing to see matches on television, to watch the roiling mass of mostly male, mostly drunk fans chanting and singing on a flat screen. It was an entirely different matter to be surrounded by those same drunk men in person.

Some of the verses the crowd shouted were sentimental and encouraging, while others were frankly appalling—like the "She said no, Roelof" and "Roelof you're a c*#t" melodies sung with gusto when Peeters emerged from the players' tunnel to take the field.

"Are they saying...?" she asked Jamie as the teams lined up for their pre-match photo.

Jamie's face was grim. "Yep. They learned those songs from United fans after he was accused of rape one of his first seasons."

Emma remembered the accusations. Peeters had been thrown in jail for a couple of weeks after a woman he met in a club accused him of raping her in a hotel room not far from the flat he shared with his wife. He insisted the sex was consensual, and many months later the court dismissed the case based on lack of evidence. It turned out the not guilty verdict was accurate—Peeters's accuser eventually admitted she had made the story up. *For publicity.*

"They don't tell you on TV what they're singing, do they?" she asked.

"Nope," Jamie agreed. "They don't."

Emma wasn't sure she enjoyed the game. "Enjoy" felt like the wrong word. The match was entertaining, yes, the atmosphere electric. The soccer itself was top notch, skilled and fast with plenty of dramatic moments. But she kept contrasting the feeling of being in the stands here with her experiences at the Olympics or the World Cup, or even a Seattle Sounders game. The atmosphere in each of those cases had been powerful, the large crowds knowledgeable and impassioned, but everything had felt much more positive and sports-focused. At women's games in particular, the crowds tended to consist of more women and children than men, and the male fans in attendance carried handmade posters decorated with slogans like, "I wish *I* could play like a girl!" Here, as a woman, she couldn't help being intimidated by the testosterone-laden air of violence simmering beneath the surface.

The fact that she was intimidated infuriated her, and by the time the game ended she barely cared that United had won. She mostly wanted to escape this environment where she didn't feel safe—and where she couldn't help thinking that Jamie might as well be wearing a bulls-eye on her jacket.

But: "Not yet," Jamie said, remaining in her seat as the people around them began to file out, muttering and grumbling about the result. The score had ended 1-2, with one of United's goals coming on an own goal by an Arsenal defender.

"What do you mean, not yet?"

"I mean," Jamie said, her voice low, "that if we leave now, we could get hurt."

"Because I'm a United supporter?"

"No, because most of these men are drunk and out for a fight. And you and I both, to be honest, make easy targets."

It wasn't anything Emma hadn't thought herself, but hearing Jamie matter-of-factly confirm the vulnerability she'd hoped she was imagining still chilled her.

"Besides," Jamie added, her tone lighter, "I thought you might like to go down to the field. You know, to meet some of the players?"

Like that, her desire to leave vanished. "Arsenal players?"

"Among others."

Emma grabbed Jamie's arm and squeezed. "Are you serious right now?"

"Completely."

"Oh. My. God." Her bucket list included seeing Manchester United play in person, but meet actual players? She had never thought to wish for that. She lowered her voice, because while the people closest to them didn't appear to be paying them any mind, there was no need to draw attention to what she was about to say: "I love you so freaking much right now."

Jamie laughed, her cheeks pink from the cooling air but also, Emma suspected, from yelling at the refs, a habit she had picked up from Ellie and Jodie. "I love you too. *Obvs.*"

The tense atmosphere in the stadium faded within minutes of the game's end as the fans filtered quickly out to the streets. Once the rows around them had cleared, Jamie led Emma down to field level.

"Oi, Green!" she called, sounding more British than American. Irish? Emma wasn't sure.

A trainer from the home side turned toward them. "Max," he said, smiling as he approached. "You made it."

"Of course I did. I only wish the outcome had been different."

"You and sixty thousand other people." He nodded to the security guard blocking their way. "They're with me, Johnny."

"I don't know," the giant, orange-clad guard said, eyes narrowed as he looked Jamie up and down.

The trainer scoffed. "Do you not recognize these women? They're on the American national team, man. Come on. Let them through."

The trainer was a fan of the women's game? Emma was fairly certain that such a species of British male was nearly extinct or, at the least, endangered. Then again, endangered status implied that they had ever existed in great numbers to begin with. They hadn't—at least not in recent history. Jamie had told her that women's football had enjoyed support during and after World War I, with one Boxing Day match in 1920 drawing upwards of *fifty thousand* fans. But a year later the FA banned women's football matches at Association club football grounds, citing strong concerns about the physical "unsuitability" of the game for women. The FA ban wasn't lifted until 1971, and English women were only now starting to catch up to other national team programs.

The guard wavered and then finally gestured at them, his mouth pinched. "Fine. But it's your neck, Green, not mine."

Behind his back Green rolled his eyes, and Emma had to hold back a laugh.

Once they hopped the barrier and were safely on the pitch, Jamie and the trainer embraced in a bro hug.

"This is Emma, by the way," Jamie said as she pulled away.

He turned to her, eyes widening. "I know! I mean, hey, I'm Nick. It's really, really great to meet you, Emma." He pronounced her name like half of Jamie's London friends did: *Emmer.*

"You, too," she said, and held out her hand for him to shake.

Nick stared at her hand for a second too long before grabbing for it, his palm damp against hers.

Jamie snickered, and Nick promptly flashed her a glare. "Sorry, dude," she said. But she didn't sound sorry at all.

Emma pretended not to notice Nick's reaction. She routinely dealt with men—and women—who tripped over their words in her presence. She had long since grown accustomed to being a minor celebrity in the eyes of soccer fans and a mild curiosity to everyone else. Since the last international tournament cycle, she and most of her teammates had faded back into relative obscurity outside of athletic circles. Currently, however, she was at the center of a very specific athletic circle.

As Nick led them through the players' tunnel and Emma realized who was waiting in the vestibule outside the locker rooms, her heart rate skyrocketed. Holy *shit*. That was Matthias Ilunga, the Belgian international who had scored more than 200 goals during his career at Arsenal. She'd had a poster of him on her closet door her senior year of high school, the year he earned FIFA World Player honors. He was the reason—other than Jamie—that she had always considered Arsenal her second-favorite British football club. Beside him was English international and United legend Adrian Evans, who had beaten Ilunga twice for World Player of the Year. They were standing there chatting with each other amicably as if it was normal for legends of the game to casually hang out after their former clubs had fought a bitter battle on the still-lit pitch.

To say that it was her turn to be tongue-tied was an understatement. The next thirty minutes slipped past almost unnoticed as Nick introduced Jamie and Emma to the retired footballers, both of whom were cordial and welcoming. Evans told her he'd watched her play in both Germany and the Olympics—talk about mind-boggling—while Ilunga brought up the turf issue at the upcoming World Cup. Even as he expressed support for the legal challenge, he shared his doubts that they would be able to achieve a fair ruling. FIFA needed new blood that wasn't rich, white, and male, he said while Evans nodded beside him; only then would real change be realized.

As current players began to emerge from the locker room, Emma found herself swept into different conversations with members of each team, some of whom asked to take photos with her and others who she asked for photo honors. Emma, naturally, stripped off her jacket and sweatshirt and posed in her old school United jersey while Jamie snapped picture after picture, eyes glowing. At one point, Nick took Jamie's phone so that Roelof Peeters could pose between them in their opposing jerseys, and Emma didn't even mind when Jamie promptly put the photo on her public feed.

When a couple of the younger guys invited them out for drinks, Emma declined politely. Conversation and selfies, yes. Anything else? No thanks. Jamie seemed to approve of this decision, and at last, after a final bro hug and many enthusiastic thanks to her trainer buddy, they headed out into the mild evening.

"So? What did you think of your first ever Premier League match?" Jamie asked as they walked down the street together, carefully not touching in front of the hordes of men and boys still lingering in the area bemoaning the fixture's result.

Emma wished she could kiss her, or hug her, or even hold her hand. But she contented herself with a smile, hoping her eyes conveyed the vastness of her delight in the day's activities. "I think it was amazing. *You're* amazing. Thank you, Jamie. I mean it. This really has been the best vacation ever."

"I agree," Jamie said, smiling back at her, eyes shining. "It totally has been."

*Best. Vacation. Ever.* They'd repeated this refrain to each other ad nauseum over the past ten days, despite the semi-regular rain and decided lack of tropical warmth. Emma couldn't remember ever gelling with someone so easily. Part of it was their shared history, she knew. But also, they genuinely loved many of the same things. They had similar senses of humor, they were both careful about what they did with and to their bodies, and any differences they had only seemed to add interest to their interactions.

And, of course, there was the mind-blowing sex. Definitely shouldn't forget about that.

It was another perfect day in a long run of perfect days, and as they lay in bed together that night, Emma found herself wondering what her teenage self would have thought if she could have popped back in time and told her about this incredible experience they would one day share.

"We should retire here," she said, and felt Jamie, on the verge of sleep, jerk almost comically awake.

"What?"

"After we've won a World Cup and the Olympics and an NWSL title. We should retire from American soccer and come over here to play."

In men's football, European players sometimes chose to retire to the American MLS, where they got to be soccer stars in the United States for a year or two before returning home to Europe. But in women's football, America still led the world in fiscal and fan support. If things continued as they were now, Emma could see American stars ending their careers in lower level European leagues for the experience of living and playing abroad.

"*We* should?" Jamie echoed.

Emma stilled, realizing what she'd revealed. They hadn't spoken of the distant future yet, sticking mainly to the weeks or months immediately ahead. But while they hadn't talked about making a deeper commitment or moving in together, in her own head Emma knew that Jamie was it for her. When she pictured herself with a house and a baby, Jamie was in the background mowing the lawn or fixing dinner. When she imagined life after soccer, Jamie was at her side, building that life with her. The only thing she didn't know for sure was if that future was what Jamie wanted, too.

In distinctly un-Minnesotan Scandinavian fashion, she nodded. "Yes, *we*. I don't want this to end, Jamie. I don't want *us* to end."

"Neither do I," Jamie said immediately.

"You don't?"

"Of course not, Emma. I've loved you for half of my life, practically."

The same was true for Emma. If they were still

together when she turned thirty-two, then she would have loved Jamie for exactly half her life. Once again, mind-boggling.

"But what about your condo?" Jamie asked, fingertips skimming a loop on Emma's arm.

She paused. Then, drunk on love and sex and a hope she'd discovered they shared: "I could sell it. In fact, I probably should sell it."

"Why? You love that place."

"I know, but we're going to need something bigger for the kids eventually."

Jamie's hand stilled on her arm. "The kids?"

"Well, yeah. Babies grow into children, you know."

"How many are you planning, exactly?"

"Only a couple. Although I suppose that's something I'll need to discuss with, you know, whoever I end up marrying and procreating with."

"Oh, now we're getting married, too?"

"It is the American dream, isn't it?"

Jamie laughed and kissed her, and Emma kissed her back, their teeth clacking awkwardly because neither of them could stop smiling.

Yep, no doubt about it: *Best. Vacation. Ever.*

# CHAPTER EIGHT

"Let me take you to Rio, to Rio," Jamie sang, dancing through baggage claim.

"We're not even in Rio," Angie grumbled.

"Close enough."

"No, it isn't. And if you don't stop singing that song, I swear to fucking god—"

"Wang," Phoebe barked, her glare pinning Angie in place. "*Language.* You know the travel rules."

"Sorry," Angie huffed, her sassy tone undercutting the apology.

Jamie relented as they collected their luggage and piled into rental vans outside the airport. Angie was right—they weren't anywhere near Rio de Janeiro. Instead, they would be spending the next two weeks hundreds of miles inland in Brasilia, the nation's capital.

The flight to Brazil had been long and bumpy, and Jamie had held Emma's hand under the cover of a thin airline blanket likely more than the coaching staff would have preferred. But it wasn't like she could ignore Emma's wide eyes and pale skin as the airplane shuddered and feinted over the exceedingly mountainous South American continent.

175

To be fair, the coaches—minus Jo, who would join them the following day—had seemed in better spirits during the flight than most of the players. Jamie, Taylor O'Brien, and Jessica North, the "Newest New Kids," as the team's PR rep was itching to christen them, were the only ones who appeared jazzed about the upcoming tournament. The team's veterans were still annoyed that the federation had agreed to Jo's plan to whittle their sacred off-season into a mere six weeks. That, or they were cranky from the overnight flight that Fitzy, the national team manager, had booked for them. Possibly both.

"Do they not care that we don't get to see our families enough as it is?" Steph griped as the rental vans rolled away from the terminal and set off into the warm, humid morning. "I'm going to have to pack three weeks of holiday prep into three days when we get back."

Jamie tuned out the "Entitled Veterans Rant Reprisal," as she thought of it, and stared out the window at the city. This was her first time in Brazil's capital. The last time she'd visited the soccer-crazed country had been in 2007 when the U-20 national team had participated in the Pan American Games. That tournament, played entirely in and around Rio de Janeiro, had gone well for the American side—until they'd encountered Brazil's full senior national team in the finals. Jamie had never forgotten the humiliating 5-0 drubbing they'd received at the hands of Brazil's up and coming star, Marisol, who had dazzled the nearly seventy thousand screaming fans with her brilliant play.

From what Jamie could see, the neatly laid-out city beyond her window was significantly different from crowded, chaotic Rio with its chains of islands and surrounding mountains. This city had been built purposefully in 1960 in the central plains region to work in tandem with the existing landscape, Emma had told her on the plane as they decelerated over Brasília. Designed by two well-known architects of the time, the new capital city was meant to serve as a central hub for the geographically diverse country.

Beside her, Emma was still studying her travel guide. Jamie leaned over her shoulder, glad that her girlfriend was such an unabashed nerd. "Let me guess—you're memorizing import/export data, right?"

"Duh." Emma shot her a small smile that normally would be accompanied by a touch but, this time, wasn't.

Jamie returned her attention to the passing scenery. *Team time*, she reminded herself. They would officially be on team time for the next fifteen days. She would need to remember that.

The route to the city's hotel sector took them past the stadium where the tournament would take place: the Estádio Nacional Mané Garrincha, Brazil's national soccer stadium. Named after a legendary striker who had helped lead Brazil to two of its record five World Cup victories, the stadium had been built in 1974 and renovated for the 2013 Confederations Cup and this past summer's Men's World Cup. Jamie may never have been to Brasilia before, but she easily recognized the stadium from television—and from Emma's guide book.

This past summer had been Brazil's second time hosting the Men's World Cup. Jamie had watched the US matches mostly with her Thorns teammates on the road or on DVR after practice or a match, but she and Emma had managed to "watch" some of the games while on the phone together. It had felt like high school all over again, except that now their phones offered video chatting.

Over the course of the tournament, they'd ended up rehashing a decade's worth of Men's World Cup moments: in 2006, Zinedine Zidane's head butt had shocked everyone, while in 2010, there had been Luis Suarez's "Hand of God" save, the French team's revolt against their coach, and, of course, Landon Donovan's last-minute score against Algeria to keep the American team's hopes alive. They'd also spent a lot of time—A LOT OF TIME—bitching about Landon

Donovan's omission from the current World Cup squad. Jamie felt that Jurgen Klinsmann had some explaining to do for swapping out "a god-damned American *hero*, Emma," for a cadre of players who had been born and raised in his own native Germany. If she ever ran into him, she intended to tell him as much. Maybe. She would at least glare at him from a distance, that much was certain.

The hotel wasn't far from the stadium, and soon the players had checked in and were ready for their traditional travel day workout. Lacey Rodriguez, the longtime fitness coach who had survived more than one change in team management, put them through their paces on a practice field at the sports complex near the stadium. Afterward they returned to the hotel for lunch and the highlight of the day: FIFA's Canada 2015 Official Draw, where each of the twenty-four teams that had qualified would learn its group competition—and travel schedule—for the following summer. Jo wasn't here in Brazil with them because she had flown to Ottawa with the other head coaches to attend the draw ceremony in person.

Once the meal had been cleared, the players pushed the conference tables to one side and arranged chairs in rows before the large-screen television mounted on one wall. Jamie sat toward the back with her friends, while Emma sat up front with Ellie and the other veterans. But as the French announcers began to read off the results of the draw, Jamie found her gaze drawn to Emma only to find her looking back over her shoulder, eyebrows quirked.

As soon as the US was named to Group D, a chorus of whistles went up around the room. Ellie turned around, glaring. "Just because it's D doesn't mean it'll necessarily be the Group of Death. How about a little optimism here, guys?"

"Right," Angie muttered to Jamie and Lisa. "Because that's how the draw works."

The selection process was incredibly tedious—thanks,

FIFA—so they passed the time between selections gossiping and making fun of the announcers. Each time a Group D selection came up, though, a tense silence overtook the room. How you came out of your group—assuming you emerged from group play at all—determined your route to the finals.

The second Group D member picked was Nigeria, ranked number thirty-five in the world. While the African team played fast and rough, they had never come close to beating the US. The next selection, however, sent a ripple of whispers across the room: Australia, exceptionally young and also fast—and currently number ten in the world. When the final ball was selected, a half-laugh, half-groan spread through the assembled players: Sweden, number five in the world. That made three top ten teams in one group.

"Well," Phoebe said, "that confirms it. D is officially the Group of Death."

Ellie elbowed her fellow captain. "Optimism, remember? I prefer the Group of Distinction!"

More groans rained out, accompanied by flying paper wads.

On screen, the camera panned to Jo again, tongue sticking a tiny bit out of her mouth as she made notes on her page, and the groans gave way to cheers and more whistles. Jamie wondered what she was writing—formation ideas? Notes on their opponents? Now that they knew their early round match-ups, the US's summer in Canada was finally taking shape.

Jamie's foot tapped spasmodically as she wondered if she would be in Canada next year as a player or as a fan. The coaches had brought twenty-four to Brazil, but would only take twenty-three to Canada. If she was the last player to be cut, she wasn't sure she'd be able to show her face, especially not if the US made it to the finals.

When the draw ended at last, the team was excused until the evening video review session. Their first game of the tournament would be against Brazil in a few days, Coach Mel reminded them, and there was much work to be done in the meantime.

"There's always much work to be done," Rebecca said as they left the conference room.

"You are correct, young grasshopper," Lisa said, and dodged an elbow from Angie. "What? Not a David Carradine fan?"

"You mean the white guy who thought it was okay to play a Chinese priest? Freaking Hollywood whitewashing," Angie said, shaking her head.

"Preaching to the choir, my dude," Lisa agreed. She was one of two African-American players in the pool currently, and often lamented the lack of racial diversity on the team.

Emma caught up to Jamie in the hallway, giving her a hip-bump by way of greeting. "What did you think of your first World Cup draw?"

"I think Germany got off suspiciously lightly, as did Japan."

"Are you suggesting the draw might be rigged?" Emma pretended to sound scandalized.

"It's FIFA. Isn't that more believable than it *not* being rigged?"

"So cynical, Max."

"I prefer the term realistic."

"Mm-hmm. Feel like taking a walk later?"

"Absolutely."

"Sweet. I'll text you." And with that, Emma sauntered away.

Jamie hurried after her friends, who had moved on to LGBTQ+ representation on the big and small screen.

"Kids' movies are the worst," she put in as the

conversation paused. "You know what they say about Disney, don't you?"

"If it walks like a gay guy..." Angie said.

"And talks like a gay guy..." Lisa added.

"Then it must be a Disney villain," Rebecca finished.

Jamie regarded the small group appreciatively. "Nice."

Her friends laughed and pummeled her affectionately.

"It's good to have you back, Nerd Squad," Angie said, slinging an arm around her neck.

It was good to *be* back. Now if only she could convince the coaches to keep her around.

Her first couple of days of training went well. Her time off from the NWSL had allowed her to recover from the busy pro season, while training with Arsenal for Champions League had kept her match fit. Not everyone in the pool could say the same. For the second winter in a row, Steph Miller came into an end-of-year camp dragging from sleepless nights and the common childhood illnesses her son had managed to share with the family. Jamie was starting to think that Ellie's plan of retiring before having babies made a lot of sense. Not that she mentioned this realization to Emma. While their relationship had grown considerably during their London holiday, they were nowhere near the point of discussing when to have their hypothetical children. For one thing, they hadn't even told Jo they were dating.

The night before the first match, Emma and Jamie stopped by the coaches' table after dinner. As they'd rehearsed, Emma smiled brightly and said, "Hey guys. Do you have a second?"

The three coaches exchanged a look, and then Jo nodded up at them. "Have a seat, ladies."

Jamie had once read that people tended to think more quickly on their feet than seated, but Emma was already accepting the seat Mel had pushed toward her. Reluctantly, Jamie took the other chair.

"So," Jo said, folding her hands at the edge of the conference table, "what can we do for you?"

Jamie nodded at Emma, who took a breath and said, her voice impressively steady, "We wanted to let you know, in the spirit of transparency, that we're in a relationship. A romantic one."

"I see." Jo didn't seem surprised. Neither did the other coaches.

Mel smiled and said, "Congratulations! That's good news."

"Oh." Emma blinked a few times. "Thank you."

"Yeah, thanks," Jamie added, relief flooding her system at the easy acceptance in their coaches' eyes. "We thought about mentioning it in September, but we weren't sure if it would be an issue, given my status with the team and everything."

"Well, thank you for your transparency, and for your continued professionalism on and off the field," Jo said. "I don't believe that either of you will have any trouble putting the team first, no matter what."

"Absolutely," Emma agreed. "I've been around this team for a while. I wouldn't want to do anything to negatively impact our dynamics."

"Same," Jamie put in. "Or, I guess I haven't been around this team for a super long time, not like Emma, but I am definitely committed to keeping any relationship issues away from the team. Not that there are any! Issues, I mean. Everything is hunky dory!" Jamie's teeth clicked as she closed her mouth to prevent any more words from escaping. *Hunky dory?* What century did she think they were living in?

Jo pressed her lips together and Mel glanced at the other assistant, Henry, while Emma gave Jamie a slightly exasperated head shake. Jamie shrugged back. It was hardly her fault that in tense situations, her mind spat out gobbledy-gook, was it?

"Uh-huh," Jo said. "Anyway, this reminds me of a conversation I was planning to raise with you two. I've been seeing some of your online posts recently—fantastic luck you two, by the way, getting to meet both Ilunga *and* Evans. That was quite the feat."

"It was lucky," Jamie agreed, though she'd pulled every string she had ever possessed to make that meeting happen.

"Jamie's being modest," Emma said. "The Arsenal organization loves her."

"You did social media work for some of the players, didn't you?" Jo asked.

Jamie nodded.

"Well, that's what I wanted to talk to you about. I noticed some things recently and—"

"Actually, Jo," Emma said, "is this something I could talk to you about in private?"

Jamie glanced at her, startled. Why had Emma interrupted their coach mid-sentence?

After a slight hesitation, Jo nodded. "Of course. Why don't you come by my room later?"

Emma agreed and thanked their coach, and then the meeting was over. Successful, if a bit mysterious. But that summed Emma up quite nicely, didn't it?

As they walked back to their own table, Jamie murmured, "What was that about?"

"Fitzy sent me an email letting me know that the federation doesn't think I'm 'utilizing social media as well as I could be,'" Emma admitted, invoking air quotes. "I just didn't want to have that conversation in front of the whole team. Or, for that matter, you."

Jamie started to say that the federation was full of it, but then she realized she couldn't actually remember the last time Emma had posted anything on her public social media accounts. And Ellie *had* said their contracts specified a certain amount of online engagement… "Well, let me know if I can help. That is kind of my thing. Or it used to be, anyway."

"I will," Emma said, her smile a little off. "Thanks, Jamie."

"What are girlfriends for?" she said sassily, pleased when Emma's smile turned more genuine.

"So?" Maddie asked as they neared the table.

Jamie gave their waiting friends a thumbs-up.

"Awesome!" Angie elbowed her as she slid back into her seat. "Blakewell lives, huh?"

"And breathes," Jamie agreed.

Emma slapped Maddie's extended hand as she took her own seat. "All good."

"Told you it would be," Angie said. "They were super cool when we told them."

"This from the one who barely slept the night before the big reveal," Maddie said. But her eye-roll was as indulgent as ever.

"On to more crucial matters," Emma announced, staring around the table. "Who snagged the last chocolate chip cookie?"

The conversation moved on, and soon Jamie did too. The coaches knew about them—officially, because apparently they weren't as subtle as Jamie had believed—and now they would just have to wait and see what kind of consequences, if any, their revelation would bring. In the meantime, they were playing China tomorrow, and then they would play Brazil. *In Brazil.* Games like these didn't come along every day. She intended to enjoy every moment.

Good thing games like this one were few and far between, Jamie thought a few days later as Emma stalked past her and dropped onto the end of the bench.

The tournament was not going well. They'd come out of the gates against China rusty and slow, yielding a 1-1 tie after a decidedly lackluster performance. Now, after going up 2-0 in the first ten minutes of the match against Brazil, they had somehow allowed the home team to score three unanswered goals. With twenty minutes left in the game, they were down a goal *and* a player, thanks to Steph Miller's second yellow card. With Marisol busting through the defense left and right and the US playing ten versus eleven for the rest of the match, the odds of drawing even were not high.

But twenty minutes was a long time, Jamie reminded herself. Anything could happen on any given day. That was the beauty—and spectacle—of sport.

She glanced down the bench at Emma, watching as her girlfriend angrily released her hair from its customary game day braid and then tied it back up in a ponytail. She wished she could say something helpful, but Emma looked like she wanted to be left alone. She hadn't played that well today or against China. She was struggling, and it made sense that Jo would sub her out. Still, to put Taylor O'Brien in her place? O'Brien was an attacking midfielder with next to no experience anchoring a back line. Jamie's least favorite thing about her former youth coach was how Jo insisted on converting offensive players to defense. Not everyone understood how to defend, as Jenny Latham had proven more than once.

The game ended 2-3, with the home team picking up three points and the US emerging with no points—and, thanks to her cumulative red card, no Steph Miller for the next game. Jamie tried not to think it, but she couldn't stop herself: With Steph out, would she maybe, possibly, get a chance to play in the final group match? She didn't linger on the question. Line-ups were beyond her control. The only things she could do in the coming days was be a team player and train hard.

Emma still hadn't made eye contact with her. Jamie watched from a distance as the team moved through the post-game handshakes and Lacey's cool-down exercises. When they were done, Emma started off by herself, head down. Jamie was about to go after her when she heard a voice call, "Maximillian!"

She turned back, quick smile nearly slipping as she realized Isabela, her Thorns teammate, was approaching with none other than Marisol, arguably the greatest player of all time—other than Ellie and Mia Hamm, of course.

"Hey, Isa," she said, giving a lame half-wave.

Isa kissed her on both cheeks like she always did, and then Jamie's heart almost stuttered to a stop as Marisol put her hands on her shoulders and kissed her cheek soundly.

"Jamie Maxwell," the international star said, offering a dazzling smile that Jamie recognized from photos showcasing FIFA's picks for World Player of the Year. "I remember you! Rio, wasn't it? The Pan American Games final?"

"Oh, uh, yeah," Jamie said. "That was me. I remember you too. Three goals, wasn't it?" She couldn't believe her mind had managed to come up with a semi-coherent reply. Usually when attractive women smiled at her she immediately forgot her own name. But this attractive woman was also one of her idols. By all accounts she should have been on the ground by now.

"I don't remember how many goals," Marisol said, waving a hand. "I always felt bad about that match. It was unfair. But anyhoo, how are you finding our capital?"

They were chatting about the city's layout when Jamie felt an arm slip around her waist and squeeze possessively. Emma.

"Hello, Mari. Isabela." She nodded at the Brazilian players, the lines on her forehead belying her professional smile.

*What was she...?* And then Jamie understood. Emma

was staking her claim. On Jamie. To Marisol and Isa, of all people. If it hadn't been such a ridiculous notion, Jamie would have been irritated. As it was, she shifted slightly, arranging her hip to put space between Emma's body and her own. She was no one's possession. Emma, more than anyone, should know that.

Marisol—*Mari*—stepped forward and grasped Emma's face, laughing as she kissed her cheeks. "Emma!" she exclaimed. "It is wonderful to see you! How is that giant little brother of yours? He must be out of school by now."

Back in the early days of the WPS, Jamie remembered, Marisol had done a stint as the leading scorer with the Boston Breakers, Emma's first pro club. Jamie listened as they talked about the old days, and then Ellie joined the group and Jamie felt like she used to when she first got called up—a star-struck interloper who definitely didn't belong in such exalted company. When Angie elbowed her on her way toward the sideline, Jamie seized the opportunity to escape.

"Holy soccer stars, Batman," she said as she planted herself in the grass beside Angie, their backs to the visitor's bench.

"No kidding," her friend answered, stripping off her socks and shin guards. "Popular much?"

"Whatever." Jamie flicked her before reaching for her bag. At least she wouldn't have to shower. The wind off the high plains had picked up that morning, and her uniform had barely gotten sweaty during warm-up.

She was stowing her cleats when she overheard Emma's name. Jessica North, her Utah camp roommate— though not this trip, thank god—was saying to O'Brien behind them, "Did you see when Jo subbed her? Slamming around the bench like the rest of us didn't even exist. Everything has always been easy for her. No wonder she doesn't lose well."

"None of us do," Taylor pointed out. "That's how we

all got here, isn't it?"

"Yeah, but there's refusing to lose and then there's being a poor sport. I bet that's how she acted when the Reign lost to KC, too."

Jamie knew she should take a breath and walk away. It wasn't like Jess North's opinion mattered. But the only breath she took was to gather the air needed to ground out, her voice withering, "Maybe you shouldn't talk shit about your teammates, especially when you don't know what you're talking about."

Jess looked over her shoulder, her mouth twisting unpleasantly as she saw Jamie and Angie behind her. "Really, Maxwell? You're actually going to sit there and defend your girlfriend to me? Kind of seems like the opposite of professionalism. Maybe we should see what the coaches think of that."

"Oh, no she didn't," Angie muttered, throwing down her shoe.

But before she could rise, another voice chimed in. "*This* coach thinks it's unprofessional to tear your teammates down behind their backs. Or, say, threaten them to their faces." Mel narrowed her eyes at Jessica. "Maybe you should think on *that*, North, preferably somewhere far away from me." As the defender stared up at the coach, frozen in place, Mel added in a dangerous voice, "*Now.*"

*Thank god for family*, Jamie thought as the two newbies scrambled away, Taylor muttering furiously to her petulant friend.

"Thanks," she offered to Mel, and then immediately second-guessed herself. Should she apologize? *Had* she acted unprofessionally, defending Emma like that? But no, she would have defended any of her friends in that situation. Some of her not-so-friendly teammates, too.

"You're welcome," Mel said, a frown still marring her sharp features. "You two okay?"

Jamie only nodded, but Angie made an impatient sound as she removed her soccer sandals from her bag. "She's lucky you came along when you did. That's all I'm gonna say."

Did Mel's lips twitch at that?

"Just so you know," Jamie said, "that was all North. Taylor was sitting with her, but she tried to shut her down."

The coach's brow lifted incrementally. "Duly noted. Chalk talk in the locker room in ten." She gave a sort of salute—not gay at all—and turned away.

"What's up with the noble shit?" Angie asked. "You and Taylor are competing for a spot on the World Cup roster. The World Cup, Jamieson!"

"What, I should have let Mel think Taylor was out of line when she wasn't?" She shook her head, remembering the oily feeling under her skin when she'd hidden her injury at January camp, the disappointment in her father's eyes when he realized she hadn't told her coaches. "That's not my style. I can't believe it's yours, either."

Angie shrugged. "I don't know. I'd like to say it isn't, but I'm not sure anymore. You have to take care of yourself, you know?"

"No, I don't know. There's no 'I' in team, Wang," she said, barely managing to keep a straight face.

Angie laughed and stood up, holding out a hand. "I love you, man. You know that, right?"

Jamie let herself be pulled up. "Love you too."

Ten minutes later, the team sat in the visitor's locker room, the sounds of the home crowd celebration still echoing from the parking lot beside the stadium. For three thousand people, they sure made a racket. Today's attendance had dwarfed their game against China, listed at a measly 300. Rumor had it that figure included both teams and their entire staffs.

Jo stood near the dry erase board, hands on her hips.

"Are you satisfied with today's outcome?" she asked, her voice unreadable, eyes lingering on each player in turn.

"No," Ellie said, voice vibrating with frustration.

"No," the rest of the team chorused.

Steph threw a USA sock to the floor. "I'm sorry I let everyone down."

Jo didn't say anything, but Ellie and Phoebe quickly assured her it wasn't her fault, it was the ref, it could have happened to anyone…

"No," Steph insisted, shaking her head. "It was a bad tackle. I was already sitting on a yellow, and I should have known better."

"Well, I should have shut Marisol down," Emma said. "I'm sorry too."

"As long as we're assigning blame," Phoebe put in, "I dove early on that last goal."

"No loss is ever one person's fault," Jo said. "It may be a cliché, but that doesn't make it any less true. We win as a team and we lose as a team. Always. We're going to have more moments like this, ladies. And that's okay. In a way, I'm glad that we're struggling. I brought us here so that we could get out of our comfort zone. As one of my old coaches used to say, adversity builds character. This feeling right now is how we get better. It's what we do from here, how we recover—if we recover—that matters."

She paused and gazed around the room. "Everyone in this room has overcome something to be here—major injuries, anxiety, trauma, loss. No one here has come to this place and time unscathed. But to me, that's what makes us stronger. In the face of adversity, you all know that you can persevere. That's what gives each one of you the heart of a champion, whether you win the game in the end or not."

She stopped and let her words sink in. "All right. Grab your bags. You can get cleaned up at the hotel."

And with that, she and the rest of the coaching staff swept from the locker room.

For a moment, no one said anything. Then Ellie stood up and stuck out her arm. "Bring it in, guys."

The group gathered around her, arms thrust into the center, bodies pressed together in the familiar ritual, and waited as she looked around the group. Finally Ellie shrugged. "What she said." She smiled as everyone laughed, and added, "No, seriously, you guys, Jo's right. Every loss is an opportunity to get better, and we are in this together, badass motherfuckers that we all are, every single one of us. Team on three. One, two, three, TEAM!"

As players began to filter out of the locker room, Jamie could feel Emma's eyes on her. But she didn't look up, merely turned away and went to wait for Angie, who, predictably, had to pee. When she checked again, Emma was already gone.

On the bus Jamie slid into her usual seat, sighing inwardly when Emma kept her gaze fixed on the foreign city outside her window, noise-canceling headphones clamped over her ears. They would talk when they were alone, and tomorrow they would get back out on the field to resume training. One practice at a time, one match at a time—or so that cliché went.

Back at the hotel, they rode up in the elevator together, Emma with her headphones still on, Jamie and the others watching the numbers pass in silence. On the sixth floor, the players stepped out and headed down the hallway en masse. Emma's room came first. Jamie hung back from the group as she unlocked her door.

"Emma," she said, raising her voice to be heard over the music.

Emma turned in her partially open doorway and regarded Jamie blankly.

"Come on, Em," she tried again.

"Oh, so now you're talking to me?" Emma challenged, finally deigning to lower her headphones.

Jamie glanced down the hallway as the elevator dinged. More of their teammates piled off, but Steph, Emma's current roommate, wasn't among this group either. "Can I come in?"

"Suit yourself." Emma ducked into the room without waiting to see if she followed.

She almost didn't. But the thing about the ice queen act was that she knew it was only a cover to hide whatever Emma was feeling. Besides, they needed to talk before their relationship was back on display in front of the whole team at dinner. No pressure or anything.

Jamie stopped near the mirrored closets, watching as Emma dropped her bag at the foot of the closest twin bed. The hotel was one of the nicer ones in the city, and yet the rooms were only large enough to fit a double bed or two twins. Still, it was nicer than most of the places she'd stayed with Arsenal.

Emma turned and faced her, expression closed. "So?"

Jamie frowned. "What was that back there?"

"What was what?"

"You know what."

Emma stared at her a second longer, and then she sat down abruptly at the end of the bed and covered her face. "I don't know," she mumbled.

"Yes you do." Jamie stepped closer, stopping in front of her and touching one of her hands. "Don't shut me out."

"I can't help it. I'm Scandinavian. It's what we do," she said, voice still muffled by her fear filter. Or maybe an all-around general emotion filter was a more accurate description.

Jamie tugged on her hands. They came away easily enough. "Seriously, what was that?"

Emma sighed, her breath sending a few flyaway curls away from the edge of her face. "I'm sorry."

"For…?"

"For being a dick."

Her phrasing reminded Jamie of a walk they'd taken nearly a year earlier when they were still figuring out how to be around each other. "No argument here."

"It's just, Mari's a legend, you know?" Emma said, her voice higher-pitched than usual. "And she was looking at you like she wanted to wrap you up and take you home with her, and I—"

Jamie choked out a laugh. "Marisol. Looking at me. Did you take an elbow to the head today or something?"

Emma's shoulders dropped. "You didn't notice?"

She started to step back but realized that might not send the right message. "Okay, first of all, you're on crack. Second of all, even if Marisol liked girls—"

"She does. She totally does."

"Even if Marisol liked girls," Jamie repeated, pretending Emma hadn't spoken, "you would have nothing to worry about. Do you honestly think I would give her the time of day?"

Emma plucked at the polka-dot quilt that matched the retro table and chairs near the balcony door. "No. But she's *Marisol*. She has a reputation, Jamie, one that makes Ellie's pale in comparison. I didn't think, okay?"

Jamie set her blown mind aside and refocused on the topic at hand. "Okay. You're not going to do that again, though, right? Act like I'm some piece of meat that you own?"

Emma's mouth dropped open. "I didn't act like that!"

"Yes, you did."

"No, I didn't!"

Now Jamie did step back. For a moment she was tempted to walk out again—*forget this shit, I'm out*—but then she pictured having to explain to their friends why they weren't currently speaking; imagined Jo and the other coaches watching them shoot daggers at each other across the conference room mere days after revealing their romantic involvement. Their supposedly issue-free romantic involvement.

Instead of bolting, she closed her eyes and channeled the voice of her former therapist, Shoshanna: *Is your anger justified?* Definitely. *Then speak from the "I" perspective and tell her how you feel.*

"When you put your arm around me like that in front of Marisol and Isa," she explained, "I felt like you saw me as a thing to be owned, not as my own person."

"Oh."

She opened her eyes to see Emma gazing up at her, expression troubled. "Oh?" she echoed.

"No, I can see that." Emma sighed. "I really am sorry. I was having a bad day and I took it out on you. I didn't mean to make you feel like that."

"Okay. Apology accepted."

"Good. Thank you." Emma looked relieved, as if she too had pictured airing their personal drama in front of the entire national team. Definitely not for the faint of heart, new relationship management policy or not.

"Thank *you*." Jamie took a breath, feeling some of the tension ease from her neck and shoulders. "Anyway, do you want to talk about the game?"

As Emma hesitated, voices sounded out in the hallway, and Jamie took another step away. By the time the door opened and Steph walked in, she and Emma were several feet apart.

"Sorry," Steph said, pausing in the entryway. "Am I interrupting?"

"No," Emma said. "I was just about to walk Jamie out."

And there was her answer. Jamie imagined barbed quills, only this time they were lodged in Emma's skin, and she was the one trying to protect the people around her from their inadvertent release.

At the door, Emma hugged her, but carefully, like she wasn't sure she should. Jamie hugged her back harder. "Apology accepted, remember?"

"I remember." Emma pulled away. "Thanks for coming after me."

"I wanted to," she said, wondering if Emma remembered that conversation on an LA roadside too. "Let me know if you want to talk later, okay?"

She nodded. "Thanks, but I think I need some time to myself."

Even though Jamie had been expecting that response, despite the fact she fully understood where Emma was coming from, she still had to work to keep her hurt from showing. "Okay, then. I'll see you later."

"I'll see you at dinner," Emma corrected, squeezing her arm.

Jamie squinted at her. "Right. See you at dinner."

She left then, running through the afternoon's events in her head as she paced toward her room. Their first real fight hadn't been over the Arsenal-United rivalry, after all. It had been over a pretty woman who Emma had somehow worried might swoop in and snatch her away—a woman who happened to be Brazil's Greatest Of All Time. Which, hello, *Marisol* liked girls? And had been flirting with *her*? This was almost as surprising as Emma behaving like a jealous girlfriend. Although in a way she supposed it made sense— Emma had once admitted that one of the long term effects of her father's death was that she sometimes worried irrationally about losing the people closest to her.

As she let herself into her and Gabe's room at the other end of the hall, Jamie couldn't help wondering how Emma's fear of loss might manifest in the future. At least they were both aware of it. Awareness was supposed to be the first step, wasn't it?

# CHAPTER NINE

The next morning, Jamie brushed her teeth hurriedly and slapped a baseball cap over her bedhead. Then she headed down the hall, fiddling with her glasses as she stopped before Emma and Steph's door. Emma had texted to invite her out for coffee in the hotel restaurant, which seemed like a good sign.

Jamie closed her eyes and whispered her shortest mantra. Twice. Then she knocked.

Emma opened the door immediately. She was smiling—another good sign. "Hi."

"Hi, yourself."

Emma hugged her, saying as she pulled back, "I love you in glasses."

"I love you in glasses, too," she replied. She could hear the shower running and added, her voice low, "I also love you out of them."

Emma swatted her arm and dragged her to the elevator, where they stood a foot apart smiling at each other, energy fairly crackling between them. Another week of enforced team time was going to be the death of her, it really was.

"So," Emma said when they were seated side-by-side at the counter near the restaurant's front window, the stadium where they'd lost to Brazil the day before visible in the near distance. "I did some thinking about the game yesterday."

"Okay." She sipped her green tea and waited.

Emma toyed with the foam at the top of her cup. "I'm not sure what was worse, my shitty performance or my shittier attitude."

"Everyone's entitled to a bad game," Jamie said.

"I know. But I haven't been playing well for months now. At least, not consistently," she amended as Jamie opened her mouth to protest.

That, she couldn't argue with. Emma did seem to have hit a rough patch. Such things happened to professional athletes, but still. The timing of this particular slump was more than a bit suspect.

"Is it... Am I distracting you?" Jamie made herself ask.

"No," Emma said quickly. Maybe too quickly.

"Are you sure?"

"Yes, I'm sure." Emma bent forward to sip her mocha, letting her loose hair shield her face. "It's nothing new. Just this stupid system Jo wants me to play. She expects me to *score*. I'm not a scorer."

"I think I might have heard that somewhere." Emma's perfectionist streak, she knew, was easily enough to knock her off her game, especially since Jo was asking her to learn new skills. "Why don't you talk to Mary Kate? I bet she could come up with some strategies that would help."

Mary Kate Kennedy was the national team's resident sports psychologist. She traveled to most major competitions with them, and some of the smaller ones too.

Emma lifted her head, expression thoughtful. "That's a good idea."

"Don't sound so surprised." Jamie brandished the

cocky smirk she knew Emma simultaneously loved and hated. "I mean, Stanford, am I right?"

"Ugh," Emma said, and then, after a glance around the mostly empty restaurant, pressed her shoulder into Jamie's and murmured, "You're lucky I love you, dork."

She returned the pressure. "Ditto, nerd."

Emma fiddled with the handle on her mug. "I'm sorry again about yesterday."

"It's okay. I don't need you to be perfect, Em, but I do need you to communicate with me, okay?"

"Yeah, I think I can do that. The communication thing, not the perfection thing."

"Same," Jamie said, smiling sideways at her. More than her heart leapt when Emma smiled back and pressed her palm against her thigh.

*God. Damned. Team. Time.*

Still, she was lucky that they were here together, especially lucky that Emma somehow loved her as much as she loved her. Marisol might be beautiful and charming and potentially the greatest soccer player of their generation, but she wasn't Emma.

Coffee with Emma was a good start to what turned out to be a fantastic day. That afternoon Jo informed her at the end of practice that she would be starting in Steph's place against Argentina. STARTING. HER FIRST NATIONAL TEAM GAME.

"I am?" she asked, somehow dazed even after willing those very words to emerge from her coach's mouth.

Jo inclined her head. "You are."

Jamie bounced on her toes as she grinned at the head coach. "Thank you, ma'am!"

"You've earned your shot, kiddo," Jo said, giving her the smile that had always seemed reserved for her, proud and big sister-like and protective in a way that Jamie had never quite been able to explain. "Now take it."

"I will," Jamie promised.

When she shared the news with Emma, her girlfriend for once didn't bother to check to see who was nearby. She simply pulled Jamie into her arms there in the hallway outside the practice facility locker room.

"I'm so proud of you!" she said, voice and breath warm in Jamie's ear.

"So am I," Jamie admitted, feeling Emma's laugh reverberate through her own chest.

"You should be." Emma smiled into her eyes. Then her gaze flickered, and that was all the warning Jamie had before she felt something small and solid smack into her from behind.

"Group hug!" Angie called, and then Jamie's other friends from her youth team days were surrounding her and Emma in a laughing embrace, and all Jamie could do was grin at Emma and hold on tight.

As she tried (and failed) to fall asleep that night, Mel's voice came back to her from a year earlier: "What we're offering you is a chance to play yourself onto this team. What you do with that opportunity is up to you." Then she remembered what Jo had said: "You've earned your shot."

Turned out the theory of marginal gains worked. Jamie had worked her ass off all summer, improving a small amount at a time on whatever she could—strength, endurance, diet, sleeping habits, and mental acuity—until now, in December, she was about to start her first national team game. It didn't matter that she was only starting because Steph had picked up a red card. It didn't even matter that Steph would likely be back starting in the next match. What mattered was that Jo was giving her a chance that she had no intention of squandering.

*Win the first five minutes*, she told herself, visualizing herself running and passing and shooting and scoring like a soccer-playing machine. *Play your ass off for the first five minutes, and then do it again for the next five. And the next, and the next, and the next after that...* Ellie had told her once that she approached big games by breaking them down into smaller chunks of time so that they didn't feel quite as overwhelming. As she pictured it now, Jamie sent out a mental thanks to her housemate, teammate, captain, mentor.

Because hard work alone hadn't gotten her to this point. Without Ellie and Emma, without Jo and Mel and all of her other coaches along the way, without her parents or her sister or her teammates from every team she'd ever played on, she wouldn't be here now in Brazil, waiting for the sun to rise on the biggest day yet of her soccer career. Her family and friends back home would all be watching her debut on YouTube, since the tournament wasn't being televised in the US. But that was okay. There would be video replays available of her first goal in a US uniform. Tomorrow, when the time came, she was going to score.

*Win the first five minutes,* she told herself again, concentrating on her breath. Win those, and she would be golden.

*   *   *

Emma had been expecting it. She had even rehearsed her reaction ahead of time, a rehearsal that, it turned out, had been unnecessary. Because Jamie's first goal for the United States Women's National Team? It was spectacular, a dead-ball strike from thirty yards out that was still rising when it slammed into the top right corner of the goal. Emma wasn't far behind her when the referee blew the whistle three and a half minutes into the game. She sprinted up and launched herself at Jamie, feeling her girlfriend's strong arms encircle her waist and lift her clear off the ground.

"Yes!" Emma shouted, and grinned up into Jamie's ecstatic face. "I knew you could do it!"

She *had* known Jamie could do it. She was just grateful

she got to be on the field with her to celebrate.

"Thanks, Em," Jamie said, eyes bright. Then Ellie was there, lifting Jamie into her arms the way Jamie had done to Emma, and the rest of the starters were piling on—Maddie, Jenny, Gabe, Ryan, Lisa, Emily, Jordan, and Phoebe, who had sprinted all the way up from her own eighteen. Even Angie and Rebecca got a hug in when Jamie stopped by the bench on her way back to their end of the field, with Jo and Mel and Henry and Steph slapping her on the back. They were all there to celebrate Jamie's first goal with the national team— first of many, Emma thought proudly as she jogged back toward their defensive end.

Argentina was one of those teams that could have been good, if only their federation would support and invest in them. These women had grown up in a culture that ate, drank, and slept soccer. Or, men's soccer, anyway. Unfortunately, their countrymen didn't appear to give a whit about the women's game. By halftime the US already had nine shots on goal and led 3-0, with Jamie accounting for one goal and one assist.

This was more like it, Emma thought as she jogged toward the players' tunnel. Jamie's play had sparked an offensive surge. Sometimes the game was like that—swap one person into a key position and a team's entire dynamic could shift. That was why she wasn't surprised when Jo told her during halftime that she was giving Taylor O'Brien the second half at center back. She'd been expecting that, too. Or, more accurately, dreading it.

This time she didn't stomp off or throw her shin guards. Today she nodded like the mature adult she was and even managed a smile. On the bench a few minutes later she tugged on a pinny and sat beside Jess North, and not only because she wanted to see the homophobic newbie squirm while she cheered her girlfriend on. She was the Better Person, damn it. High time she started behaving like it.

The bench afforded her a much clearer view of

Jamie—and the rest of the team too. But her eyes were drawn back to her again and again mostly because Jamie was having a coming out game to remember. She was everywhere, her energy and confidence limitless as she raced end to end, supporting her teammates and setting them up in between launching shots of her own. She scored once more in the second half and assisted Ellie on another, and Emma didn't think she was biased in any way to conclude that Jamie Maxwell was the reason they ended up beating Argentina 7-0. Well, as much as any single person could be the reason for a soccer team to prevail.

"Thanks, guys," Jamie said that night as she sat in Emma and Steph's room, drinking champagne with a large percentage of the team. They had insisted on toasting her goals—and Taylor O'Brien's, as well, because the Notre Dame grad had scored her first national team goal today too. On a set piece. While playing in Emma's position.

But tonight was not about Emma or Taylor freaking O'Brien. Well, it was a little about O'Brien. Mostly, though, it was about Jamie and her amazing, glorious performance. Again, not that Emma was biased.

"Yeah, but it was against Argentina," Jamie apparently felt the need to point out after Ellie made a fittingly grand toast to her prowess.

"Oh, hell no, Rook," Jenny Latham said. "I don't care who we played. When you personally account for more than fifty percent of the offense, you get to feel good about yourself without qualifying anything. Got it?"

"Yes, ma'am," Jamie said, smiling despite the older player's dressing down.

She was so beautiful and doing so well at seizing the day and making it hers that it wasn't Emma's fault she had trouble keeping her hands to herself after a couple rounds of champagne. Steph gave them alone time before curfew, and Emma didn't have to work that hard to coax Jamie into a quick, private celebration on her squeaky twin bed. Hooking up illicitly reminded her of high school, and for a moment she felt transported back in time to the year when she had dreamed about being with Jamie, knowing she probably would never get the chance. But here they were in Brazil, both playing for the national team, and Jamie had just scored her first goal in her first ever start. *And* they were legitimately in love.

It was almost unfathomable in the very best way possible.

The following morning, the team went right back to work. A win against Argentina was all good, but that game was in the books, and now they needed to prepare for the last match of the tournament. Brazil had emerged from group play on top with the US second, so they would play for first place honors while China and Argentina would contest third place. The rematch presented an uncommon opportunity, Jo told them: an immediate chance to redeem their loss in the game they'd let slip through their fingers a week earlier.

Training the next few days was intense. Emma knew she needed to fight to show she deserved her starting spot, but instead of rising to the challenge, she got stuck inside her own head again, doubts swirling in an endless cycle. In a half-field scrimmage the day before the rematch, she hesitated a second too long on a Jenny Latham cross and ended up colliding with Ellie. As the ball sailed overhead, they both hit the ground.

"Fuck," Ellie cursed, rolling up to her feet. She tried to take a step but froze, her face contorting in obvious pain. She swore again more quietly and limped away.

"Elle," Emma said, following her, "wait. Are you okay?"

"I'm fine," Ellie said, voice terse.

But she left the field to confer with a trainer, and as the

game continued, Emma lost track of her. It wasn't until the end of the scrimmage that she heard the news: Ellie had sprained her ankle and was out for the match against Brazil.

"I'm sorry," Emma said that night as she sat on the end of Ellie's bed, shoulders hunched miserably.

"Blake," Ellie said, adjusting the ice pack on her ankle, "it's a contact sport. Shit happens."

"I know, but—"

"Did you hurt me intentionally?"

"Of course not! But I should have—"

"Jesus, Emma. Can you please stop making this about you? I'm the one who's hurt here."

Emma winced. "Oh, yeah. Okay." Was that what she was doing? Did she routinely make everything about herself?

"Now, take my mind off my stupid ankle. What did Jo say?"

Jo had called Emma up to her room after dinner to discuss the following day's game. She wouldn't be starting, Jo had explained, because the coaches wanted to see what Taylor O'Brien could do with ninety minutes against a quality opponent. Also, frankly, Emma seemed a bit burned out, Jo had added. The rest might do her good. Recharge her batteries before a World Cup year, or some such bullshit.

"Do you think she's right?" Emma asked Ellie. "*Am* I burned out?"

"It's possible. I know I have been at various points in my career. But Mel has been looking for a back-up for you and Lisa for a while now, and besides, Phoebe has very particular feelings about who plays in front of her. Between you and me, you don't have anything to worry about."

"I don't know." She stared at the muted television, where a Brazilian club game was playing in steady rain that had turned the field into a mud pit. "Jo says I need to score more. Or, I guess, score at all, since I never have for the national team."

Ellie's forehead furrowed even as she smiled. "She said that?"

"See?" Emma let her chin hit her chest. "I'm not a scorer! Everyone knows that."

"Not your dad."

"What?" Emma peeked up at her.

"Didn't you tell me once that your dad compared you to Mia Hamm?"

He had. Over smoked salmon latkes at the Experience Music Project in Seattle Center one night, Emma's father had counseled her not to focus on the destination so much that she missed the journey. Among other things.

"Yes, but that's what dads do," she said. "They believe the best of you in the face of overwhelming odds to the contrary."

"Not my dad." Ellie gazed at the silent television. "Mine told me I would never amount to anything. He said of all his children, I would always be his biggest disappointment."

Emma had known that Ellie wasn't close with her parents. Known, too, that both her mother and father struggled with her "tomboy" tendencies. This, Emma had understood, meant they were homophobic, a fact that had only been reinforced when she met them in real life. But she'd never realized how deep the gulf between them ran.

"I'm sorry," she said softly, moving uninvited up the narrow twin bed to slip her arm through Ellie's. "That sucks."

"Yeah. It does." Ellie laughed as she made room for Emma, her voice slightly hoarse. "I think that's why breaking the scoring record would be such a big deal. Maybe then he'd realize he was wrong about me."

With every goal Ellie crept closer to Mia Hamm's scoring record. At her current rate, she should break it before the World Cup. Or, well, she *had* been on target to do so before Emma wrecked her ankle.

"Ellie, he's wrong about you whether you break the record or not," Emma said, leaning into her friend's shoulder. "You have to know that your worth doesn't depend on a number. We all follow you because you're an amazing person and an even better leader, not because of how many goals you score."

Ellie lifted an eyebrow. "So you say. But I'm pretty sure the goal-scoring helps."

Emma's fists clenched. Realistically she understood that if Ellie didn't believe she was more than the sum of her soccer career, there was nothing anyone could do or say to change her mind. Except maybe her father.

"So what you're telling me," she said, "is that I'm a shitty goal scorer because my dad wasn't a total asshole?"

This time Ellie's laugh sounded more genuine. "Yes, Blake, that's exactly what I'm telling you." She paused. "Do you want to do some extra work on offense during January camp? I bet we could convince Jamie and Angie to stay after practice. Maybe some of the others too."

"You would do that?" But the idea didn't really surprise her. As she'd told Ellie, she was an awesome leader, not to mention generous to a fault.

"Emma. The '99ers may be the ones who told me to work on my defensive skills, but in case you've forgotten, you and Tina are the ones who actually taught me how to play better defense. Besides, it isn't like I haven't seen you helping out other players."

"Okay, then," Emma said, touched. "I would really appreciate it, Elle."

"No problem. I mean, assuming my ankle heals in time for January camp..." As Emma groaned, Ellie elbowed her. "Kidding! I'll be fine. Takes more than a little sprain to keep me down."

The screen flickered, and they glanced back to see a goal celebration. During replays, the door opened to reveal a whole gaggle of well-wishers who wanted to check on their team captain—and leading scorer.

"That's my signal," Emma said. With a final attempt at an apology that Ellie only waved away mock crossly, she excused herself and went to check on Jamie before curfew.

As she got ready for bed later that night, Emma couldn't get Ellie's words out of her head. For her own father to call her his biggest disappointment? How did you get over something that hurtful? Emma may not have always gotten along with her father, but the night he'd compared her to Mia Hamm he'd also told her that she and her brother were what he was proudest of in his own life. Not his surgical patents or the thousands of children whose lives he'd saved with his pioneering techniques. No. She and Ty were his true legacy.

*Thanks, Dad*, she thought, casting her thoughts out into the universe in the hopes that he was still out there somewhere, in one form or another.


Jamie didn't start against Brazil the next day either, but she did play in the second half. That was more than Emma could say. As Jo had promised, Taylor O'Brien played the entire match, which ended in a scoreless draw. In the event of a tie the team with the better group stage finish was crowned the victor, so Brazil took top honors. Still, the game was an improvement over their previous meeting if only because they didn't give up any goals. Lisa had kept the defense organized, and Taylor's speed had come in handy a few times when Marisol attempted to split the four-back.

Emma couldn't remember the results from September's round of fitness testing. Was Taylor faster? *Should* she be starting on a regular basis?

"Dude, no way," Jamie insisted on their "walk" that night. Brazil had a certain reputation, and that meant that team members were required to travel in groups. Instead of going out on their own as they'd done in Utah, they had taken to setting up on adjacent treadmills in the hotel fitness room most nights after dinner, careful to keep an eye out for visitors.

"I don't know," Emma said. "I think she might be. She's definitely better offensively."

"Well, she *has* played offensive midfielder for most of her life. If you ask me, Jo takes the idea of versatility to an extreme."

It was nice to know that Jamie thought that, too, even if her role as Emma's girlfriend meant that she was required to say such things.

"Besides," Jamie added, "Jo didn't say anything last night about it being permanent, did she? You said she was giving you a break, not replacing you outright."

"No, you're right. She didn't mention the future." In fact, she'd left the door wide open, a fact that didn't make Emma feel any better.

Jamie checked over her shoulder before asking, "Did she say anything to you about us? You know, anything relationship oriented?"

"No. I told you, she just wanted to let me know I would be sitting today."

"She really didn't say anything about me at all?"

"No, Jamie. Unless you count the part where we gushed about your goals against Argentina." Emma didn't mention that they'd talked at length about Jamie a week earlier, the first time Jo had called her up to her room. She had no intention of telling Jamie the truth about that conversation anytime soon.

"Oh. Well, good. I was a little worried, after the other Brazil game."

Honestly, Emma had been, too. "I think if there was a

problem relationship-wise, Jo would tell us. She seems like the direct type."

Jamie laughed. "That's an understatement. This one time the U-16s were playing in Florida and a bunch of us wandered off without telling anyone where we were going. Holy crap, was there hell to pay."

"You broke the rules?" she said dryly, recalling teenage Jamie's propensity to skateboard while high.

"Shut it, Blake." Jamie walked for a minute with her shoulders back, posture a thing of beauty until, all at once, she caved in on herself. "Can I ask you something?"

"Of course."

"It's going to sound stupid."

Emma scoffed. "I doubt that."

"No, really." She lowered her voice and said all in a rush, "Am I somehow stealing your luck? Because it's beginning to feel like only one of us gets to have good soccer karma at a time."

And, okay, maybe her warning was accurate, although *absurd* was a better word choice than *stupid*. Emma shook her head. "Come on, Jamie, that's not how this works."

"Logically I know that, but we're professional athletes. I think we're entitled to a little superstition. You've been starting all this time, and then I show up and you get benched?"

Of course someone who believed in soccer deities would think that way. Besides, Emma remembered, Jamie had her reasons for thinking in magical terms. Very good, legitimately terrible reasons.

"I really don't think that's what's happening here," Emma said carefully. "Do you?"

"No. I guess not." Jamie toyed with her treadmill's control panel, slowing the pace and then speeding it up again. "Do you remember Shoshanna?"

She nodded. Like she would forget the therapist who had basically saved Jamie's life one week at a time.

"Whenever I used to say things like that, Shoshanna would tell me that I'm not that important to the universe. But still, it feels like that in my gut."

"Have you thought about calling her? I know it's been a while, but it might be worth checking in considering everything that's been happening."

Including the things she didn't know about. If Emma's online situation worsened like it had with Sam, it would probably be wise for Jamie to have a solid support network in place. Besides, while Jamie had said she'd worked through most of her intimacy issues during previous relationships, she sometimes still got quiet after they had sex, drifting off into an interior maze where Emma couldn't reach her, could only hold on and wait for her to find her way out. Sometimes she didn't until the next day, and a couple of times she'd appeared to be lost to her thoughts for longer than a day, although it was difficult to gauge sometimes given how much time they spent apart. Would that happen more or less if they occupied the same space permanently?

"Huh." Jamie glanced over at her. "Not a bad idea, Blake."

"Don't sound so surprised," Emma said. "I mean, UNC, am I right?"

Jamie laughed, her eyes crinkling in that way that Emma loved, and suddenly the world didn't seem that bad.

That is, until she got back to her room and lay in the dark, ear plugs not quite blocking out Steph's nearby breathing and the never-ending traffic sounds of Brazil's capital. She couldn't stop replaying the look in Jamie's eyes when she asked if she was the reason Emma was losing playing time. If Jamie blamed herself for something that wasn't remotely her fault, Emma could only imagine the depths of her self-flagellation if she knew that the photo she'd posted of them in their Premier League jerseys had set off Emma's would-be stalker again.

That was what Jo had wanted to talk about the night they revealed their relationship, not Emma's lack of online activity. Contractual obligations were Fitzy's purview, which was why the email had come from the team manager. Jo was more concerned about her players' safety and well-being. Because while Jamie hadn't yet clued in to Emma's Twitter problem, the coaching staff had.

"I assumed Jamie knew too," Jo had told her when Emma came up to her room that night.

"No, and I don't want her to."

"What about her friends on the team? Won't they try to talk to her about it?"

"I asked them not to mention it either." Accustomed to dealing with their own trolling issues, Ellie and Maddie had readily agreed, while Angie and Britt had told her they already ignored most online commentary.

"Is that really the best decision, Emma? It's only a matter of time before she sees one of these tweets."

"There are things you don't know, Coach. Information that isn't mine to share. But if you knew, I think you'd understand why I want to protect her from all of this."

At that, Jo had balanced her pen on two fingers like a teeter totter. "I appreciate that you don't want to give away Jamie's confidence," she'd said finally, glancing up at Emma meaningfully, "but I think I might understand why you're so protective of her. Pete Tyrell, one of her old club coaches, and I go way back."

Emma's eyes had narrowed. Pete was the coach who'd taken Jamie's club team to Lyon. Was Jo saying she knew about Jamie's assault? But Jamie had never told Pete what happened the last night of the trip, so how could he have told Jo?

All of a sudden it had hit her. "Her parents," she said

softly. "They *told* him?"

"They were upset," Jo explained, "as any parent would be. I think her mother needed someone to blame. When he found out what happened to Jamie, Pete blamed himself too. No coach wants something like that to happen to the kids on their watch. Well, no good coach. I think you and I both know there are people who can't be trusted around kids."

Emma had nodded, her eyes misting over. "She doesn't know he told you, does she?"

"No. It's her business. If she wants me to know, she'll tell me."

After dropping her bombshell, Jo had asked Emma if she'd contacted the authorities about her online harasser. Emma explained that technically, the guy on Twitter hadn't done anything illegal, and she was hoping it stayed that way. That was good, Jo had agreed. Still, she thought that Emma should meet with Caroline Jankowski, the team's PR rep, during January camp. Whether she included Jamie in the meeting or not was up to her. But the federation had experience with these matters, and Jo felt certain that Caroline would be able to offer advice and access to additional resources.

Emma had realized that night that Jo was on her side, and Jamie's too, with the full weight of US Soccer behind her. It made a difference, as much as Emma might wish it didn't. Three years ago, she hadn't reported the incident with Sam because she'd chosen not to press charges, and her contract only required her to inform the federation of official police reports. Now she wondered: If she had asked for help back then, would things have gone differently for her and Sam?

Before she could go too far down that rabbit hole, she reeled herself back to the present. The situation was under control. She and the coaching staff were on the same page, and Jamie hadn't been distracted by Emma's online drama. When Jamie had asked her about the meeting in Jo's room,

Emma had only shared Jo's suggestion that she meet with the PR rep to discuss social media strategy. She hadn't let on what that conversation would likely entail: a review of the kinds of online behavior that were illegal under state and federal statutes versus the sort that simply had to be endured, without recourse to official channels.

From everything Emma had read, the latter type of harassment was far more common—and preferable, too, because in most cases it went away on its own. That was what had happened last time, after she and Sam broke up and the furor around the last World Cup finally died down. Hopefully that would be the outcome this time, too—except that they wouldn't lose to Japan in the World Cup finals and she and Jamie wouldn't break up. Right. The power of positive thinking.

She closed her eyes, shutting out the little voice reminding her that another World Cup was only six months away. Positive god-damn thinking: They would win the World Cup and ride off into the sunset. *They would win the World Cup and ride off into the sunset.* THEY WOULD WIN THE WORLD CUP AND...

She punched her pillow, but quietly so as not to wake Steph, and tried to think of something else to worry about—tomorrow's return trip across the bumpy Brazilian atmosphere, for example. That was it. She settled into the familiar fear, almost welcoming its pull. After all, gravity and potential mechanical failures were things over which she had long since accepted she had zero control.

# CHAPTER TEN

Snuggled up on her parents' couch in front of a roaring fire, Jamie sighed for approximately the thousandth time since arriving in Berkeley the night before last. From the dining table across the room, Meg pelted her with popcorn in a surprisingly accurate throw.

"Hey!" Jamie picked the popcorn off the couch and tossed it in her mouth. No use letting good food go to waste. "What was that for?"

"For mooning over your girlfriend like a lost puppy," Rhea supplied, fingers moving rapidly over her own popcorn string.

"I'm not—" Jamie started, but then she stopped. Maybe she was.

"Dude," Meg said in that half-mocking, half-affectionate tone only a sibling could muster, "why don't you go visit her?"

"I am. New Year's at the Space Needle, remember?"

This would be the first time in memory that Jamie failed to attend New Year's at the Embarcadero with her parents and the Thompsons. While she knew she would miss being with family and friends, she was hoping that ringing in the new year with Emma would mark the start of an era. The idea of watching Seattle's fireworks with Emma from her deck made Jamie feel more grown-up than almost anything else she'd done this year. Except, maybe, buying her own car, and even then her parents had co-signed the loan.

Maybe 2015 would be the year she could finally claim financial and emotional independence from her family of origin. It would definitely be the year she turned twenty-seven, anyway.

"I meant go see her in Minnesota," Meg said. "She's there until right before New Year's, isn't she? I assume you have frequent flyer miles up the wazoo, with your recent jet-setting lifestyle and all."

Jamie sat up on the couch, frowning. "I can't just show up on her mom's doorstep."

"Why not? She did here last year, didn't she?"

This was an excellent point. Also, hadn't Emma all but asked her in London to "show up unannounced" sometime in the near or far future?

Becca's mom poked her head into the combined dining/living room. "How are the popcorn strings coming, girls?"

"Fine, Mama Ruth," Meg said cheerfully.

"Good. Because the eggnog is spiked, ready, and waiting. Well, not for you," she added with a smile at her daughter-in-law. Her very-pregnant-with-twins daughter-in-law. After hanging out with Tina Baker when she was pregnant the previous winter, Jamie hadn't expected Rhea to be quite this huge. Then again she was carrying an additional human being in there.

Incidentally, Becca kept calling the babies their BOGO twins—as in, Buy One Get One free. They'd gone through a sperm bank in LA that was apparently considered top-notch but that also charged quite a bit for their services.

"Turns out it's expensive to be sperm-challenged,"

Becca had complained earlier. Rhea did not seem amused by this term nor by her wife's nickname for their unborn daughters. Unsurprisingly, this did not prevent Becca from repeating both ad nauseum.

Ruth turned to Jamie. "And what exactly are you doing, young lady?"

"Offering moral support?" Jamie hazarded from her cozy spot by the fireplace.

She'd gone outside earlier to help with the annual hanging of the lights, but too many light-hangers was an actual thing, she'd discovered. Instead of incurring another person's wrath, she'd retired to the living room and built up the fire. For the sake of the greater good, of course.

Becca's mom pursed her lips. "Is that what the kids are calling it these days? Well, I suppose you're still suffering from jet lag."

"Right. Jet lag," Jamie agreed.

"More like lovesickness," Rhea murmured snidely to Meg, who hid her laugh behind a handful of popcorn.

Jamie was about to stick her tongue out at her sister and Rhea when the door to the front porch opened, revealing Becca dressed in her usual thousand layers, including a faded 49ers balaclava. Becca hated cold weather so much that Jamie had been shocked she'd chosen NYU for college, and even more surprised when she stuck it out all four years. Rhea was a large part of the reason she hadn't transferred back to the West Coast after her first New York snowstorm. They'd met at the library during their first week of classes, though it had apparently taken them a couple of years to figure out they belonged together. Still, they'd been together ever since, and now their "we" was about to expand.

"Yo, ladies, the 2014-15 Maxwell-Thompson Street Light Show is ready for your viewing pleasure," Becca announced. "Drop your popcorn balls and—wait, are you lying down on the job, James?"

"Dude, no!" Quickly she rose, shedding her blanket. "I was tending the fire so you could warm up when you came back in."

Becca stared at her suspiciously. "Right. Let's get the viewing over and the eggnog-sipping by the fire started!" Her gaze shifted to her wife and gentled immediately. "How are you, sweetheart? Can I get you anything?"

"I'm fine," Rhea said, sounding uncharacteristically annoyed. "I have to pee. I'll be out in a minute."

As Rhea heaved herself up from her seat at the dining table and headed for the downstairs bathroom, Jamie was fairly certain she saw Becca's shoulders fall slightly. In the years they'd been together, she'd never witnessed such tension between them. It was probably just the babies wreaking havoc. Pregnant women supposedly experienced mood swings that made PMS seem like nothing. She pictured Emma, her belly round (but not as large as Rhea's, preferably; Jamie wasn't sure she could handle twins), her face twisted in grouchiness for months on end. It would be hard, but at the end there would be the babies—BABY—making everything that had come before worth it. She hoped.

Outside, the assembled members of the Maxwell, Thompson, and Kirschoff clans waited for Rhea to join them before Jamie's mom did the honors, flicking the master switch to the massive light strings hung around the gutter, the trees in the front yard, and even the bushes that lined the walkway. It was pretty amazing, Jamie had to admit. But then, it always was. Her parents took their holiday lights seriously. It was the ideal blend of her mother's artistry and her father's tech wizardry, they claimed.

Did Emma's mom decorate her house in the Twin Cities with lights, or was that something she'd given up after Emma's dad died? Assuming they'd hung lights in Shoreline at all.

"Earth to Jamie," her dad said, gazing at her

expectantly.

"Oh, sorry," she said. "It's great, as usual."

"Wishing you were in Minnesota right about now?" Meg asked.

"Not at all," she lied. No doubt unconvincingly—she'd never been much good at it.

"Why would anyone want to go to Minnesota in December?" Becca asked, shivering at the mere thought of such ridiculousness.

"Because she'd have Emma to keep her warm," Meg answered.

An assertion that Jamie couldn't argue with.

It was a perfect Maxwell-Thompson family holiday celebration, with the usual outdoor lights extravaganza followed by eggnog around the fire place, the informal party attended by good music and the scent of shortbread, gingerbread, and sugar cookies baking in the kitchen. Jamie enjoyed the family and friends time as ever, but this time she was only half present. The other half of her mind was, as her sister alleged, in Minnesota.

Always in the past, no matter what her relationship status, she'd spent Christmas in this house with her family. And always, in the past, that had been enough. Last year, she and Clare had been planning to spend the holiday together for the first time when the national team called, signaling the end of their relationship as far as Clare was concerned. Jamie had ended up booking a flight that left London on Christmas morning, though with the time difference, she'd still managed to get home midday.

Now, a year later, she was at home again, rehashing the same arguments about the consumerism of American holidays and which was better: shortbread or gingerbread cookies. (*Pumpkin pie*, obviously, Jamie thought, rolling her eyes to herself.) And yet it wasn't the same. She missed Emma, a familiar sort of ache that all at once felt unnecessary. Why weren't they together right now? Why weren't they splitting time at each other's family's houses over the holidays—Christmas with one, New Year's with the other—like Meg and Todd, Becca and Rhea, and even Emma's little brother Ty and his fiancée? The main difference was that the other couples had been together longer than they had, but in point of fact, Jamie and Emma had known each other far longer than any of the others had. The only reason they weren't together right this second snuggling on the couch beside Meg and Todd was that it had been her turn to do the asking, and she'd chickened out.

When Todd went to grab his guitar to start the caroling portion of the evening's entertainment, she excused herself briefly to make a call.

*Carpe diem, biatch*, as Angie would say. Angie, who was home in New Jersey with her family while Maddie celebrated separately in Chicago with hers. But that was more by necessity. Neither of their families approved of their "lifestyle choice." Unless they were prepared to have an Orphans' Christmas, they didn't have the option of being together at the holidays.

A voice at the other end sounded, and she clutched the phone tighter. "Hi, it's Jamie," she said. "I have a favor to ask."

She was beginning to feel like she spent half her life in airports waiting for luggage to crawl past at either abysmally slow or psychotically fast rates. In this case, at the Minneapolis airport, the current rate was Way Too Slow. But at last, as it usually did, the baggage carousel spit out her suitcase and duffel. She sent a quick text and headed outside, stopping directly as pre-arranged beneath the glowing "1" sign.

And, hell's bells, it was COLD. She huddled deeper into her puffer coat, trying to remember if its insulation was good to zero degrees. How was this temperature even possible in mainland America? Seemed more suited to the Yukon Territory, honestly. At least baggage claim exited onto a covered drive. The exposed roadway up on the ticketing level was, presumably, even colder.

Fortunately—thank the good lord in whom she did not believe—she didn't have to wait long. Soon a sedan slowed in front of her and ejected a tall, poshly dressed man from the passenger seat.

"Holy shit," she said. "You're super tall."

He grinned down at her. "Well, I *was* only thirteen the last time I saw you."

"Shut up," Jamie said, laughing as she pulled him in for a hug. "It's good to see you, Ty."

"You too, Jamie." Before they could freeze to death, he helped her deposit her bags in the trunk. "Back seat okay?"

"I don't care as long as it has heat," Jamie assured him, sliding into the thankfully warm car and slamming the door. "Jesus. I mean, hi," she added as she realized the woman in the driver's seat was watching her.

"Hi," the woman replied, smiling somewhat shyly. She was even prettier in person than on Facebook, Jamie realized. *Well done, Ty.*

Ty folded himself into the front passenger seat. "Jesus Christ on a pogo stick, it's freaking cold! Oh, Bridge, this is Jamie. Jamie, meet Bridget, the kind and amazing woman who has agreed to share her life with me."

"Don't you mean certifiable?" Jamie teased.

"I resemble that!" Bridget exclaimed, casting her a mock glare.

And yeah. She would fit right in with the Blakeleys.

Bridget placed the car in gear and started away from the curb, maneuvering around haphazardly parked vehicles and baggage-laden people in varying stages of dress, from the heavily bundled to the barely bundled at all. Jamie was definitely going to borrow a hat and gloves—assuming she left Emma's mom's house at all before their flight to Seattle in two days' time. It was brief enough of a visit that she might be able to get away with staying inside.

"Congratulations, by the way," she said, projecting her voice into the front seat.

Bridget smiled at her in the rearview mirror as Tyler said over his shoulder, "You mean on the Longest Engagement Ever$^{TM}$?"

Jamie bit her lip. "They told you they call it that?"

"I overheard them," he admitted. "Not the most tactful of people, my family."

"Speaking of, does Emma know?"

"Nope, not a clue." His smile was smug, and reminded Jamie a bit of his older sister when she was especially proud of herself for some bit of geekery or another. "Mom claimed we ran out of beer, so as long as Em doesn't go check the garage stash, we should be set."

That was good, Jamie told herself as she nodded at Ty and glanced outside at the frozen Minnesota landscape. Why was she so nervous, then? Because everyone who knew Emma knew how she felt about surprises. Sure, she'd said in London that Jamie was always welcome, but had she meant it?

As Bridget guided the car across the city, Jamie sincerely hoped she had.

She only managed a glimpse of Emma's mother's "new" house as they drove up the long driveway on the non-lake side. Still, she saw enough to realize that while the property might not be quite as imposing as the old house overlooking Puget Sound, it was impressive all the same with its wide, snow-covered yard and peaceful setting across the street from a good-sized lake. Her attention wasn't on the house itself, though. She was more concerned with the people inside.

Bridget stopped the engine and cast Jamie an encouraging smile. "Ready?"

*No.* Why had she ever thought this would be a good idea? Ty had said his mother was fully supportive, but what if she was only being polite? What if she didn't want Jamie invading their family time? It wasn't like they got all that much of it these days.

Too late for second thoughts now. "Ready."

Giggling and shushing each other, Tyler and Bridget led the way into the mudroom off the garage. There Jamie paused while her chauffeurs and fellow confidants continued into the house.

"I thought you were getting beer," she heard Emma say.

"Oh, right," Ty said, and opened the door again, nodding at Jamie.

Showtime. She took a breath and stepped past him into an open plan kitchen that immediately reminded her of the house in Seattle. "Surprise!"

Emma's mom was at the sink while Emma was perched on a stool at the breakfast bar. She stared at Jamie, her mouth open in shock, and then she was throwing herself off the stool and crossing the space between them in a matter of steps as she squealed, "Jamie! I don't believe you!"

By now Jamie was accustomed to Emma's weight— and enthusiasm. She absorbed the impact of her body easily, relief washing over her in an almost literal wave as she squeezed her eyes shut and buried her nose in Emma's loose curls.

"Merry belated Christmas?" she asked.

"I'll say it is," Emma said, and then kissed the corner of her mouth quickly, the touch barely there and then gone again. She gripped Jamie's hand as she turned to shoot what passed as an accusing glare around the room. "You guys were in on this, weren't you?"

Everyone laughed and nodded, and then Emma's mother stepped forward, reminding Jamie of the night she'd arrived in Seattle for Emma's father's funeral. Mrs. Blakeley had a little more gray in her blonde-brown hair now, and her face and figure were fuller than they'd been back then, but her smile was as welcoming as ever.

"Jamie," she said, embracing her in a hug that was steady and firm. "I am so pleased you could be here with us. It's wonderful to see you and Emma in the same space and time again, my dear." With a final squeeze, she stepped back, still beaming at her.

Jamie felt herself blush. She wasn't used to such a warm welcome from a partner's mother. Her previous girlfriends' parents had almost uniformly failed to hide their dismay that instead of a man, their daughter had brought her home to meet the family.

"Thank you, ma'am," she said, falling back on formality to cover her awkwardness.

"Oh, sweetheart, call me Pam. Now, you're just in time for lunch. Where are your bags? Emma, help her with her bags, will you?"

"Absolutely," Emma said, grabbing the keys from her brother and tugging Jamie toward the garage. She hadn't let go of her hand yet, rendering her mother's hug a bit cumbersome but totally fine as far as Jamie was concerned.

"I can't believe you're here," Emma said as they freed the bags from the car's trunk.

"I can't either," she admitted, following her girlfriend back inside the house. "Good surprise?"

Emma flashed a smile over her shoulder. "The best."

*Whew.*

They headed up a staircase that opened onto a landing

with a bookshelf and a comfy arm chair. Emma led her down the hallway to the right, away from the kitchen side of the house, and waved her into a small, neutrally-decorated bedroom. Jamie had barely set the bag down when she felt herself being shoved unceremoniously onto the double bed. Laughing, she rolled over as Emma climbed on top of her and settled astride her waist.

"I can't believe you," she said again, smiling down at Jamie.

"I think you already said that."

"Doesn't make it any less true." Emma leaned forward, her hair encircling their faces, and kissed her.

"Wait," Jamie said after a while. "We have to get back down there."

"No we don't." Emma's hand drifted lower.

"Emma!" She gasped as she felt warm fingers slip inside her shirt. "They'll know what we're doing!"

"So what?" Emma nipped her earlobe, her breath doing amazing things to Jamie's ear and neck just as her fingers were doing elsewhere. "Between team time and family time, I haven't been alone with you in entirely too long."

She had a point, Jamie realized, shutting her eyes against the sunlight streaming in the window as her own hands gripped the hem of Emma's sweater.

Lunch could wait.


Returning downstairs with Emma in prime post-orgasm glow was every bit as mortifying as Jamie had anticipated, but other than Bridget and Ty exchanging an amused glance, the fallout wasn't too bad. Emma's mom acted as if she didn't know that her daughter had thrown Jamie on the bed upstairs and had her quick but satisfying way with her, a pretense that Jamie could appreciate. Soon they were seated around the dining room table at the front of the house overlooking the lake, and Jamie was fielding the same kinds of questions Emma had faced from her family in Utah: "How are your parents and sister? How was Christmas in Berkeley? How's Portland? And what have you been up to since we last saw you a decade ago?"

Jamie answered the questions as openly as she could, which was quite openly seeing as this wasn't the first time she was meeting Emma's family. Then she turned the conversation back on Pam and Ty, asking about their current lives as well as the years since they'd last seen one another—and about future plans, too. Like Emma's brother and his fiancée, Ellie and Jodie had been dodging questions about setting a date for a while now too. Jamie figured it didn't hurt to ask.

"We've decided to have it after the World Cup," Ty explained. "Probably at New Year's since we know there won't be any games that week."

"Wait, what?" Emma's half-eaten tuna sandwich sat frozen in her grasp.

"You heard me," Ty said, tilting his chin upward in the same stubborn, slightly challenging way Emma had.

"You put a hold on your wedding because of me?" Emma clarified.

"It's not a big deal." Ty's frown matched hers. "We aren't in a huge hurry, so we thought next year would work. You know, like maybe we'll have two amazing things to celebrate in the same year? And if not, well, hey, there's guaranteed to be one awesome party in 2015. Am I right?" he added to Jamie.

Automatically she held her hand up for him to slap. It had been years, but she had always thought of Ty almost like a younger brother, one she didn't have to share a roof—or a bathroom, thankfully—with. The familiarity and sense of connection came back now as easily as it had been forged back in the day, only this time they were talking about weddings instead of funerals, a conversational upgrade she was sure they were all only too happy to accept.

Except, possibly, Emma. "I'm sorry," she said. "You shouldn't have to plan your wedding around my availability."

Ty rolled his eyes. "Get over yourself, Em. We're not planning around your schedule. We're doing what works for us, and if it means you can be there too, all the better. Right, Bridge?"

"Right." The younger woman nodded at Emma. "If we want you to be part of our day, it only makes sense that we take the World Cup into consideration. Besides, we were hoping to be in Canada next summer… If that's okay with you?"

"Of course it's okay," Emma said, her frown smoothing out. "I would love if it you guys were there. Assuming I'm on the team."

Jamie gazed at Emma in surprise. Had Jo told her she might not get her contract renewed in 2015? Sometimes new coaches cleaned house, but to get rid of a player like Emma when she was at the top of her game would be insane.

"I thought the new coach was merely resting you in that last match," Pam said, her frown a mirror image of her children's. "Did something else happen?"

"No," Emma admitted, poking at her sandwich with a finger. "But no one's job is secure. That's a given at this level."

Jamie released the breath she hadn't realized she was holding and reached for her glass of water. Emma was just being Emma.

Pam appeared to agree. "That sounds like nerves, honey. I'm sure you'll be in Canada next summer. As will I— Roger and I have already put in for the time off."

Though Emma's family was too polite to ask, Jamie felt the need to address the elephant in the room. "I'll be there too, one way or another," she said, aiming for plucky and upbeat.

The moment of silence that fell over the table was— well, awkward, until Emma's mother came to the rescue. "I don't doubt that for a second, sweetheart."

That made one of them.

As they finished lunch, the assembled group made a plan to explore The Cities. Ty and Bridget had only arrived the previous day after spending Christmas in Boston with Bridget's family, and Emma's mom said she wanted to show Jamie some of the sights, same as she'd done with Bridget on her first visit to Minnesota. Jamie resisted the urge to dwell on Emma's mom equating her with her future daughter-in-law and instead focused on the potential to-do list: ice cream at Sebastian Joe's in Minneapolis, a visit to an outdoor sculpture park, dinner at a downtown restaurant, and a drink at a St. Paul "ice bar."

Exploring the great outdoors in near subzero temperatures was questionable enough, but ice cream and drinks at an ice bar, whatever the heck that was?

Out of the corner of her mouth, Jamie asked Emma, "Is your mom joking about ice cream?"

"Minnesotans never joke about something as serious as ice cream," Pam declared as she and Bridget loaded lunch plates into the dishwasher. "Besides, it could be worse, you know. Twenty-five degrees is positively balmy."

*Could be worse.* Had she actually said that? Next thing you knew she'd be saying, "Oh fer cute," a phrase that Emma claimed her relatives habitually invoked at the holidays.

"It's too bad you won't be here in a few weeks for Icebox Days in International Falls," Pam added.

"Icebox Days?" Jamie echoed. "That sounds— interesting."

"Suck-up," Ty muttered, smirking at her.

Jamie flipped him off, lowering her hand quickly as

Pam turned away from the sink. Had she been busted? No, she didn't think so. *Whew*.

"It's a winter festival in the northern-most town in Minnesota," Pam explained.

As she went on to describe the various and sundry competitions in the tiny town's festival—a frozen turkey bowling game, a toilet seat toss, and a moonlight ski race, cross country because apparently there weren't many hills in the state that could support a downhill course—Jamie shifted closer and whispered to Emma, "Do you think the extreme cold has addled people's minds here?"

Emma murmured back, "More like mind over matter. It takes incredible powers of concentration to trick your brain into not noticing you're about to freeze to death."

Their first stop was, in fact, the ice cream shop in Uptown only fifteen minutes from Emma's mother's house. For a Saturday in late December, the tiny shop was remarkably crowded in Jamie's opinion. They waited in line to place their orders, and then they waited in line again to pay. They were still waiting when a table opened up in the corner, so Jamie and Ty went to stake their claim.

Jamie was dragging a fifth chair to the small circular table when Ty said, "I'm glad we have a moment. I wanted to say something."

"Fire away." She dropped into the chair she'd retrieved and sucked on a spoonful of Oreo vanilla, watching him curiously.

"Okay. Well, the thing is, my sister is fairly crazy about you. Don't know if you've noticed?"

She smiled, hoping it didn't seem too giddy. "The feeling is entirely mutual."

"Good. Right. Well, I wanted to tell you that I'm psyched you guys are finally doing the couple thing."

"Thanks, Ty," she said, touched.

"Sure. But at the same time, if you do anything to hurt her," he added, hazel eyes narrowing and lips slanting dangerously, "I will hunt you down and make you regret the day you were born."

Jamie stared at Emma's brother, aware of brightly colored posters lining the walls behind his glaring visage and the scent of chocolate and strawberries wafting incongruously between them. And then his face cracked and he started to laugh, pointing his waffle cone at her.

The little fucker. Although really the fault lay with her. She should have known the old Ty was still in there somewhere.

"Holy shit," he gasped in between laughs, "you should have seen your face, Max. Classic!"

Reluctantly she smiled, and then she punched him in the shoulder. Hard. "Dickwad. I can't believe I thought you would give me the shovel talk."

"That makes two of us." His laughter finally faded, and he lifted his eyebrows at her. "Anyway, it's more you having to be careful of what Emma brings to the table, isn't it?"

"What are you talking about? Your sister is awesome."

"No, of course she is. I meant the Sam thing."

*What* Sam thing? But before she could ask, he smiled over her shoulder. Jamie glanced back to see Emma leading her mom and Bridget through the dense clump of tables to their corner. As they approached, she tried to remember what Emma had said about her relationship with Sam. Not much, she didn't think. They'd always been so pressed for time together that neither had wanted to spend it talking about past relationships. Besides, whatever had happened between Emma and her ex-girlfriend wasn't really any of Jamie's business.

"How's your Oreo vanilla?" Emma asked, sliding into the seat beside her.

"Fantastic. What about you? How's your Lavender

Truffle?" she asked, not bothering to keep the disgust from her voice.

"Incredible. Want a taste?" Emma waved her cone under Jamie's nose.

"Ew!" she said, flinching away. "Gross. There's no way that's real ice cream."

"Now you're drawing a line between real and fake ice cream?" Ty said. "Okay, Sarah Palin."

The conversation switched gears from dessert items to politics, and Jamie settled back, content to listen to Emma's family's banter and check out the shop's other patrons. The group at the next table caught her attention. With their matching red hair and stocky builds, they looked like three generations of Vikings descendants. While Jamie was observing them, the thirty-something dad of two freckle-faced cherubs shot the older man a glare and said, his voice carrying clearly over the din of the shop, "Come on, Dad, that's a giant load of you-know-what kind of hooey."

Jamie blinked rapidly. "Did you hear that?" she asked Emma, her voice low.

"Uh-huh."

"Can you translate? Because I'm not sure I know what hooey is, let alone—"

"—the you-know-what kind of hooey?" Emma finished for her. "Sorry, I don't speak Minnesotan. I'm a Seattleite, remember?"

"Thank god," Jamie replied fervently.

"What are you guys talking about?" Ty asked.

Emma kept her voice low as she repeated the conversational tidbit they'd overheard, and soon everyone at their table was trying to contain their laughter—even Emma's mom, a native Minnesotan.

Jamie finished off her dish of Oreo ice cream, her thigh pressed into Emma's. While it was colder outside than should ever be allowed, the shop was warm and bright, as was the company. Maybe ice cream at Christmas in Minnesota wasn't such a crazy idea after all.

"Admit it," Emma said, burrowing into her side under their bed's flannel sheets and down comforter that night, "you had fun today."

"I did," Jamie agreed. "When I wasn't freezing my ass off."

From Sebastian Joe's they'd moved on to the Walker Art Center (indoors) and Minneapolis Sculpture Garden (outdoors), where they'd wandered shivering along trails that offered views of downtown Minneapolis and, notably, a giant spoon sculpture with a cherry on top until Ty and Bridget made the mistake of attempting a snowball sneak attack. Emma and Jamie had ended up kicking their butts, of course—not only were they professional athletes, but they played a team sport. Together.

After Ty and Bridget conceded defeat, the group had headed downtown to Emma's mom's favorite used bookstore. The next stop was sushi, where the excellent quality of the fish had surprised Jamie, given their land-locked location. Roger, Pam's "gentleman friend," as Ty and Emma referred to him in snooty English accents, joined them for dinner. He was a nice guy and clearly adored Emma's mom, and as another plus he claimed to believe that soccer was superior to most other American sports.

The last stop of the day was the aforementioned ice bar, where they sat in an outdoor courtyard on huge blocks of ice that were covered in blankets, their drinks resting on carved ice tables, a large fire roaring in a nearby firepit. Ty and Bridget kept singing Olaf's song "In Summer" from *Frozen*, and despite its exaggerated Great White North vibe, the ice bar was an entertaining way to end the evening. Although with Emma by her side and spiced wine warming her insides, Jamie probably could have frozen to death quite happily.

"Your ass feels fine to me," Emma said now, her wandering hands dipping lower to demonstrate the truth of her statement.

Jamie fought her off. "Keep your fingers away from me! They are literally like ice. And I should know after today's itinerary."

Emma followed her across the bed. "But you're so warm! You know you love being my heater."

"Normally, yes. But this kind of cold isn't normal. Would it kill your mom to turn up the heat?"

Emma relented, relaxing against the pillows again. "She likes to sleep cold. Otherwise she says her hot flashes keep her up all night."

Jamie's mother was currently in the throes of menopause too, so she understood the need for a cool house. She moved closer to Emma and lay facing her, head pillowed on her elbow. "You're not planning to move here, right? Because that would be a total deal-breaker for me."

"Uh, no. I'm a Left Coaster for life, babe. Which is too bad because I think Ty and Bridget are planning to settle on the East Coast."

"That's a bummer." Suddenly she remembered Ty's prank at the ice cream shop. "You're not going to believe what your brother did." She relayed the story, pretending to be offended when Emma laughed at her. Not *with* her this time, but definitely *at*. "What is it about your family and friends threatening me, anyway? First Maddie and now Ty. Anyone else I need to worry about?"

"Dani," Emma said immediately. "Definitely Dani."

"I feel like if she ever gave me the shovel talk, it would be dead serious." She winked, proud of the pun. "Get it?"

"Yes, Jamie, I get it. How could you think Ty meant it,

though? Maddie, yes, but my little brother?"

"He was sneaky," she defended herself. "He sucked me in, telling me how happy he was that we're together."

"I could see that." Emma clasped Jamie's free hand. "You've always been a Blakeley family favorite too, you know."

"Your mom and brother, maybe. Your dad was less than thrilled at the prospect of me being in your life, if you'll recall."

Emma's grip on her hand loosened. "I recall."

Normally Jamie didn't bring up Emma's dad, but cuddling with her in her mom's house at the holidays brought a sense of easy intimacy. Maybe that was why she finally voiced the question she'd long been curious about: "Do you think he didn't like me because I'm gay, or because I look like a boy? Or both?"

Emma looked away. "I don't know. I was barely speaking to him then."

"Oh. Right." It was possible Jamie was the only one feeling a heightened sense of intimacy. Or maybe she simply shouldn't be asking Emma about her late father so close to Christmas. The holidays were supposedly difficult for families who'd lost someone, no matter how far in the past the loss might be.

Beside her, Emma moved restlessly. "I really don't know, Jamie. I was too angry with him my senior year to care much about what he was thinking or feeling."

"You had every right to be angry. He cheated on your mom and walked out on you and your brother. Even if he did come back, there's no taking away what he did."

"I know. I get that it's justified anger and all of that, but it still sucks that he died thinking I hated him."

"He died thinking you were angry with him," Jamie corrected, smoothing her fingers over Emma's soft cheek.

"Still shitty, but there is a difference."

Emma closed her eyes and leaned into her touch. "Yeah. I guess you're right."

"Hello, of course I'm right."

Emma's eyes flicked open and she smiled. "Goofball."

"*Your* goofball." Jamie pressed a gentle kiss to her lips.

"My goofball," Emma agreed, tugging her closer. "Love you, James."

"Love you too, Em."

A moment later Emma murmured, "I have an idea about how to warm you up. Want to hear?"

"As long as it doesn't involve hooey of any sort…"

Emma cracked up, and then she kissed her.

Her ideas, Jamie thought contentedly just before they both fell asleep, were pretty freaking awesome.

# CHAPTER ELEVEN

The kitchen was occupied the next morning when Emma and Jamie returned from a brisk, snowy run around Lake Harriet.

"Good morning, girls," her mom said, closing her newspaper with a smile. "I had no idea anyone else was up this early."

"No rest for the wicked," Emma said, smiling back. Minnesota was starting to feel more and more like home—or a second home, anyway. She had a feeling that would be true of any place her mother chose to live.

"How is it out?"

"Not bad," Jamie said. "I still have feeling in all my extremities, so that's a plus."

"Speaking of extremities," Emma said, swatting her affectionately, "you can have the first shower."

"Well, yeah. I beat you, remember?" she said with that swagger that always made Emma's heart go all aflutter.

Her mother was watching them, so she only huffed and turned away. "In your dreams, Maxwell."

"You're the one who's dreaming, Blakeley."

"You wish." Emma tossed her a banana from the bowl

on the kitchen island. "Now get going before the smell of sweat kills my mom's appetite."

Jamie's eyes widened, and then she skedaddled from the kitchen as fast as her tights-encased legs would take her.

"Emma," her mother admonished, "that wasn't nice."

"Hate to tell you, Mom, but I don't think 'Minnesota nice' is a thing in Seattle." She crossed to the refrigerator and, after rummaging through its extensive interior, emerged with a carton of eggs. "French toast?"

"If you're cooking."

"I'm cooking."

As Emma had known she would, her mom moved from the table by the window to a stool at the breakfast bar to keep her company.

"How was the trail around the lake?" she asked as Emma assembled various bowls and utensils.

"Mostly clear. It's warmer today, so we decided to run outside instead of taking turns on your treadmill."

"Ah."

"Which," Emma prodded, glancing over her shoulder as she cracked an egg into one of the bowls, "is a little bit dusty, I noticed."

"It's the holidays," her mother said, waving a hand. "I'll get back to my routine once you kids go back to your lives, but for now I want to be with my children. Is that so bad, Emma?"

"Nice try, Mom," she said, adding more eggs to the mixing bowl, "but I think you can spare a half hour for a workout. It's not like I haven't made time to exercise since I got here."

"That's different, honey. Your job depends on how fit you are, whereas mine most definitely does not."

Emma moved to the sink to wash her hands. "Why don't you join a tennis club? They play indoors year round, don't they?"

"I thought about it, but with my work schedule, it's hard to commit to anything that requires regular attendance."

"I know it's hard," Emma said, drying her hands. "But that doesn't mean you should just give up. You and Dad used to be so active, and now..." She trailed off as she stacked bread on a cutting board. She didn't want to make her mother feel bad about herself. She simply wanted her to be healthy. Or, healthi*er*.

"We were younger back then, honey. We had enough energy to work sixty-hour weeks and still attend your games *and* take Ty to the skate park. I'm not that young anymore. It's normal for a woman's metabolism to slow down at my age. It's the life cycle of the body at work."

"I know," Emma repeated, adding a dash of cinnamon to the egg-milk mixture. And she did understand that, in theory. But when you spent ninety-five percent of your time with professional athletes, your notion of what constituted a "normal" body tended to end up skewed.

Her mother sipped her coffee. "This is nice, by the way, just the two of us. I'm sorry I had to work so much before your brother and Bridget got here."

"It's fine," Emma said. If there was one thing she understood, it was the importance of work. "It gave me a chance to get to know Roger better. Has he always been a soccer fan, or have you been training him?"

"I might have trained him. You'll be happy to know he's now an official Manchester United fan."

"Well done, Mom," Emma said approvingly.

"Speaking of soccer, how are you? You appear very fit, although admittedly it's hard to tell with all the layers."

"Ha ha." She shot her mother a mock glare before adding butter to the oversized non-stick pan warming on the burner. Her mom had such nice kitchen gear. Maybe she should invest in some quality pots and pans herself. Right.

Because she was home so often.

"Another residency camp starts soon, doesn't it?" her mom asked.

"A week from today." Emma felt her shoulders tense and tried to relax them, knowing her mother would notice.

If she had, she didn't mention it. "How's the new coach working out, really?"

As she dunked several slices of bread in the soupy mixture, Emma experienced déjà vu—hadn't her mother asked nearly the same question the last time Emma was home for the holidays? And hadn't Emma sat at the breakfast bar dithering over being at January camp with Jamie, who was still the same lovely person she'd always been only, unfortunately, with a serious, live-in girlfriend? Now somehow a year later, Emma was the serious girlfriend, albeit not of the live-in variety. Yet.

"Jo is fine," she said. "Good, I think. Better than Craig, definitely. Since she played for the federation and has been coaching in the system for a while, there's a layer of knowledge and understanding that he simply didn't have."

She spread the melted butter around with a spatula and then used a fork to transfer the sodden pieces of bread from the mixing bowl to the pan. They sizzled briefly before settling into being cooked. Emma fiddled with the flame height. She missed cooking with gas. Electric stoves were so imprecise. Her off-campus house in North Carolina, where she'd first learned to cook spaghetti and steamed vegetables for twenty, had contained a huge old gas stove. So had her loft in Boston. Built in a historic building that once housed a factory, the apartment had come with radiators and gas appliances. Seattle, meanwhile, was the land of electric appliances. That was one of the only downsides to her home state, as far as she was concerned.

"How does Jo compare to Marty?" her mother asked.

Emma shrugged and turned to face her, leaning against

the oven handle. "She's similar, but more systematic, I guess. Deliberate and structured whereas Marty was more the wing-it type." She hesitated. "It wasn't only the last game, though. I didn't get as much playing time overall in Brazil."

"I noticed," her mom said, hands clasped around the ceramic mug Ty had made her in tenth grade art class. "Could it be retaliation for your efforts around the turf issue?"

"I don't think so. If it were, she'd have to bench half the team. And anyway, Ellie says that as a former player, Jo supports any push toward equitable treatment."

"All right then. That leaves you not getting involved with scoring."

Emma nodded. "Yeah." Despite their insane work schedules, she and her mom talked and video chatted regularly. As a result, her mother was well-acquainted with most of her recent national team troubles.

"So what's your plan, honey?"

She turned back to the burner and checked the bread. Ready to flip. "Ellie offered to work with me during January camp. Jamie and Maddie did, too."

"Sounds like your people are rallying around you."

She hadn't thought of it like that. "I guess they are."

"I'm not surprised. I've always liked Ellie and Maddie, and Jamie is obviously wonderful."

"Obviously."

"You two seem happy," her mom commented.

She smiled over her shoulder. "We are. Or I am, anyway."

"I think it's safe to say she is too. Took you long enough to find your way to each other. It was all I could do last Christmas not to shake some sense into you. I swear, Emma, it felt like you were doing your best to avoid the happiness being dangled directly in front of you."

"I wasn't avoiding it," Emma insisted, but the protest

sounded weak even to her ears. She checked the bread. It was ready, so she added it to a plate warming in the oven and transferred additional slices to the pan. "Anyway," she added, casting about for a new subject, "Ellie told me some things about her family I didn't know."

"What kinds of things?"

Emma filled her mother in on Ellie's relationship with her parents, particularly her father.

"That poor young woman," her mom said. "I had no idea."

"Neither did I. Actually, it reminds me of something Jamie said. About Dad."

"Oh?" Her mother's tone was slightly confused but open, a combination that gave Emma the courage to continue.

"You know how he didn't like Jamie? Well, she asked me if I knew why, and I realized I don't." She cleared her throat. "I was just wondering—do you?"

Her mother was silent for a moment. "I wouldn't say your father didn't *like* Jamie," she said finally, plucking at a linen napkin on the bar. "He thought she seemed like a good kid. A smart kid, maybe a bit wild, but not unlikable."

That couldn't be right. Emma placed the finished slices in the oven and switched off the burner before turning to face her mother. "Then why did he tell me over and over again that he didn't think our friendship was a good idea? The last time we talked about her, in fact, he thought Jamie and I were dating. When I asked him if that would be so bad, do you know what he said?"

Her mother shook her head, brow creased in a way that Emma recognized instantly. It was the same look she and Ty got, too, when they were upset.

She stopped. What was she doing? It was Christmas, and she was upsetting her widowed mother over something that had happened a lifetime ago. She turned back to the stove and relit the burner. "Never mind. It's not important." She added more butter to the pan and dunked more bread in the mixture. A few more pieces and the bowl would be dry.

"Don't do that, Emma," her mother said, voice rising slightly. "I know that our family isn't always the best at communication, but this is clearly important or you wouldn't have carried it with you all these years."

Emma stared down at the stovetop. "I don't want to upset you. It's the holidays."

"And you and I have what, five minutes more, tops, before your brother or Roger or someone else comes down those stairs? Talk to me, Emma, while we still can. Please."

"Fine," she said, transferring the final pieces of toast to the pan before turning back to her mother. "The night he took me out to dinner at Seattle Center, Dad told me that he didn't want me getting involved with 'someone like Jamie.' So I told him she had more integrity in—I think it was her elbow, or maybe her little toe? Either way, more than he did in his entire body."

She still remembered his expression when she'd stormed out, leaving him by himself at his favorite restaurant. She used to feel so special when he would take her out for a father-daughter dinner date. But by then, he was spending more time away than at home. Rather than allow what she'd perceived as his rejection of who she was—who Jamie was—to hurt her, she'd found refuge in anger.

"And you thought that meant he didn't like Jamie?" her mother asked. "That he was opposed to your relationship with her because she was a girl?"

Emma nodded, swallowing against the tightness in her throat. Before her mom could say anything else, she turned and flipped the bread in the pan. No need to set off the fire alarm. Although it would serve her brother's lazy ass right to be awakened by the alarm, hard-wired through the house and serviced by a company with the local fire department on speed dial.

"Oh, sweetie," her mom said, abandoning the breakfast bar and coming closer. "I'm so sorry. I knew that you two had argued, but I didn't know what about."

"You don't have to be sorry. It's not your fault he was homophobic. May he rest in peace," she added, flashing a wry smile at her mother. Enough time had passed that they could sometimes invoke dark humor about his passing.

Her mom wrapped an arm around her shoulders. "That's just it, though—he wasn't homophobic. Do you want to know why your father worried about your friendship with Jamie? Why we both did?"

They *both* did? "Yeah, I think I do."

"When your dad met Jamie's mother at Surf Cup, the night you two took off without telling anyone, Sarah told him that Jamie had suffered a recent trauma and that she was worried she might do something to hurt herself. That was your father's first impression of Jamie—of a troubled girl whose mother thought she was capable of self-harm."

Emma frowned. *Had* Jamie considered harming herself? It didn't seem like something she would do, but Emma hadn't gotten to know her until a few months after France. Then again, Jamie's mom hadn't handled the assault or its aftermath well at all. Case in point, violating Jamie's privacy in order to yell at her club coach.

The french toast was done, so she added the last slices to the warming plate and turned off the burner. Then she settled back against the counter beside her mother, facing out toward the lake.

"I didn't know that," she admitted.

"You have to understand, Emma, that as a parent your first concern is always going to be your own child's safety. Peer groups are so important in adolescent mental health; all the research says so. Your father and I used to stay up late at night worrying about Dani's brother's influence, or about one of the girls on the soccer team who we knew was having problems. We could make sure you were well fed and that you got enough sleep and had adequate emotional support, but the one thing we were powerless to affect was who you and your brother chose to care about. It was what we worried about most while you were in high school. It'll probably be the thing that you worry about most with your kids someday, too."

Emma flashed to a slightly older Jamie dressed like Emma's dad used to in a sports jacket and tie, recording their future daughter's soccer game from the sideline. It was a nice image, almost nice enough that she wished she could skip over the intervening years and be there now. But in the future she imagined, their kids were still young enough that she and Jamie didn't stay up late at night worrying about their peer groups.

"You honestly think he didn't dislike her?" she asked. "That he was only worried about collateral damage?"

"I do. And that's a good way of putting it." Her mom slipped her arm around Emma's shoulders again. "He wasn't homophobic, sweetheart. He may not have known how to talk to you about it, but I truly believe he would rather have seen you end up with a woman like Jamie, sweet and sensitive and so in love with you, than that awful boy you dated your senior year—what was his name again?"

"Justin Tate," she supplied, and made a face. "He was awful, wasn't he?"

"Justin Tate?" her brother echoed from the doorway. "Why in god's creation are you talking about that massive douchebag so early on a Sunday morning?"

"Language," their mother said, frowning mildly in Tyler's direction. "And it's not early."

"Sorry, Mom," he said, and came over to kiss her cheek. "I meant d-bag." Then he punched Emma in the arm. "Dork."

She whacked him back. "Nerd."

"What smells so good?"

"Emma made french toast."

"Sweet. I love it when my sister serves me breakfast."

"Just for that, you don't get any," Emma declared.

"Yes I do."

"No you don't."

"Mom, Emma's being mean," he whined.

"Children," she said mock exasperatedly, and then hugged them both to her sides. "It's so good to have you home at the same time, and with your partners, too."

Emma didn't point out that Minnesota wasn't her home. To his credit, neither did Ty.

Whereas Saturday had been about showing Jamie the city, Sunday was mostly an indoor day. Specifically, a Mall of America day. Emma couldn't believe they were doing it, but once Jamie heard Ty say there were roller coasters, giant slides, and a zip line, there was clearly only way to spend the afternoon. Other than the slides and zip line, Emma and Bridget stayed on the ground chatting while the rest of the crew—including their mother and Roger—went on every ride, even the SpongeBob and Teenage Mutant Ninja Turtles rides.

This was the most time Emma had ever spent with Bridget. She loved her brother, but it was nice to converse with his future bride all on their own. Bridget, however, seemed less enthralled with the alone time, responding to Emma's questions about her family and her childhood in the Boston suburbs with short, monosyllabic answers until finally she turned to Emma and blurted, "I have to ask you something."

Emma, who had been relaxing against the railing near the TMNT ride entrance, straightened up. "Oh. Okay."

"It's—god, I used to watch you play on television, and now…" She stopped. "I'm sorry. I'm being weird, aren't I?"

Frankly, she was. "Why don't you just ask me whatever it is?" Emma suggested.

Bridget nodded. "Okay. Here goes. Emma, would you consider being one of my bridesmaids? I understand if you can't. I mean, you barely know me, and—"

"I would be honored," Emma said, smiling at the younger woman.

"You would?"

"Completely. I would love it." She started laughing. "I totally thought you were going to ask me something else."

Bridget tilted her head. "Like what?"

"Like, what it's like to play in a World Cup, or if I've ever hung out with the NBA players at the Olympics…"

"I *have* always wondered if you guys get any say over uniform design," Bridget volunteered.

"Unfortunately, no. The federation thinks we're far too opinionated as it is. And in this case, they would be correct." Emma couldn't even imagine the amount of "discussion"— i.e., straight-out arguing—that would be involved were they to be given input into their uniforms. "Anything else? We are about to be sisters, so if you have any other questions about the national team…"

"Are you serious?" Bridget asked, fidgeting with the strap on her purse.

"As long as you promise not to leak anything I tell you to *Sports Illustrated*."

Bridget's questions covered familiar territory, but Emma answered more honestly than she usually did as she confessed that her primary emotion after making her PK in the 2011 World Cup quarterfinals was enormous, overwhelming relief; that losing to Japan a week later was the worst disappointment she'd ever experienced on a soccer

field and yet, at the same time, how gratifying it had been to
see the tears of joy on the face of Ichika Yamamoto, her
Boston Breakers teammate who had lost an aunt and young
cousin in the tsunami; that it was surreal and not as good for
the ego as one might suppose to see her own face in
magazines and on television; and that she felt grateful usually
and overwhelmed occasionally by the responsibility inherent
in being a role model for young girls.

"Thank you," Bridget said as the rest of the family
approached. "Not only for agreeing to be in our wedding but
also for letting me fangirl all over you."

"Of course," Emma said, and slipped her arm around
the younger woman's shoulders. "I'm thrilled to have a part
in your wedding. And I promise, you can always ask me about
soccer. We're family. Or we will be soon, anyway."

Ty and Jamie were riffing off something that had
apparently happened during one of the rides, but he paused
as he saw them standing together. "Everything okay?"

"It's all good," Emma assured him, giving Bridget's
shoulders a squeeze before releasing her.

"Very good," Bridget added, smiling up at Ty as he
kissed her cheek.

"Hey, you." Jamie stopped next to Emma and began to
drift in as if to kiss her, too. Then she caught herself, eyes
widening. "Oh. Whoops. Sorry."

Emma glanced around to see that no one in the vicinity
appeared to be watching them and leaned forward, pressing
her lips quickly to Jamie's cheek. "No worries. Where to
next?"

She didn't think anyone saw the gesture. They'd been
tucked between ride entrances, nearly hidden by the huge
Teenage Mutant Ninja Turtles display, and yet as they walked
through the mall, she felt the old anxiety begin to crystallize.
Ty and Jamie were strutting along with their arms around
each other, singing over and over again, "Yo ho! Look out

below, look out below, when you hear them call, 'Timber!'"
The song came from the Log Chute ride that had featured
giant, animatronic—"and super creepy," Jamie insisted—
versions of Paul Bunyan and his great blue ox, Babe. Bridget
was laughing, and her mom and Roger were smiling
indulgently, but Emma couldn't stop worrying about who
might have seen that ill-conceived kiss, or how a blurry photo
or shaky video might find its way online and be noticed by
Twitter user EmBlakily77, the most recent handle to hijack
her mentions.

"Paul Bunyan supposedly cut down half the forests in
the Midwest," Bridget pointed out. "Not much of an
environmentalist's hero, is he?"

"Yeah, Mom," Ty said, lifting an eyebrow at their
mother. "Not exactly the most environmentally-conscious of
states you're from, is it?"

"I didn't mean—" Bridget started, but their mom
stopped her.

"Don't worry," she said, patting the girl's arm. "Ty and
Emma like to tease me about my home state. I don't take it
personally. I happen to know more about Minnesota than the
two of them will ever allow to penetrate their narrow minds."

"Dang," Ty said to Emma. "Did you hear that?"

"She's just jealous that the Vikings suck and the
Seahawks rock," Emma said.

Ty high-fived her and the conversation moved on to
NFC rivalries, but Emma still couldn't escape the jittery
feeling she remembered well from the last few months of her
relationship with Sam. She'd thought she left it behind for
good when she and Sam broke up, but the old paranoia was
definitely flaring up again.

It wasn't long before Jamie dropped back to walk
beside her. "You okay?"

She nodded quickly. "Fine. Just tired."

"You sure?"

"I'm sure. I'm glad you're here."

And she was. Only, she wished they were back at her mom's house right now watching the NFL or Premier League and yelling at the refs together, their only audience people she was related to. Or maybe back in London where female footballers flew beautifully if problematically under the radar.

It wasn't like they could hide out at home or in foreign capitals forever. But as strangers swirled around them in the largest mall in the country, Emma thought it might be nice for a little while, anyway.

Despite the fact they'd gone to bed early, four-thirty still came way too soon the following morning. The six-thirty AM flight violated Emma's self-imposed travel rules, but it was the only non-stop to Seattle that she and Jamie had been able to switch to that had two seats available in business class. On the plus side, Jamie had taken minimal persuading to borrow enough frequent flyer miles to upgrade her fare.

"Twist your arm?" Emma had joked, and Jamie had simply kissed her, presumably to shut her up. A win-win as far as Emma was concerned.

The town car she'd reserved showed up on time, and even Ty roused himself long enough to see them off, his eyes red-rimmed and cheeks stubbly. As Emma hugged Bridget warmly, she saw her brother do the same with Jamie, their mom standing in the background by herself. And she thought as she sometimes still did, *I wish you were here, Dad.*

Then they were dragging their bags out to the car and collapsing in the warm back seat, where soft music played as the driver navigated the mostly deserted streets between Lake Harriet and the Minneapolis airport. The terminal was busier than the traffic had been, but they made it through security and to their gate in plenty of time, where Emma dozed while Jamie played a video game that Ty had convinced her to download. Some things hadn't changed at all since they were teenagers.

On the plane, Emma asked the older businessman in the seat next to hers if he would mind switching with her "friend," and he agreed readily, though he did give Jamie a side-eye once he realized who he was trading with. Jamie nestled in beside her in time for take-off, during which she held Emma's hand and distracted her from the unnatural act of airplane flight by quizzing her about their New Year's Eve plans with Dani and her boyfriend.

Almost as soon as the seatbelt button dinged, Jamie was up in the aisle, stretching her legs and back and even throwing in a few jumping jacks.

Emma started laughing. "Ty was right. You are like a puppy."

"Takes one to know one." Her head shot up. "Wait. You and Ty were talking about puppies? Is that what you got me for Christmas? A puppy?!"

When Jamie had asked if they could exchange gifts the night she arrived, Emma had had to burst her bubble and tell her that her gift was back at home in Seattle. Now she watched her girlfriend, waiting for the logistics of the situation to sink in.

"What?" Jamie asked. Then her shoulders drooped. "Oh, I get it. You haven't been home in a month, so that would make it a dead puppy, wouldn't it?"

"I promise, I'm not giving you a dead puppy for our first Christmas together."

"Might be kind of hard to explain to the kids later. What is it, then?"

Emma's heart fluttered at Jamie's casual reference to their future progeny. "Like I'd tell you, Maxwell."

"Fine," she said, and pouted, her lips eminently kissable.

Emma didn't press her in return. Knowing Jamie, she'd

cave and tell Emma what she'd gotten her. (*See*, Emma thought. *I like* some *kinds of surprises.*)

After a few tai chi exercises, Jamie sat back down. They chatted about Christmas presents they'd given and received both this year and in the past, which led somehow to reminiscing about the flight to Seattle they'd shared after Jamie's first residency camp the previous December. Perhaps because she hadn't yet consumed enough coffee, Emma found herself confessing that when the flight attendant told her what a cute couple they were, she hadn't bothered to correct him.

"Well, we are," Jamie said. "So you were having impure thoughts about me even then, huh?"

Emma swatted her shoulder. "No! Well, maybe a few. But I'm not the one who thought—" she lowered her voice in case anyone within a ten-foot radius was listening "—that someone was trying to get me to join the mile high club." As Jamie grinned and lifted her eyebrows suggestively, Emma recoiled. "Not a chance. Talk about a violation of the personal conduct clause."

"It was worth a shot."

Dang it. Now she really was having impure thoughts.

Emma retrieved the deck of cards her mother—er, *Santa*—had put in her stocking. "Anyway, didn't you promise to teach me your favorite card game?"

"That's right." Jamie's smile turned competitive. "Let's see what you got, Blake."

Over the next half hour, Jamie taught her a game called Bastard that she claimed to have played obsessively with Britt back in their Arsenal Ladies days, whiling away many a rainy English night. But Emma, who was "a god-damned natural," according to Jamie, kept winning, and winning, and winning some more. Eventually Jamie threw her cards down on the tray so hard that it shook the business-suited traveler in front of them. After Jamie apologized to the stranger, they agreed that maybe card games weren't the best way to pass the flight.

"I asked my mom about my dad yesterday," Emma announced. The words sort of flew out. Once again, she blamed her non-caffeinated state.

"You mean about me?" Jamie asked.

"Yeah. It turns out he didn't dislike you. My mom says he was worried about me getting too close to you because..." She paused, her brain finally cluing in to the decided lack of wisdom in broaching this particular subject at this particular time and place. A bit late to change courses now, though, so she rushed ahead: "She said your mother told him you'd recently experienced a trauma and weren't, um, in the best place."

"She told your dad about *France*?" Jamie demanded. "Before you and I were even friends?"

"Not in any detail. Though the words self-harm might have been used. I think." Emma nearly clapped a hand over her mouth. Jesus. What was her problem?

"You think." Jamie flexed her fingers against her thighs. "Wow. I did not see that coming, and yet, I totally should have."

"At least now we know he wasn't being homophobic," she offered.

Jamie frowned at her. "No, he just thought I was going to embroil you in some tragic lesbian suicide plot. That's not homophobic at all."

When she put it that way... "Right. Valid point."

"Gee, thanks." Jamie's tone was curt and she looked away, chewing on her thumb nail.

Emma reached for her hand and tugged it down, smoothing one finger over the nail's jagged edge. "Don't."

"Seriously?" Jamie pulled her hand back, her expression settling into something harder than Emma was used to. "Things don't always have to be perfect, Emma."

"I know that."

"Do you? Because I'm not so sure."

"Is this about me beating you at cards?" Emma asked, and then wished she hadn't as Jamie snorted, eyes pinning her in place. "Okay, so it's not about the cards."

Abruptly Jamie stood. "I'm going to the bathroom," she said, and stalked away, her movements short and choppy.

*Great.* Emma glanced out the window, for once unconcerned that she was in a large metal container a mile above the earth. Mostly.

When Jamie returned from the bathroom, Emma tried to catch her eye. "Hey."

"What." It came out flat, unquestioning.

"What did I do?"

"Nothing." Jamie rummaged through her backpack.

Emma tamped down the urge to throttle her girlfriend. It was her own fault for bringing up a sensitive subject when they were stuck on an airplane surrounded by strangers. "Don't shut me out, Jamie," she said, channeling her mom from the previous morning. "I can't fix it if you don't tell me what's wrong."

"Not everything has to be fixed, Emma. That's sort of the point here." Jamie gave her a look laced with something like contempt. No, Emma corrected herself—with *actual* contempt.

"Fine. Not everything has to be fixed," she said shortly, and reached for her headphones. She dialed up a recent playlist, turned her head to the window, and closed her eyes.

Normally she slept better with Jamie beside her, but not this time. This time she couldn't get her mind to quiet, couldn't get the image of Jamie staring at her with such condescension out of her mind. Her father used to say, "The best defense is a good offense." The phrase echoed in her mind now, and she pictured Jo Nichols and the last video review session in Brazil, when Jo had criticized Emma's lack of offensive production in front of the whole team. She'd said complimentary things as well, and Emma wasn't the only one who felt the sting of her critique. Although perhaps words like "criticize" and "critique" weren't entirely accurate. Jo was a straight shooter, a direct communicator, but not unnecessarily harsh like Jeff Bradbury, their old coach. She simply pointed out what she observed, and if the player had done well, then the observation was positive; if they hadn't, her commentary reflected that fact.

Beside her, Jamie shifted restlessly, her knee jumping. She was clearly upset, and the recognition thawed some of the coldness in Emma's chest.

"Hey," she said, reaching for her hand.

But Jamie moved out of her reach. "Leave it, Emma." Her voice cracked slightly, and she turned her head away.

For the next hour, Emma read an ebook Ellie had recommended on fostering a scoring mentality, glancing at Jamie every so often to see if she might be ready to talk. But Jamie remained quiet through the rest of the flight, only relenting when the plane bucked semi-violently as they descended toward the airport runway. But even then she held Emma's hand almost furtively, her eyes forward as the plane landed and taxied to the terminal.

At baggage claim she played on her phone while they waited for their luggage, and then she stared resolutely out the window on the cab ride back to Queen Anne. Emma played on her own phone, relieved to see that her social media accounts were blissfully quiet even as she contemplated her next move with Jamie. Would she listen if Emma apologized? Maybe Jamie was PMSing. She was so fit that she didn't get her period regularly, but that didn't mean her hormones couldn't act up. Still, Emma didn't imagine that any query after her possibly fluctuating hormones would be well received.

When they reached the condo, Emma dropped her bags in the hall and turned on a light. It wasn't even lunch time on the West Coast, but winter clouds hung low and thick, lending the city an air of twilight.

"So?" she said, tone even as she turned to face her girlfriend.

"So." Jamie watched her, expression maddeningly neutral. "I think we should talk."

Oh, god. Was this a "We need to talk" moment? Emma swallowed nervously and led the way to the couch in the living room. They weren't about to break up, she assured herself. Jamie wasn't about to walk away from everything they had. They loved each other and had for years upon years. People in love didn't break up over a single conversation. Did they?

"I'm sorry," Jamie said once they were seated.

Emma braced herself for what was coming next: *I can't do this anymore*, or maybe *It isn't you, it's me*. She hadn't seen this coming. Should she have seen this coming?

"I shouldn't have reacted like that," Jamie continued, and Emma felt the relief pour through her, raw and almost frightening in its intensity. "You were right. I was cranky about losing the stupid card game. I think the thing about your dad just touched a sore spot."

"I'm sorry too," Emma said quickly, words almost tripping over themselves. "I should have been more sensitive. A crowded plane wasn't the right place for that conversation."

Jamie nodded. "Thank you for acknowledging that. I get that from your perspective it was good news, like, 'Hey, my mom said my dad wasn't a homophobe after all, yay!' But to me it sounded like you were taking your parents' side. Like you thought I belonged on the outside of your family and not on the inside."

Emma frowned. Why did there need to be sides of any

kind here? Her father was long gone, and she and Jamie were adults, living their lives away from their families. She almost said as much, but then she heard her mother's voice in the back of her head reminding her of the importance of listening to and empathizing with other people, especially when they were upset. She thought about how Jamie's voice had cracked on the plane, how it had felt to ride through the Seattle traffic beside her but apart, how shockingly fragile their connection ultimately was. If she wanted, Jamie could hop on a train or a bus to Portland and they wouldn't have to speak again until January camp. If then. From experience, Emma knew it was possible to avoid someone at residency camp, even if that someone was the person you cared about more than all the others combined.

She took a breath and reigned in her defensiveness, because this was not the time for a good offense. Instead she asked, "Why did it feel like that to you? That I was putting you on the outside of my family, I mean."

Beside her on the couch, Jamie ran a hand over her short hair, leaving the longer swoop in front disheveled. "Do you know that not one father of anyone I've ever dated has reacted well to meeting me? They've all been somewhere on the negative spectrum—either shocked, or confused, or outright hostile. Not once has a girlfriend's father smiled at me and told me it's nice to meet me. The mothers, either— except yours, and we weren't dating when I met her."

Emma frowned. "That sucks." By contrast, she couldn't remember a single instance of a partner's parent treating her with anything other than easy acceptance— except Jamie's mom. But, again, they hadn't been dating back then.

"It does suck," Jamie agreed. "Your mom is the first one to hug me right off the bat, and I did feel welcome this weekend. But then you tell me that she doesn't think your dad was homophobic even though he was officially on record as saying you should stay the hell away from me? I guess it feels like I can't win with the whole parental approval thing."

Again Emma's first reaction was to blurt out that Jamie didn't understand, that she hadn't heard her mom's explanation about research and peer groups and worrying late into the night about your children's friends' potential inability to navigate a difficult world. But that was an explanation best left for later because Jamie wasn't talking about Emma's parents. She was trying to tell Emma how it felt to be her in that admittedly difficult world.

"I'm sorry," she said again, reaching out hesitantly to touch Jamie's hand. "The last thing I want is to make you feel like an outsider in my family. My mom does care about you, and she's genuinely happy that we're together. So is Ty— which I think you already know."

Jamie turned her palm up and wove their fingers together. "No, you're right. I think this is just my baggage talking. Or, you know, one luggage set of many."

Emma released a laugh that was more a vent of tension than amusement, gripping Jamie's hand tightly. "Join the club, my friend."

"The woman-loving-woman emotional baggage club?" Jamie queried, a hint of a smile curling her lips.

"That's the one." Emma hesitated. "Is this just about parental approval? Because I sort of get the feeling there's more to this whole outsider thing."

Jamie traced the tendons along the top of Emma's hand. "I've always felt like I don't belong in very many places. That's one of the things I love about soccer. It's not about how you look or feel on the inside, it's about how hard you work and what you bring to the team. Because off the pitch?" She shook her head and leaned back against the couch, staring up at the ceiling. "Things are never quite as simple."

"You're right, they aren't," Emma agreed. "Especially on cold, dark mornings when you have to be up at four-thirty AM…"

Jamie narrowed her eyes, but playfully. "Excuse you. Are you suggesting I don't do well on cold, dark, early mornings?"

"I was talking about myself," Emma said. "But sure, we can go with you."

"How about both of us?"

"Sounds accurate." She rested her chin on one hand. "If neither of us does well in the cold and dark, maybe we should rethink the whole retiring to Northern Europe plan."

"Couldn't be much worse than the Pacific Northwest, could it?" Jamie nodded to the wall of windows, where the Space Needle was lit up against the dusky afternoon. Then she moved closer and hid her head in Emma's shoulder. "Does that mean you still love me enough to want to retire with me?"

"What?" Emma craned her neck to see Jamie's face. "Are you kidding me, Maxwell? If a decade of you freezing me out wasn't enough to kill my feelings for you, what makes you think a couple of hours would get it done?"

"I wasn't freezing you out," Jamie muttered. Then, as Emma remained pointedly silent, she added, "Fine, I was. But it was your own fault for beating me at cards."

"I can't help it if I'm a 'god-damned natural, for eff's sake,'" she air-quoted. Jamie tried to pull away, but Emma wrapped her arms around her and refused to let go. "I love you, Jamie. That's not going to change."

"I love you too." Jamie paused. "Though I think I might love you even more if you feed me."

Food and coffee, Emma thought, practically salivating. "Your wish is my command," she said as they unfolded from the couch.

"No it isn't."

"No, it isn't. But how about we open Christmas presents after lunch? Will that make up for the cold, dark, early morning?"

"Hells yes," Jamie said, perking up immediately. She cast her gaze about the living room. "Where is it? I thought you said it was here."

"It is here. Just not in this room." Emma was glad she'd had the foresight to place Jamie's gift in the bedroom before she left. It was almost as if she had hoped Jamie would visit her in Minnesota and then fly home with her—because it was exactly like that.

Jamie pretended to sniff the air. "Hmm, no dead puppy smell. That's a relief. I give up. What is it?"

"Food and hot beverages first, then presents."

"Aw," Jamie whined, and Emma had a flash of Christmas Yet-to-Come: Jamie and their future children racing each other to see what Santa had brought them. Would Jamie let the kids win? Seemed unlikely.

Life was good, she thought as she tugged Jamie toward the kitchen, the worry and overwhelming sense of fragility dissipating like fog from the Sound. More importantly, *they* were good, and soon there would be presents.

She couldn't wait to see Jamie's face.

# CHAPTER TWELVE

To be honest, this was not the face Emma had expected.

"What the hell is that?" Jamie demanded, her brow thunderously low.

"It's a bicycle."

"Obviously."

"You asked." Emma rested the gift in question in the corner against the recliner. "What is the problem? I want to be able to go for a bike ride with my girlfriend. Is that so terrible?"

"I already have a bike," Jamie said. "One that I'm guessing cost a third of what this does."

A quarter would probably be more accurate, but Emma decided not to mention it. "Yes," she said fake patiently, "but it is currently in Portland, is it not?"

Jamie stared at her. "So you're saying this is a second bike for guests?"

Emma stared back. "Is that what you want me to say?"

She folded her arms across her chest. "I think so."

"Fine," Emma huffed. "In that case, yes. For your Christmas present, I bought myself a second bike so that we can go on bike rides when you visit. Is that acceptable?"

"I guess," Jamie said grudgingly.

Two minutes later she was reading the manual, eyes wide as she discovered the various bells and whistles on her new hybrid road bike. That, Emma thought, watching her, was the face she had expected. She enjoyed Jamie's enthusiasm for a little while longer before finally saying, "Hello. Still waiting over here for my present."

"Oh, sorry!" Jamie scrambled up and made a beeline for her luggage in the hall, where she paused and glanced over her shoulder at Emma. "It's not... it's nothing like what you got me."

Emma winked at her. "That's okay. I don't need a new bike."

"Neither do I," Jamie pointed out. She rummaged through her carry-on and stood back up, a paper bag in her hands. "I didn't wrap it. Wrapping paper is bad for the environment, you know?"

"It's fine. I don't need wrapping paper, either."

Jamie sat down beside her on the couch, hesitated, and then handed the bag over.

It wasn't one present but three. The first was a flat box with a silver photo frame inside. Curious, she turned it over. It was a double four by six frame, hinged along the horizontal edge, and inside—

"No way," she said, laughing as she found herself staring into her teenage self's eyes. The photo on the left was of the two of them at the beach ten years ago almost to the day, arms around each other's shoulders, smiles wide and untroubled. They had been so young, hadn't they?

On the right side of the frame was a more recent shot she didn't remember being taken, from the night in May their teams met for the first time. They were seated on the bench at the brew-pub they'd gone to in downtown Portland afterward, shoulders pressed together, heads turned toward each other, smiling dreamily. It was a stunning shot—the definition of heart eyes.

"Ellie?" she asked.

"Yep. I was moaning about not having a good enough picture and she was all, 'Hey, I might have something on my phone.' The asshat."

"Total asshat," Emma agreed. "What was that beach called?"

"Stinson."

"That's right." She skimmed her fingers over their younger faces. They hadn't changed all that much, and yet, that day felt like it had happened to two entirely different people.

The second gift was a notebook full of coupons. Upon closer examination, Emma realized Jamie must have created them in one of the many photo software programs on her laptop because they contained their names and other personal details. She leafed through the bound notebook, each page sporting a different entry. There were massage coupons, date night coupons that let Emma pick the restaurant, movie coupons that gave her the power to choose the movie—even if Jamie objected, according to the fine print. There were even a couple of coupons that let Emma skip her turn to drive to Portland and make Jamie come to Seattle instead.

"I love it," she declared, wiggling her eyebrows somewhat wickedly.

"Crap," Jamie said. "I've created a monster, haven't I?"

"Muahaha! You have no idea."

Emma reached through tissue paper for the last item in the bag. And then she stopped as her eyes fell on the cover of a book she had long since given up for lost. "You kept it," she breathed.

"Meg did, actually. She found it in her room last week. I thought you might like it back."

Emma set the book on her lap and traced its well-worn

cover. *The Mountains of California* by John Muir—her father's favorite book. She opened it and, sure enough, there was his sloped, impatient handwriting: "Emma ~ May you one day share our family's love of the mountains with children of your own. Much love, Dad."

She blinked back the inevitable tears. "Thank you. I love everything."

"You're welcome," Jamie said, and kissed her sweetly. "I love you."

"I love you too. Merry Christmas, Jamie."

"Merry Christmas, Emma."

The day went on outside the condo, but they stayed where they were, mugs in hand, legs touching under a fleece blanket that bore the Sounders logo. Despite her earlier inclination, Emma ended up telling Jamie what her mother had said about peer groups and their influence, and Jamie seemed better able to listen this time.

"That does make sense," she admitted, rubbing her thumb over the faded UNC decal on her mug. "Even I can see it over the massive chip on my shoulder."

"You don't have—" Emma started, but then she stopped as Jamie gazed at her. Because, yeah, she sort of did. "That reminds me. Can I ask you something?"

"Fire away."

"You said earlier that you love soccer because it doesn't matter how you feel on the inside. Does that mean you feel different on the inside? Like, are you...?"

"Trans?" Jamie supplied. "Yeah, I fall under the umbrella. But I don't feel like a man trapped in a woman's body. I'm actually lucky because I love my body. It's been good to me with soccer and everything else. I think I feel more like an androgynous person living as a woman, if that makes sense."

Emma thought hard, trying to grasp the difference.

"Okay, apparently that doesn't make sense to you," Jamie said, half-smiling.

"I'm sorry. I'm not trying to offend you."

"Babe, it takes a lot more than that to offend me." As Emma squinted and tilted her head sideways, Jamie amended, "Usually. On non-cold, non-early mornings. Anyway, have you ever heard of the genderbread person?"

Emma hadn't, so Jamie found a PDF on Google and they spent the next few minutes discussing the differences between gender identity, sexual attraction, gender expression, and biological sex. As they talked, Emma discovered that she didn't know nearly as much as she'd thought she did going into this conversation. The diagram helped immensely, and she downloaded it onto her phone for future reference.

The fact that Jamie considered herself genderqueer—a blend of both male and female rather than one or the other— wasn't news. But until now, Emma hadn't fully understood what that identity meant to her.

"A few of my friends in college would have preferred to have been born biologically male," Jamie told her, "but I'm glad I was born female. Being a man is way more risky."

Emma frowned. "How can you say that? What about France?"

"It's because of France I'm saying that. I would rather be a rape survivor than a potential rapist, Emma. That may sound harsh, but I had a friend at Stanford who transitioned, and he said testosterone should be registered as a chemical weapon because it basically produces weaponized human beings."

That sounded about right, Emma thought, picturing various comments she'd observed or fielded herself on social media platforms where misogyny ran rampant. But the Internet wasn't the only or even the main place where women were vulnerable. Look at Jamie. Look at the girls and women all over the world harassed and assaulted on a daily basis, some of whom were targeted for rape as part of "official military strategy." Weaponized humans, indeed.

"Can I ask *you* something?" Jamie added.

"Of course."

"Did Sam identify as genderqueer?"

For the second time in as many days, that was not the question Emma had been expecting. "Not when we were together. But she never really liked the word queer. The kids in her neighborhood on Long Island used to play a game called Smear the Queer, and she said she could never quite get that connotation out of her head."

"That would be difficult to forget." She paused, and when she spoke again, her voice was quieter. "So what really happened with you two, anyway?"

Emma took a sip of her long cold coffee. Temperature wasn't everything. The beverage still tasted good, still gave her that slight, pleasant jolt of energy. In Boston, where summers were hot and humid, she used to drink her body weight each week in iced coffee. Or so Sam had always said.

"The World Cup happened," she told Jamie. "There was so much scrutiny, and I was on the road even more than usual. Sam finally decided it wasn't what she wanted."

This was the official story Emma had developed after Sam's exit, and it was accurate as far as it went. Only a few people—Dani, Maddie, a handful of others—knew it wasn't the entire story. Jamie wasn't one of those people. But right now, she was looking at Emma as if she might be.

"That's it?" she asked. "She left because you were away too much?"

As she hesitated, Emma was struck by the sense that they had been here before. Not this exact situation, but close. Except that when they were kids, Emma had lied by omission to protect herself. Now she was doing it to protect Jamie. Either way, it was not the brightest thing she'd ever done. She needed to tell her the truth. She *wanted* to tell her. Just, not yet. Jamie still had occasional bad days, still suffered from PTSD triggers and probably, she'd admitted to Emma, always would. But for the most part, she had moved past the assault. For the most part, she was a happy, healthy human being. Emma couldn't bear to be the person who might set her back. For now, she wanted that specific set of emotional luggage to remain packed away as long as it possibly could.

She couldn't lie to Jamie, either, so she dodged: "Why are you asking about this now?"

"Ty said something about you guys the other day."

Ty had adored Sam. Was it possible he knew why she'd left? "What exactly did he say?"

"Nothing specific, only that I should be worried about what you brought to the table. When I asked what he meant, he said 'the Sam thing.' That was it."

Well, shit. He definitely knew. The realization made Emma squeeze her arms in close to her sides, as if she could ward off the memories of her terror for Sam—and herself— by becoming physically smaller, less visible.

"Something did happen with Sam and me," she admitted. "Something that was pretty terrible at the time. One day fairly soon I imagine I'll feel like talking about it. But honestly, I'd rather not right now. If that's okay?"

Jamie's knuckles whitened as she clutched her mug in both hands. Then she shook her head. "You don't owe me your past, Emma. There are plenty of things from previous relationships that I probably won't ever tell you."

Emma eyed her skeptically again. "Really?"

"Oh." Jamie cleared her throat. "Well, maybe not. But only because you're cute and I'm not very good at saying no to you."

"You're cute, too," Emma said, and kissed her, tasting the bitterness of green tea on her lips. She pulled back and rested their foreheads together. "Thank you."

Jamie didn't ask her for what. She simply nodded. "You're welcome."

Emma settled against her. "I know we should go work out—the beep test is less than a week away, yegads—but I would love a nap. What do you think?"

"Work-out, shmerk-out. I second the nap option."

Emma felt Jamie's arms tighten around her, and she relaxed even more, closing her eyes and luxuriating in the feel of her girlfriend's warm, strong body against hers. They would be okay. 2015 might not be perfect any more than 2014 had been, but it *was* going to be good, if Emma had anything to say about it. They would win the World Cup and ride off into the sunset. *They would win the World Cup and ride off into the sunset.* THEY WOULD WIN THE WORLD CUP AND RIDE OFF INTO THE SUNSET!

This time, she believed it. At least, she did with Jamie curled around her, the two of them keeping each other warm and safe as they dozed the afternoon away.

*   *   *

On the last day of the soon-to-be old year, Jamie sat in the recliner in the corner reading as Emma stood before the sliding glass balcony door, her back to the living room. Or rather, she tried to focus on the *Star Wars* novel she'd downloaded to her iPad, but her attention kept returning to her girlfriend, whose shoulders were hunched as she stared out across the city skyline, phone to her ear.

In the near distance, Jamie could see people and machines crawling over the Space Needle, readying it for the big event later that night. She was psyched she would get to see the Seattle fireworks from Emma's condo this year. Last year she'd been newly single when she rang in the start of 2014 in San Francisco, and even then part of her had wondered how Emma was celebrating, whether or not she had someone to kiss at midnight. This New Year's Eve, Jamie would be the someone kissing Emma at midnight—a surreal concept, but considerably less so after dating her the past eleven months.

"Okay," Emma said into the phone. "I guess that's it then. Thanks for all your work on this, Ellie. I'm sorry we couldn't get it done." She listened for a moment. "Don't worry, we won't. You and Jodie either, okay? Happy New Year." She ended the call and turned, tossing her phone at the couch where it bounced once before settling.

"So...?" Jamie gazed up at her without much hope.

Emma twisted her hands together. "It's over. We're dropping the suit."

"Shit. I'm sorry." Jamie set her Kindle aside and patted her leg in invitation. Soon Emma was seated on her lap, face tucked into her neck. Jamie readjusted their combined weight and murmured, "So FIFA's still being a giant bag of dicks?"

Emma exhaled a short laugh into her skin. "Yes, the bastards." She gazed up at Jamie, serious again. "Their attorneys made it clear that even if the court orders them to provide grass, they won't comply."

"What? They can't do that, can they?"

"They can and they would, which means this lawsuit has zero chance of affecting any change. General consensus among the players is that with the tournament so close, we need to shift our attention away from politics and back to the game."

"I can't believe they're still refusing to negotiate on this. What the hell? It's not even like it would be that expensive. There are companies who would love the exposure."

"Preaching to the choir, babe." Emma waved at the Kindle. "How's Luke Skywalker and fam?"

"They're not in it yet. I'm not that far in, though."

Rhea, Becca's wife, had recommended the novel *Aftermath*, first in a trilogy set in the period between *Return of the Jedi* and *The Force Awakens*, after Jamie had mentioned how much she'd loved the new teaser trailer for *TFA*. Another good thing about 2015: for the first time in ten years, a new *Star Wars* movie would be in theaters. And this one, rumor had it, offered a female main character who—no offense to Princess Leia Organa or Queen Padme Amidala—was a total badass. Jamie couldn't wait for the fan fiction that would be written about the new character, since lord knew there weren't likely to be lesbians in the latest trilogy either.

"Any girl-on-girl action?" Emma asked.

"Sadly, no."

"Wow, and you're still reading it?"

"It's *Star Wars*," Jamie said, as if the reason for reading were obvious.

The *Star Wars* franchise was an institution that each generation connected with in its own unique way. Jamie didn't require queer characters to enjoy the story—although if Daisy Ridley's lead (or any other non-Imperial female character, for that matter) in *The Force Awakens* ended up being into women, that would only make the franchise that much greater in Jamie's estimation. Still, she wasn't holding her breath. She doubted she would survive if she did.

With effort, she set the awesomeness that was *Star Wars* aside and steered the conversation back on topic. "How do you feel? About dropping the lawsuit, I mean."

"Pissed off. Frustrated. Their behavior is completely unacceptable. But at the same time..." She toyed with the strings on Jamie's hoodie. "It's not a shock, is it? They made it clear from the start that they weren't going to budge, and sure enough, they haven't."

"Maybe not a shock, but it is disappointing."

"You're right. It's a huge disappointment. In fact, I'd call it a giant load of—"

"—you-know-what kind of hooey," Jamie finished with her. "You know the best way to show the boys at FIFA how wrong they are? Fill the seats and dazzle the global audience."

For once at a women's event, that would be possible. The announcement had come while they were in Brazil—an early holiday gift, the team had agreed—that Fox was planning to broadcast 200 hours of World Cup coverage. That figure worked out to somewhere between six and seven hours of television coverage *per day* during the month-long competition. Not only would the 2015 World Cup be the largest women's cup in history, with twenty-four teams instead of the usual sixteen participating in group play, it would also have the largest potential audience of any previous women's soccer tournament. Ever.

Emma nodded. "FIFA refuses to spend money on us because they say no one cares about the women's game. I hope we make them eat their fucking words next summer." She paused and took what Jamie assumed was meant to be a calming breath. "Anyway, enough about the giant bag of dicks. Ellie said not to let them affect our New Year's Eve. Captain's orders."

Jamie tapped her chin thoughtfully. "But does she have jurisdiction here? Because I'm pretty sure we're not on team time now."

"Good thing, too." Emma moved forward until her lips were only inches away. "Because we have just enough time for me to ravish you before Dani and Derek get here."

"We do, do we? In that case…"

The ravishing had to take place in the shower because they'd spent the first half of the day at the soccer academy in Tukwila where Emma trained in the off-season. Since they were planning a mostly exercise-free New Year's Day, they'd put in an extra-long workout today, taking advantage of the mild temperatures and rare rainless skies. Clear skies that would, Jamie hoped, make tonight's fireworks show even better.

She was still pulling on her collared shirt when the doorbell rang. Emma was in the bathroom working on her make-up, so Jamie buzzed Dani and her boyfriend up and then speed-buttoned her shirt, barely getting it tucked in and her red and silver striped bow-tie fastened before the familiar knock sounded.

"Hola, babes," Emma's best friend said, bursting through the door with her usual sassy smile, a bottle of champagne in each hand.

"Hey guys!" Jamie hugged Dani with one hand and accepted a champagne bottle with the other. She waved slightly at Derek, who stepped forward to give her a warm hug.

"Where's Blake?" Dani asked, stripping off her jacket.

"Still getting ready." Jamie chose to ignore Dani's knowing smirk. "Can I take your coats?" she asked, playing host as if the condo was her home too. She spent more time in Seattle than Portland these days, so it wasn't that far from the truth.

When Emma emerged from the bedroom a few minutes later, Jamie watched her approach, taking in her hair falling around her shoulders in a cascade of loose curls, her thigh-length scoop-neck dress—*red for the holidays, dontcha know*, she had said earlier—and the black leggings that emphasized her muscular legs. Legs that had been wrapped around Jamie's waist only a little while earlier…

Dani elbowed her. "Breathe, Max."

Good advice, really.

"You look beautiful." She kissed Emma's cheek, careful not to smudge her lipstick.

"So do you." Emma smiled as she took in Jamie's tailored gray dress pants, red bow-tie, and collared shirt— dark green, she'd told Emma earlier, because "together we make Christmas." Emma had laughed at her cheesiness, but in a good way, Jamie was pretty sure.

"Happy New Year!" Dani said, and surged forward to hug Emma. "Now let's get drunk!"

And with that, the dinner party had officially begun. Jamie wasn't sure that it technically counted as a dinner party, seeing as it was only three-thirty. They'd decided to start early in order to achieve their goal: bingeing the first three episodes of *Star Wars* before midnight.

"Technically, we're watching the *middle* three episodes," Jamie noted as she loaded *A New Hope* into the DVD player. Derek nodded in agreement while Emma and Dani only stared blankly at her. "You know, because four through six were released first, with one through three following later? *The Force Awakens* will actually be episode seven."

Dani glanced at Emma. "You're right. She *is* an even bigger nerd than you."

"Ha, ha," Jamie said, side-eyeing Emma's best friend.

"Oh, I wasn't joking, Max."

Emma patted the couch cushion next to her, and Jamie settled in beside her, bending forward momentarily to stick her tongue out at Dani. The other woman only rolled her eyes and nestled in against her boyfriend.

This was awesome, Jamie decided a few minutes later as John Williams's famous score echoed through the surround speakers. She was tired and loose from their epic workout, both at the training facility and in Emma's shower, and they were cuddling on the couch together, Emma's best friend and her boyfriend here with them, and the original *Star Wars* movie was on Emma's television, the opening words arcing dramatically away into the star-pricked backdrop of space. Jamie had seen this movie a dozen times, and the beginning still gave her goose bumps.

Beside her, Emma reached for her hand, and Jamie sighed in contentment. It was still early, but already this was shaping up to be the *Best. New Year's Eve. Ever.*

They managed to keep their hunger somewhat at bay by feasting on Trader Joe's popcorn and Dani's fruity champagne concoctions, but as soon as the movie ended everyone agreed that it was time for dinner. Derek had volunteered to make his mother's famous candied yams and cornbread, while Jamie contributed a kale and wild rice salad. Emma baked a huge salmon filet, and Dani—well, she kept the alcohol and conversation flowing.

By the time they sat down to dinner, Jamie was tipsier than she could remember being in months. Good thing she and Emma weren't planning on working out the following day. She had a feeling they would be sleeping in. Sleeping it off? Whatever.

Dinner vacillated between silence as they feasted on the "gorgeous spread" to noisy laughter as Emma and Dani attempted to one-up each other with intimate revelations intended to wow their respective partners.

"I'm not the one who nearly got Pearl Jam lyrics tattooed on my ass," Dani teased at one point.

"Not my ass!" Emma protested. "It was the small of my back."

"I believe I also talked you out of a Manchester United tattoo," Dani revealed.

Jamie pretended to bow to her. "You have my eternal gratitude. I don't think I could date a woman with a Man U tat."

"Oi, now, don't be bashing my boys," Emma said.

Dani snorted. "Don't tell me you're becoming one of those wankers who uses British slang and calls soccer 'football' and the field a 'pitch.'"

"Um, I'd like to point out that 'wanker' is British slang," Emma said. "Besides, it's called 'football' in the entire rest of the world, and I would argue that 'pitch' makes significantly more sense than 'field.'"

"She is dating a bonafide English footballer," Jamie said.

"A *former* English footballer," Dani corrected.

"Still current for a few more months—we made it to Champions League quarterfinals in March."

"That's right," Derek said. "Congrats, man. Who else is through?"

"Paris-St. Germain, who we play next, Bristol Academy, Frankfurt, Wolfsburg, and a couple of Swedish teams you've never heard of. Oh, and Lyon."

Jamie's lips pursed as they always did whenever she had to say the word *Lyon*. If Arsenal and Lyon both made it out of the quarterfinals alive, that would set up a semifinal meeting between the two clubs in April, and then she would have to decide if she was ready to set foot in the French city where she'd lost a part of herself all those years ago. As if 2015 wasn't already shaping up to be one unremitting test of her emotional fortitude… Maybe Emma was right. Maybe it was time she called Shoshanna.

Beside her, Emma covered her hand, and Jamie could see the unspoken support in her eyes. Immediately the tension settling over her loosened, and she nodded back. All Emma had to do was touch her and she relaxed. It was like a Pavlovian response—or the opposite, maybe. Weren't there studies that showed touching a dog lowered one's blood pressure?

Wait, who was the dog in this scenario? Jamie felt another giggle building. Yeah, might be time to slow down on the whole booze-guzzling thing.

"Did you say in March?" Dani lifted a brow in a way Jamie used to find intimidating. "What about the—what do you guys call the Algarve?"

"The Golf and Wine Cup," Emma supplied.

"Right. Won't Champions League interfere with that?"

"Assuming I make the roster for the Algarve," Jamie said, hearing the edge in her own voice, "no, it wouldn't. Champions League is later, at the end of the month."

"You'll make the roster," Dani said confidently. "Have you seen you play, Jamie? Because I have. They'd be idiots to leave you off the team, and Jo Nichols is no idiot. That Craig guy, maybe, but not her."

Maybe it was the champagne talking, but Jamie felt a rush of warmth. She'd played against Dani in college, and from what she remembered, Dani was more than a decent soccer player herself. Her assessment—especially her opinion of "that Craig guy," as Jamie was fairly certain he would now forever be immortalized in her brain—carried more weight because she was Emma's friend, not Jamie's, and also because she called things like she saw them.

They finished off almost every bit of food they'd prepared, with only a couple of servings left of the cornbread and kale salad. Jamie had purposely made extra salad so they would have leftovers on New Year's Day. She was hoping she and Emma wouldn't have to leave the condo at all. They hadn't had a day to lay around reading and watching movies since their spontaneous European vacation. Although knowing them, they would plan to do nothing and then end up going for "a short run" that would take them across the Ballard Bridge, through Fremont, and back up Queen Anne Hill. You know, just to stretch their legs.

"What is it about lesbians and kale?" Dani asked as they cleaned up the kitchen. "Jasmine, Derek's super gay sister, has it with practically every meal, I swear."

"It's true," he agreed, wiping down the stove and counter with a rag. "She's like a kale disciple who proselytizes its wonders every chance she gets."

"It's in the lesbian contract," Jamie said. "If you're bi, you get to choose between kale and spinach."

Emma, drying dishes while Jamie washed, cracked up. Then she alertly caught the chunk of cornbread Dani lobbed at Jamie's head and popped it in her mouth.

"That fell on the floor," Dani said smugly.

Emma froze, but then she shrugged. "Your stomach acid kills almost everything anyway."

It was Jamie's turn to crack up. That line was one that Meg liked to pull out at opportune moments, as Emma had learned in person that fall in Utah.

Once the kitchen was clean, they started *The Empire Strikes Back*, but only got halfway through before pausing to watch the ball drop in New York. Afterward, they made the mistake of flipping around the channels, distracted by fireworks shows from various parts of the globe where it was already 2015. By the time they remembered they were on a movie-viewing schedule, they'd run out of time to watch the third movie—as, they agreed, they were probably always going to do. They finished *The Empire Strikes Back* and turned the TV to local coverage, chatting amongst themselves as the newscasters interviewed the crowd assembled at the Space Needle down the hill from Emma's street.

"Hey," Dani said at one point, "we could always go down to Seattle Center and ring in the new year with the masses. What do you guys think?"

Jamie noticed Derek looking almost panicked at his girlfriend's suggestion. Which was weird, but who was she to judge other people's irrational fears? Then again, navigating a crowd of drunken strangers wasn't exactly her thing, either.

"I don't know," she said. "Isn't Seattle Center more for people from the suburbs?"

Dani tossed her long hair, nearly hitting Derek in the face. "Fine. It was only a thought."

Beyond her, Derek nodded slightly at Jamie as if she had done him a solid. Weird again. She would have to remember to ask him about it later.

Shortly before midnight, they bundled up in fleece and scarves and went out on the balcony to enjoy the cool, clear weather as the countdown to 2015 continued. Emma played the TV through her blue tooth speakers so that they would be able to hear the music accompanying the fireworks. As the clock ticked down, Jamie thought of her parents and the Millers holding down the same square of waterfront park in San Francisco, Becca and Rhea with them because Rhea wasn't going to let something like being absurdly pregnant make them miss a time-honored family tradition despite Becca's worry that someone might bump into her and hurt her and/or the babies. Jamie missed being there with them, but at the same time she was thrilled to be here in Seattle with Emma, leaning against her balcony railing arm in arm watching the lights flickering across the city, waiting for the clock to strike midnight so that they could celebrate the end of one year and the beginning of another where they should be: together.

And then the TV announcer was shouting out the final countdown, and the lights along the base of the Space Needle were going off in time to the chant, and she thought she could almost hear the crowd below in Kerry Park shouting, "…Three, two, one, midnight!" as the top of the Space Needle lit up all aglow and the first fireworks shot up into the dark sky, heralding the start of a brand new year.

Emma turned to her, smiling. "Happy New Year!" she said, voice surprisingly clear given how much she'd had to drink.

Jamie, who had changed to water hours earlier, smiled back. "Happy New Year," she echoed, and then leaned in for a slow, sweet kiss, fireworks lighting up against her closed eyelids.

"I love you," Emma murmured against her lips.

"I love you too."

They stayed like that, hands interlaced and foreheads touching, until Emma's eyes widened and she reached to turn down the speakers. Jamie turned to see Derek down on one knee holding out a ring box to Dani, who stared at him almost aghast, one hand over her mouth.

"Danielle Marie Romano," he said, his voice warm and rich, "I love you more than I ever thought I would love another human being. When I think of my future now, I see you beside me every step, and I wouldn't want it any other way. Will you do me the honor of spending the rest of your life with me?"

There was a pause, longer than Jamie thought any of them expected, and then Dani nodded. "Yes," she said, smiling at last as she reached for his hands and pulled him to his feet. "Yes! Derek, yes, of course!"

As Dani slipped on the ring and kissed her boyfriend— *fiancé*—Jamie glanced at Emma, who she found watching her with an unreadable expression that Jamie thought, actually, she knew exactly how to read.

A wave of adrenaline washed over her, and she pictured herself kneeling in front of Emma, holding out a box with a ring inside engraved with a phrase she had never forgotten, even if the piece of jewelry that had contained it was long since lost: "I'll be your anchor if you'll be mine." This time her initials would come first and Emma's second. Or maybe it would be Emma who proposed to her, because how did you decide who asked whom when there were two brides or two grooms? That was another thing about being queer—you got to make up the rules as you went along.

Another explosion rocked the Space Needle, red and blue and white lights seemingly falling all around it, and Jamie blinked away the remnants of her daydream. This wasn't the right time to think about proposing. They hadn't even been together for a year yet, and the honeymoon was still going strong. Better to wait and see how they handled the hills and valleys that undoubtedly lay ahead before making a decision about their future.

Even as the rational part of her brain recited this argument, Jamie knew in her heart that for her, Emma was it. She just wasn't entirely sure what lay in Emma's heart. She knew Emma loved her and in theory wanted a future together. But Emma still kept secrets, still insisted on holding parts of herself carefully separate. And even though Jamie wanted to give her the benefit of the doubt, she couldn't help worrying.

"Did you know about this?" Dani demanded. She had left Derek's side and was gripping Emma's shoulders now, almost shaking her in her excitement.

"No, I swear!" Emma laughed giddily as she hugged her best friend. "I'm so happy for you guys!"

"You'll be my maid of honor, won't you?" Dani was practically jumping up and down, Emma still in her arms.

"I would love to! You're getting married, Dan!"

"I'm getting married!"

Jamie slugged Derek on the shoulder. "Congrats, man."

"Thanks," Derek said, and gave her a bro hug, a relieved smile on his face. "I owe you big time, by the way. If we had gone down to Seattle Center, I would have had to come up with a whole new plan. There's a ton of pressure on the proposal. Have you seen all the videos on YouTube?"

"Can't say I have, but happy to help." She squeezed his side, glad she wouldn't have to deal with proposal pressure of her own anytime soon.

They stayed outside to watch the rest of the fireworks over the waterfront, music playing on the blue tooth speakers in time to the light show overhead. Jamie positioned herself behind Emma, who leaned back against her, hugging Jamie's arms to her chest. As Derek and Dani did the same, Jamie tried to burn the moment into her brain, to make a memory that would stick in her mind's twisting, complex pathways. A memory that, she hoped, would symbolize the start of a new life for a new year.

Except that this particular new life already had deep roots that had, she was almost certain, been there for years in the recesses of her brain, waiting for the chance to emerge again.

The sound was irritating, but familiar. Emma's alarm. Or her phone. Or the alarm on her phone.

Jamie nudged Emma in the ribs. "Your phone," she muttered, opening an eye to check the clock on the bedside table. Ten-thirty. So not that early after all. "Em, it's your phone."

"Five more minutes," Emma groaned, and rolled over to go back to sleep.

"No, babe, your phone is ringing." Nothing. "You have to answer it." Still nothing. Sighing, Jamie reached across her and checked the caller ID. Oh, *shit!* She dropped the phone, wincing as it landed on Emma's back and she yelped. "It's Jo. Dude, answer it!"

Within seconds Emma was sitting up in bed, phone to her ear as she rubbed her eyes and said, voice unfairly cool and collected, "This is Emma."

Jamie was close enough she could hear Jo say, "Emma! Happy New Year. Hope I'm not calling too early?"

"Not at all," Emma said, giving Jamie a look that said otherwise.

"Good. Well, I just wanted to confirm that you're available for January camp. It starts next Monday and goes through the twenty-fifth this year. I know it's longer than usual, but we have a lot of work to do."

"I'll be there," Emma said, running her free hand over the red tartan comforter cover they'd picked out together at the Williams Sonoma Home store in the U District. Emma may have paid, but Jamie still considered it their first major joint purchase.

"Great," Jo said. "I'll let you go then. I hope you're looking forward to 2015 as much as I am."

"Absolutely. Happy New Year, Coach." She hung up

and tossed her phone to the foot of the bed.

"January camp, huh," Jamie said when Emma lay back down beside her.

Emma ran her fingers over the Sanskrit tattoo on her right bicep. "I think you mean 'Death Camp,' don't you?"

Jamie was still chuckling when her own phone rang. Immediately her laughter died out, and she sucked in a breath as she read the caller ID: *Jolene Nichols.*

"Your turn," Emma said, her voice soft. "You got this, Jamie."

"Right. Okay." This was it. This phone call could determine the course of her future with the national team. Did she have to answer it? Maybe she didn't. Maybe she could... Before the thought could coalesce, she hit the call button, holding tightly to Emma. "Hello?"

"Jamie? It's Jo Nichols. Happy New Year, kiddo."

She couldn't prevent the tremor in her voice as she answered, "Thanks, Coach. You, too." She bit her lip, waiting. Would she be invited to camp, or was Jo calling to let her down easy, to tell her that the coaching staff had decided to go in—*ugh*—a different direction?

"As you know," Jo said, "January camp starts next week. I'm calling to let you know that we appreciated all of your hard work last year and would like you to join us to start out the new year. What do you say?"

"Yes!" she exclaimed, and then gave Emma an apologetic look. Her girlfriend only smiled and hugged her tighter.

"Wonderful. We'll add you to the confirmed list. Here's the thing, Jamie," Jo added, her voice dipping lower. "We're hoping to have the World Cup roster mostly figured out by the end of the month. As you know, you are one of a handful of players who are solidly on the bubble right now. So I need you to start 2015 the way you ended 2014. I need you to show us why we couldn't possibly think of leaving you off that roster. Can you do that? Can you come to California prepared to give the next few weeks your all?"

"Yes, ma'am!" she practically shouted, lowering her voice as Emma flinched beside her. "I mean, I'll try, Coach."

"Good," Jo said. "Then I'll see you soon. Enjoy the next few days, Jamie. It's probably the last bit of rest you're going to get for quite some time."

"I will," she promised. In her mind, she didn't only intend her reply to mean that yes, she would enjoy the next few days. She also meant it as an affirmation of the hard work ahead, of the trials she would endure, of her willingness to accept the challenge Jo was offering.

Somehow, she suspected Jo understood.

"I'm rooting for you, Jamie," she said before they hung up. "Don't let me down."

"I won't."

Emma was shaking her head as she set her phone down, and Jamie glanced up at her. "What?"

"That woman loves the shit out of you," Emma said, and pressed forward to kiss the corner of her mouth. "I mean, I totally get why."

"Oh," Jamie said, feeling her cheeks turn pink. "Well, I have known her for a while..."

"Almost as long as you've known me." Emma hesitated, staring at her intently, and Jamie had the feeling she was about to say something important, something that could change both of their lives. But then she blinked, kissed Jamie again, and started to slide out of bed.

"I'm thirsty," she announced, pulling on the robe her mother had given her, purple with tiny Minnesota Vikings helmets all over it. When Jamie had asked her why she, a staunch Seahawks fan, had kept what was obviously a gag gift, Emma had admitted it was the comfiest item of clothing she'd ever owned. So, for now, it stayed.

In the doorway, she paused. "Want to go for a quick run? You know, to get the blood flowing?"

Jamie smiled. "Sounds perfect."

"Coolers." Emma started to turn away, but then she stopped again, a smile warming her eyes. "Happy New Year, James."

"Happy New Year, Em."

She watched Emma disappear into the hall, and then she stretched, contracting the muscles in her back and shoulders all at once and releasing them again. Emma might be the psychic one in this relationship, but Jamie had a feeling 2015 would be amazing. On the relationship front, she and Emma were steadily building a future together; Dani and Derek had a wedding to plan; Ty and Bridget were actually getting married; and Ellie and Jodie would have to someday pony up and tie their own knot. On the entertainment front, *Pitch Perfect 2* was set to open in mid-May and *The Force Awakens* was coming out at the end of the year. Oh, and there was that whole soccer thing happening up in Canada, too—the one Jo Nichols had just told her she had a shot at playing in.

She closed her eyes and lay back in Emma's bed, murmuring her mantra to calm the suddenly crazy, hopped-up beat of her heart. But it was no use. The familiar words had no impact on her nervous system.

After a moment she gave up, kicked the comforter cover away, and jumped out of bed to face the first day of the newest year. *We got this*, she told herself as she reached for one of Emma's hoodies.

*We got this.*

# ABOUT THE AUTHOR

Kate Christie lives with her family near Seattle. A graduate of Smith College and Western Washington University, she has played soccer most of her life and counts attending the 2015 World Cup finals game in Vancouver as one of her top five *Favorite. Days. Ever.*

To find out more about Kate, or to read excerpts from her other titles from Second Growth Books and Bella Books, please visit her author website at www.katejchristie.com. Or check out her blog, *Homodramatica* (katechristie.wordpress.com), where she occasionally finds time to wax unpoetically about lesbian life, fiction, and motherhood.

To receive updates on the fourth book in the Girls of Summer series, visit https://katechristie.wordpress.com/mailing-list/ and sign up for Kate's mailing list.

Made in the USA
Middletown, DE
05 December 2020